# Women's Wiles

# Women's Wiles

## Cambodian Legends

### Collected by Guillaume Henri MONOD

---

Based on his original 1922 publication:

*Légendes cambodgiennes:*

*que m'a contées le Gouverneur KHIEU*

Translated and Expanded by

**Solang UK**

Edited by

**Kent DAVIS**

DatAsia Press

MMXIII

**About the Cover:** *La Femme aux Poules - Woman with chickens*, circa 1912 by **George Groslier** (1887-1945)

Born in Phnom Penh on February 4, 1887, the rich Khmer land infused itself in George Groslier's soul. He grew up to devote his life to his birth country and its people, founding Cambodia's National Museum and its School of Fine Arts, both of which continue their educational missions today.

His cover painting gives us an intimate glimpse of village life that resonates with M. Monod's opening tale of an unfaithful wife who beseeches a *neakta* (spirit) to rid her of her unwanted husband. To her surprise, the spirit orders her to "find yourself a broody hen and eggs, cook them, and give them to your husband to eat!" As you will soon read, the outcome is totally unexpected...making it a perfect folktale of Cambodia.

**To learn more about Southeast Asian folktales and culture visit:**
**www.NagaPrince.com & www.Devata.org**

**DatASIA Press**

**ISBN 978-1-934431-21-4 (paperback)**

Library of Congress Control Number: 2012932881

**First Edition**

**Printed simultaneously in the United States of America and Great Britain.**



**Production Credits**

1922 French Translator & Editor - **Guillaume Henri MONOD**
2013 English Translator & Cultural Consultant - **Solang UK**
Editor - **Kent DAVIS**
Text design - **Daria LACY**
Cover design - **Rebecca KLEIN**

Special thanks to **Thierry Groslier**, for sharing his grandfather's painting, to **Antoine Groslier** for his cover photo, and to **François Doré** – founder of the **Librairie du Siam et des Colonies** – for his guidance and kind help exploring the captivating world of French colonial literature.

*Avec notre gratitude à nos épouses, Beling et Sophaphan, compagnes dévouées de nos longues randonnées au Cambodge.*

*A ma femme*
*Compagne de mes longues randonnées*
*au Cambodge.*

*To my wife*
*Companion on my long treks*
*in Cambodia*

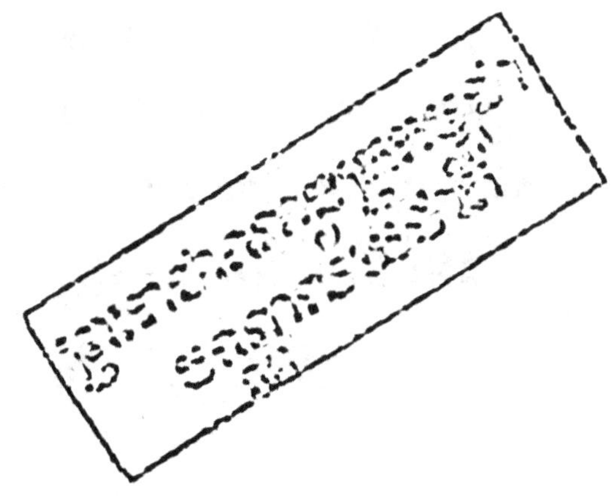

# Table of Contents

## APPENDICES

This 1914 map shows the region during Monod's era.
The black stars locate Angkor and Tuk Meas (see Foreword).

# Foreword

In this life, some seventy four years ago, I was blessed to have been born in Tuk Meas, a town in the southern part of the ancient Kingdom of Cambodia. Curiously, the name of my birthplace means "gold boat" yet today it is thirty kilometers from the Gulf of Siam, a vast sea that merchants and pilgrims have crossed for thousands of years, traveling between China, India and beyond. Certainly many legends crossed that sea, entertaining countless pilgrims on their journeys.

When I was a boy of six in March 1945, I still remember one hot day when I stood on the bridge over the Tuk Meas River with two classmates during a midday school break. Like many youngsters drawn to adventures of days gone by, we were discussing the origin of the Tuk Meas name. Local legends we had heard told of a gold boat that once sank in the river, just two hundred meters upstream from the bridge where we stood! Where was it going? Did it carry a king or queen with their treasure? And how did it come to sink here, so far from the sea? No one knew.

The source of the Tuk Meas River is in Phnom Totung, about five kilometers northwest of the town. From there it flows south, with its waters rising and falling with the tides of the Gulf of Siam throughout the year. One day when the river was dry, so I heard, a French-led team of Cambodian workers came to dig in search of the gold boat. Suddenly, a violent thunderstorm erupted, flooding the excavation and scaring the workers away. I don't recall anyone daring to dig there ever since. But even this anecdote is a legend. At that time, information—particularly about the French authorities—spread as unsubstantiated rumors.

Was there really a "gold boat"? Could an historical event lie at the origin of this tale? We heard the story from Buddhist monks, our parents and from our grandparents who were born before the French came to our land. Growing up, I never heard the story outside our tiny Tuk Meas community.

In addition to my fortuitous birthplace, I was blessed to have a father who was a Buddhist monk in his youth. In addition to knowledge of Buddhist scriptures, monks had access to a wealth of legends and folktales. To gain merit, they spent time copying literary texts, inscribing the letters on specially prepared palm leaves with a special steel stylus. In the early 20th century, Buddhist monasteries were the centers of learning, as they had been for many centuries. It was in such a monastery where my father attained the respected title of *achar*, and he was regarded as a learned man.

Now, I wish I could remember more folktales that my father told me at my bedside during my tender years. I regret not having asked the village elders for more details...especially about the gold boat! Reading Monod's collection sparked my youthful memories and made me wonder anew how much truth may be hidden in the ancient legends of our people.

Archaeologists say that the area near Tuk Meas was the heart of a kingdom the Chinese called Funan in the distant past. No local texts or inscriptions record the name of the kingdom. Even legends don't mention what local people called their land, but the indications are that this kingdom gave birth to the civilization that became Angkor itself. Few facts are certain. But I know it is a good place to be born.

The town of Tuk Meas was the administrative center of Srok (district) Banteay Meas (Gold Barracks). These "gold" names evoke memories of a yet unidentified region of Southeast Asia that ancient Indians knew as "Survarnbhumi" (Land of Gold). Certainly this coastal location and its rich names imply there were wealthy commercial centers here in ancient times. Tuk Meas is also on a transit road between the ancient port of Peam (now

Hatien in South Vietnam) and Angkor Borei (Vyadhapura), presumably the ancient capital of Funan. According to French archaeologist Louis Malleret, the former name of Peam was Banteay Meas. A canal at that port led to Moat Chrook (now Chau Doc, Vietnam) enabling Siamese warships to reach the Mekong River when they attacked the Khmer capital of Lovek north of Phnom-Penh.[1]

In September 1945 more welcome warriors passed through our town: allied troupes celebrating the end of World War II came ashore through the port of Hatien (formerly Peam) and drove colorfully decorated trucks, tanks and armored vehicles through Tuk Meas, right in front of my school. We all lined the roads for an hour or more, waving at the parade of cheerful, white-faced soldiers. My memory of the colorful tiny flags covering those military vehicles remains as fresh as if were yesterday. Being a small country boy of six, I saw those flags as decorative pennants rather than symbols of nations who won a war in Southeast Asia. But it seems I have always known that important travelers have passed this way since the dawn of time. I feel it was near here, so close to my home, that the oldest origin legends of the Khmer people arose.

In his extensive study of Cambodian dance, *Earth in Flower*,[2] Paul Cravath analyzed variations of our country's origin myths over a period of sixteen centuries. The oldest account was recorded in the third century by Chinese envoy Kang Tai, after he returned from a visit to the land of Funan, now the coastal area of modern Cambodia. Kang Tai reported that, in the beginning, Funan was ruled by Queen Liu Ye. A man named Hun Tian from an unidentified foreign land had a dream instructing him to travel to Funan with a magic bow and arrows. Upon arriving in Funan,

---

1 Malleret, Louis. 1959. *L'Archéologie du Delta du Mékong. Tome Premier : L'Exploration Archéologique et les Fouilles d'Oc-èo.* Ecole Française d'Extrême-Orient, Paris, Vol. XLIII, pp.13-33.

2 Cravath, Paul. 2007. *Earth in flower: the divine mystery of the Cambodian dance drama.* Holmes Beach, FL: DatAsia.

Hun Tian dominated the queen by force (there are many variations) and, when she was subdued, they married and had many children enabling the land to grow to prosperity.

Chinese accounts often expressed different ideologies, particularly in male-female relations. While the temples and history of Cambodia clearly show attitudes of respect and equality for female rulers, divinities and women in general, Chinese accounts clearly favored male protagonists. I explore this and similar issues of Chinese perspectives in my revised translation of Zhou Daguan's account of his 1296 AD visit to Angkor.[3]

A more popular account is that of a pious Hindu Brahmin named Kaundinya who also followed a dream to our land. According to a Sanskrit inscription in Champa dated 657 AD, Kaundinya traveled from India to the shores of Cambodia. There he met Soma, the semi-divine daughter of the King of the Naga who had chosen to live on earth. The *naga* are a mythical race of serpent beings who live in the sea or beneath the ground and control all the earth's wealth. They have the ability to assume human form and Soma has assumed a form so beautiful that the Brahmin instantly fell in love. He asked the *naga* king for her hand in marriage and received his blessing, allowing Soma and Kaundinya to form a new dynasty and become the progenitors of the Khmer race.

A similar, though less well-documented, genealogical legend is associated with the kingdom of Zhenla to the north of Funan. In that version a Hindu Brahmin or "Maharishi" named Kambu Svàyambhuva sailed from India to land on an island distinguished by a giant Thlork tree (*Parinari annamensis*), a species native to Cambodia. There he met the

3 Uk, Solang and Uk, Beling. 1999. *Zhou Daguan - A Record of Cambodia's Land & Customs*. Sandy (Bedford): www.AuthorsOnLine.co.uk.

heavenly *apsara*[4] Mera who—like her semi-divine counterpart Soma—also chose to live on earth; together they propagated the Khmer race. The unions of the local women, Soma and Mera, with the spiritually powerful Indian men, Kaundinya and Kambu Svàyambhuva, both hold significance in establishing the divine lineage of the royal dynasties who later built the famous city of Angkor.

The legend of Kaundinya-Soma became intertwined with that of Kambu-Mèra and evolved into the legend of *Preah Thong Neang Neak* that many Cambodians regard as Cambodia's genesis. Kambu Svàyambhuva became known as Preah Thong and Mèra, Neang Neak. In this variation they still meet on Kok Thlork Island but a new detail emerges: when the *naga* king blesses them he celebrates their marriage by drinking the sea and creating our rich land, which they called Kampuchea.

Here I pause to consider my home from the God's-eye view of Google Earth. Since the dawn of time, the mighty Mekong River has been expanding its delta here with rich soils from the Himalaya Mountains. As I observe the hills dotting this plain it becomes quite easy to imagine them as islands that were once surrounded by water when the sea was higher or the land was lower. Again, I ponder how much actual history may be hidden in our legends.

All our ancient tales come to us today because of the rich oral tradition among Cambodian families. Fathers passed stories to sons, mothers to

---

4 *Apsaras* are youthful, beautiful female spirits in Hindu and Buddhist mythology who are associated with water, mist, rain and clouds. In Hindu mythology they are renowned for their skill as dancers (and temptresses), appearing as entertainers in the heavenly court of the god Indra, accompanied by court musicians, known as the Gandharvas.
According to the Hindu scriptures of the Bhagavata Purana, Vishnu Purana, and Mahabharata, *apsaras* manifested from the *Samudra Manthan* (Churning of the Ocean of Milk), along with other magical entities and objects. And there, on the east wall of Angkor Wat, is carved the world's largest portrayal of this event, with *apsaras* in flight above the scene. To learn more about them, and the 1,800 *devata* (demi-goddesses) seen at Angkor Wat visit www.Devata.org.

daughters, grandparents to grandchildren, and so has gone, generation to generation. Like the fables of Aesop,[5] our ancestors kept these tales alive and retold them frequently because most serve a practical purpose. Cambodian folktales give listeners (more recently readers) useful tips and lessons about everyday life: how to analyze; how to foresee the consequences of our actions; how to judge; how to conduct business; how to interact with our fellow human beings...and even how to woo a mate and have a happy marriage.

Still, most historians only put their faith in written accounts. This is why the eyewitness report of Chinese traveler Zhou Daguan in 1296 AD is seen as the most credible description of Angkor. Zhou spent one year in our great capital, recording fantastic sights and events within the empire, at least as far as he understood them as a foreigner. During his stay, he noted that the people of Angkor wrote on animal skin or palm leaves, which explains our lack of a written history. None of those fragile records survived the insects, tropical climate and wars that finally led to the abandonment of Angkor in the 14th century. All that remained were inscriptions on stone temples, and those primarily dealt with administrative matters and praise for the kings who built them. No popular literature from the golden age of Angkor was written in stone so it vanished. Or did it?

I believe those ancient storyteller's tales—faithfully passed down to us by our ancestors and recorded in writing in recent centuries—must also be considered. In 1975, Khmer linguist Saveros Pou documented two stone

5 *Aesop's Fables* (also called the *Aesopica*) are a collection of instructive folktales thought to have originated in Greece in the 6th century BC. Whether there actually was a man named Aesop is debatable, but the fables have delighted and educated people for thousands of years. To read more than 650 of the stories, visit www.AesopFables.com.

inscriptions as the oldest example of our written literature.[6] This votive text, written in verse, dates to the Saka year 1623 (1701 AD).[7]

Possibly an even earlier example is the "Angkor Wat Poem" by a poet named Pang. Some Cambodian scholars date this to 1542 Saka (1620 AD), but this is contested because it mentions two anachronistic political entities: the Kai-Soen Vietnamese and the French. In 2006, researcher Khing Hoc Dy noted that the Kai-Soen only became known as such in the 18th century. It is also doubtful that the French were widely known in Cambodia in 1620. It was only in 1662 that French catholic missionaries from the *Société des Missions Etrangères de Paris* settled in Ayuthaya, then capital of Siam.[8]

Earlier, I mentioned how Buddhist monks made merit transcribing old texts and stories. These written sources appear in two forms: manuscripts inscribed on specially prepared palm leaves and those hand-written on "*kraing*", a thick paper made from barks of mulberry trees, folded like an accordion. In recent centuries, Buddhist monasteries and the royal palace library in Phnom Penh have preserved many of these written manuscripts, with archivists dividing them into general categories: history; justice; rural life (fishing, hunting, farming and nature); and customs and beliefs (family life, spiritual tales...and tales of spirits!). As you'll soon discover, the stimulating plots and intriguing mysteries often include more than a bit of humor.

After France established the Protectorate of Cambodia in 1863, early French administrators such as Étienne Aymonier and Jean Moura began

6 Pou-Lewitz. "VII. Inscriptions modernes d'Angkor 34 et 38." *Bulletin de l'Ecole française d'Extrême-Orient.* Tome 62, 1975. pp.283-353.

7 The Saka calendar originated in India and is still in use in Cambodia today as the official royal calendar. Adding 78 years converts dates to the Western calendar.

8 De Choisy, François-Timoléon. 1687. *Journal du Voyage de Siam Fait en 1685 &1686.* Genève : Olizane (republished 2006).

exploring the archives, and translating popular legends that shaped the morals and ideals of Cambodian society. In 1898, our author himself arrived to follow his compatriot's example, pursuing his own empathetic study of our culture during nearly three decades of residence.

As Mr. Monod relates in his own introduction, his friend Governor Khieu inspired his appreciation for this rich body of oral literature. Ultimately, he transcribed and translated a selection of tales, drawing from each of the thematic categories mentioned above. In 1922, he assembled these as a single volume, *Légendes cambodgiennes: que m'a contées le Gouverneur Khieu*, giving French readers a wonderful glimpse into the breadth and depth of Cambodian imagination and culture.

My goal in translating this work into English is to share these vibrant legends with new audiences. In this process I did my best to refine the original accounts by clarifying details and adding information from other Cambodian sources. The more I read, the more I felt that these old tales may indeed contain seeds of truth from ages past.

So as you embark on these adventures please keep in mind that—hidden between the lines —you may find clues to solve historical mysteries that still abound in our beautiful land of Cambodia.

**Solang Uk**

Rheinfelden, Switzerland

July 10, 2013

# Introduction

***Les peuples sont comme le rossignol de la chanson;***
***Ils chantent bien tant qu'ils ont le cœur gai.***

***People are like the singing nightingale.***
***They sing well as long as they have cheerful hearts.***[1]

**Anatole France** (née François-Anatole Thibault) 1844-1924

Cambodian customs endure because everything is based on extremely ancient folktales that have become, in the minds of many Cambodians, the nearly sacred origin of their traditions.

Governor Khieu, a brilliant man, has a deep knowledge of Cambodian literature.[2] He laughs about it sometimes, but gladly talks about it. It is my great pleasure to have had many long conversations with this Khmer gentleman, during which I tried to probe, with his guidance, the depth of the ancient Cambodian soul that is so mysterious to us in the West.

In selecting the tales that I offer here, I tried to diversify the types in order to give a general idea of popular Cambodian literature. Some stories may appear childish, such as "The Father-in-Law Who Chooses a Son-in-Law". Others like "Kung the Courageous"

---

1 Translator's Note: There are no nightingales in Cambodia but there are a variety of other songbirds including the *Bombicilla garrulus, Emeberiza schoenicius, Emberiza hortulana, Lanius excubitor, Passer montanus* and the *Phoenicurus phoenicurus.*

2 Monod's Note: The texts of several tales were lithographed in Saigon in 1878 (Khmer texts, with summarized translation by Aymonier). This work being unavailable today, I could not check the variants he presented with these texts from Governor Khieu.

demonstrate true psychology. "The Male and the Female Partridges" utilizes ideas on Cambodian cosmogony.

All amuse while relating interesting information on Cambodian manners, customs, psyche and religious ideas. All evoke the richness of Khmer imagination that likes to accumulate a series of incidents, making increasingly complicated situations and, ultimately, to skillfully resolve the difficult plots, as in "The Adventures of Alev," for example.

Finally, I think that the legend describing the foundation of Angkor is of great interest. The present-day Khmers, incapable of conceiving the prodigious activities of their great builder ancestors, think that the construction of this immense and admirable monument was the work of supernatural intervention. As with their other folktales, they enlivened this one with amusing incidences to indulge their poetic spirit.

My intention with these texts is not to devote myself to a scholarly work on the subject of Khmer *Sastra*.[3]

I do not believe that one can assign authenticity to any version of these tales that have been verbally told from person to person or written down by several people, sometimes with significant variations. I intend to recount them as they have been told to me.

First I try to present, as much as possible, the story's charming naivety, the courtliness of the Cambodian language as well as the

3 Translator's Note: The Sanskrit word *sastra* means theory, doctrine or book of scripture, but has evolved to include documents for leisure reading as well, i.e., literary texts. Texts in Khmer literature from the 19th century up to the 1950s were mainly written on leaves of talipot palm, and were known as *Sastra sloek rit*. Besides the Royal Records (kept in the royal palace), the ordinary *Sastra* were recorded and re-copied by hand by Buddhist monks in various monasteries throughout the country.

often infinitely gracious and delicate images that only the Khmer artistic wit knows how to illustrate.

I can hardly believe that I captured the clarity of the expressions or the subtlety of the jokes that sparkle in these tales. I only hold the pen to write, under Governor Khieu's dictation, the translation of the tales as he told them to me. I love these stories so much that I never dared add or omit a single word.

**Guillaume Henri Monod**

**1922**

# Women's Wiles

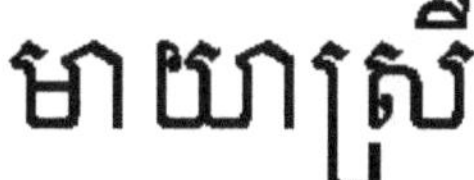

*Meayea Srey*

# Women's Wiles

## មាយាស្រី

### *Meayea Srey*

In the histories of far antiquity, there lived together a husband and his wife. They had no children. After some time, the wife took a lover who she regularly brought into her conjugal home to sleep with her.

One day the husband went out to search for tubers in the woods.

At the hottest time of the day, he went to rest in a small hut made for the *neakta*.[4] It happened that on the same day his wife — blinded by passion for her lover and overcome by an intense desire to get rid of her husband — brought offerings to the *neakta*. The husband, therefore, was quite surprised to see her entering the *neakta*'s hut.

"What is she searching for here?" he thought to himself.

He hid himself behind the *neakta* statue and waited in silence.

The wife lighted incense sticks and prayed to the *neakta*:

---

4 Translator's Note: According Narang Nouth and B. P. Groslier (2003), the *neakta* is drawn from the ancient Cambodian concept of *Me-Ba* (female male unity – past ancestors) that became the Spirit Protector of the water and the land. Every village has at least one *neakta* hut housing a piece of stone or statue representing the spirit. The Khmer dictionary defines *neakta* as the combination of *neak* (a person) and *ta* (an elder). *Neakta* is a term of address to a male guardian spirit; *neakdaun* for female spirit. The worship of the neakta in Cambodia predates the adoption of Hinduism and Buddhism and is still alive and strong today.

"I no longer want my husband. I have taken another man. I beg the *neakta* to make my husband die. In gratitude for your act, I will make an offering of a pig."

Disguising his voice, the husband replied from his hiding:

"If you have a lover and you wish to make your husband die easily, return to your home, find yourself a broody hen and eggs, cook them, and give them to your husband to eat. Then he will die!"

Convinced that this advice was really given by the *neakta*, the wife hurried back home. She took a broody hen and eggs, and cooked them with the intention to give to the husband to eat. She hoped to live with her lover afterwards.

At dusk, the husband returned. He asked:

"Have you something for me to eat? I am very hungry."

The wife brought him a pot of rice with the cooked hen and eggs.

The husband gobbled everything down. Then he pretended to be sick, and began to moan and groan. Finally, he lay still and feigned death. Convinced that her husband had passed away as the *neakta* had said, the wife opened the door to let her lover in, and they went to sleep together.

While the two lovers were having affectionate conversation, the husband sat up, called his wife, and said:

"I am cold and shivering. Go to get some water, put it over the fire for me to have a bath."

The lover, terrified by the husband's awakening and with no possibility of escape, went to hide in an empty earthen jar nearby, and waited for the husband to go back to sleep.

*La Femme aux Poules* — George Groslier, circa 1912.

The husband saw the lover's little trick, but he kept quiet and pretended to know nothing. He shouted to his wife:

"I'm cold, I'm cold. Hurry up, heat the water, I'll take my bath. I may die soon."

Hearing her husband imploring death, the wife was quite happy to see that her prayers were really answered.

When a large pot of water was boiling, the husband said to his wife:

Go find a pitcher[5] of cold water to mix with this hot one."

The wife went out with a pitcher to get cold water. As soon as she was out of sight, the husband got up, took the pot of boiling water and emptied it into the earthen jar where the lover was crouching, killing him instantly without a sound. His job done, the husband went back to lay down and continued to play sick, and moan.

On her return, the wife saw the lover's head sticking out of the jar due to the tightening of his burned muscles. In low voice, she said to him, "Get down! He's not asleep yet!"

Her lover didn't move so she pushed him down into the jar. One ear came off, and stuck between her fingers. She realized that her husband had killed her lover by inundating him with the boiling water, but she didn't say a word. She put the cover over the jar and took the cold water to her husband. The husband decided not to take bath. He said to the wife:

"I feel better now. Let's go to sleep."

ಐ ❀ ೞ

---

5 Translator's Note: In Cambodian, *k'a-ôm* is a clay pot in a shape of a stubby pitcher with a somewhat narrow neck and lip, but without pouring spout or handle.

The next morning the wife, not knowing how to get rid of her lover's body, pondered:

"In this village, there are four burglars who always break in to people's houses day and night. I'll make those petty thieves take away the corpse, and they will abandon it in the forest."

She went to borrow several *sampot haul*[6] and silk blouses, and hung them around the house as if to dry.

The four thieves saw this display and thought to themselves:

"How could this woman who we believed to be quite poor, possess such things? Surely, we will come at night to steal them from her."

In the evening, the woman took down the fabrics she had hung to dry, folded them up, and returned them to the people who lent them to her. Afterwards, she took a rope and securely tied down the lid of the jar with her lover's corpse inside. The job completed, she went out.

Seeing the house empty, the four burglars snuck in, searching every corner, but didn't find anything worth stealing. They tried to open the jar, but the cover was tightly fastened. They thought:

"All the valuable objects are certainly in this jar. Let's not waste our time trying to open it here. Let's take it as it is."

They slipped two bamboo poles under the rope, put the ends on their shoulders, and carried their loot into the woods.

When they were far enough from the village, they cut the rope and opened the jar. In the dark, one thief reached his hand in and felt the hair of the dead man. He shouted:

"Oh! It's full of silk yarn!"

---

6 Monod's Note: A *sampot* is a rectangular piece of cloth that Cambodian men and women wear like a baggy skirt or trousers. *Sampot haul* has different colors and is made of silk.

The second took his turn, he felt the detached ear, the eyes, and the nose, and shouted:

"It's a corpse!"

The third thief did not believe him, in turn put his hand in, touched the chest, and realized that it was actually a dead man. All four ran away in rage, realizing that they had been fooled by the woman who made them tire themselves out carrying away a corpse. They said among themselves:

"We will scout around for this woman. If we meet her alone, we will catch her and beat her up to teach her a lesson so she gives up the will to cheat us again."

✿

Sometime later, the woman headed to the river to do some shopping because a Chinese bazaar junk had docked at the quay.

On her way, she came face to face with the four thieves who rushed towards her all at once, insulting her and beating her soundly. But she said:

"And so! If you beat me, what benefit will you get from that? Come with me instead. I'll receive money that the Chinese owes me. When I get paid, we'll share my money."

The four thieves gave in to this suggestion and went along with the woman. She told them the following:

"You all stay on the bank while I go down to the junk.[7] When you see my hand signal come on board and you'll get a lot of money."

---

7 Monod's Note: Cambodians say the opposite of what we say in the West, i.e., to "go down" to a boat, and to "go up" to land from a boat. This is because the riverbanks in Cambodia are always higher than the water level, and one has to go down the bank to board a boat.

She descended to the junk and said to the Chinese boat captain:

"The four men I brought with me are my slaves. If you want them, I'm ready to sell them to you."

The Chinaman replied:

"Of course I want them. How much are you asking for?"

"Two silver *baht* for each man." [8]

"I'll give you one and a half *baht* for each."

"I accept", said the woman. "While you have them come aboard I'll go back up the bank. But be careful, they will want to follow me. When they're aboard, you must chain them securely."

The Chinaman paid the woman the agreed price. She emerged from the back of the junk's canopy [9] and signaled the thieves to come down while showing them the money she just received. Convinced that she was calling them to get their share, the thieves descended while she vanished under the canopy. As they barely got on the boat, sailors grabbed them and chained them below deck.

During this time, the woman left the canopy on the opposite side, climbed up the quay, and disappeared.

ꕥ

8 Translator's Note: The terms *baht, bat, tical* and *riel* were all used in Cambodia and Siam to denote a monetary unit based on a measure of silver weighing approximately 15 grams. The French introduced the terms *franc* and *piastre*. Since King Ang Duong's time, (circa 1860) Cambodia struck coins simultaneously bearing the terms *riel, peso* and *piastre*. Cambodia used the riel or tical as their local currency, but began referring to it as the franc under the French Protectorate. Upon gaining independence in 1953 Cambodia again began using the *riel* as its currency. After 1993, Cambodia recognized the US dollar as legal tender, but the local Khmers still call it the riel in their trading.

9 Monod's + Translator's Notes: Monod used the French *rouffle* for a structure covering part of the boat deck that serves as working and living quarters.

Nightfall caught the women while she was still far from her village. Afraid of tigers, she dared not continue her way in the dark. She climbed up a big tree alongside the trail, huddled up in the tall branches, and went to sleep.

Chained up below the deck of the junk, the four thieves talked among themselves:

"This woman is really clever. After making us carry the corpse into the woods, now she had sold us to the Chinese. Will she always have the last laugh on us?"

With a strength doubled by their anger they struggled with the chains. Finally they broke free, got back to the quay and escaped into the night.

By chance, the thieves arrived at the very same tree the woman had climbed! In turn, they also decided to climb up to spend the night. Three of them settled on the main branches. The fourth climbed all the way to the top where he found the woman. Boiling with anger, he said to her:

"Ah! Here you are, wretched woman! This time your game is up, you will die. You duped us before. Now save yourself if you can!"

The woman made her silver bars shine in moonlight and said quietly:

"Be quiet, so the other three won't know that I'm here! Take me as your wife. We have money to live. I know how to provide you more. You would benefit more by keeping me as companion rather than hurting me."

The thief didn't say another word. He moved nearer the woman, wrapped his arms around her, and said to her:

"*Aun*, you are indeed a shrewd woman.[10] Twice you've tricked *bang*.[11] But our destiny has made us to be man and wife. For the two of us, our lives will never have to depend on others."

Having said so, he covered her with kisses. She let him do anything without resisting. Then she said in a sad tone:

"*Aun* is afraid that *bang* does not sincerely love her. As for *aun*, I love you with all my heart."

"*Bang* really loves you. You don't know how *bang* feels. Do you want *bang* to take an oath? What do you want *bang* to do to prove *bang*'s love?"

"If you love me to the point of having just one heart and soul, let's kiss with our tongues."

She stuck her tongue out first and bent towards the thief who embraced her. He stuck his tongue out in turn. She moved closer as to embrace him and then bit the man's tongue with all her strength until it was ripped off! She then pushed him away with both arms and he fell from the treetop screaming inarticulately.

On hearing this commotion, the other three thieves thought the Chinese and his boat crews were searching for them. They jumped out of the tree shouting:

"Look out! Let's run! The Chinese are chasing us!"

---

10 Translator's Note: *Aun* is a polite term generally used to address younger people (male or female) or young children. In romance, a husband will address his wife (or a man, his lover) *aun*, meaning darling or sweetheart.

11 Translator's Note: *Bang* is the counterpart to *aun*, used when addressing older people. In romance, the wife calls her husband (or a woman calls her lover) *bang*, meaning darling or sweetheart. Furthermore, Cambodians rarely use 'I' in familial conversations. Depending on their ages and social status, interlocutors use specific terms such as *bang*, *aun*, *son*, *father*, *uncle*, *grandmother*, etc., instead of 'I' and 'you'.

The thief with the clipped tongue tried yelling to them:

"The woman is in the tree! Come to get her!"

But with his torn tongue the words were unintelligible and his companions only heard "*lol lol lol!*" Not understanding a word he said, the other thieves thought a Chinaman was speaking and they ran even faster, escaping into the woods.[12]

The woman climbed down from the tree, wrapped the silver bars with her *krama*,[13] and returned home to live peacefully ever after with her husband.

---

12 Translator's Note: When Chinese immigrants try to speak Khmer their accent is usually quite difficult for Cambodians to understand.

13 Translator's Note: The ubiquitous Cambodian shawl made of woven cotton (or silk) that country women wrap around their heads or men around their necks wherever they go.

# The Father Who Chooses a Son-in-Law

## ឪពុកក្មេករកកូនប្រសា

*Aovpuk Khmek Roeus Kaun Prâsa*

# The Father Who Chooses a Son-in-Law

# ឪពុកក្មេករើសកូនប្រសា

*Aovpuk Khmek Roeus Kaun Prâsa*

It is said that a long time ago there lived an old man and an old woman with a remarkably beautiful daughter.

In what country did they live?

I do not know. This tale had been passed from mouth to mouth until it reached me.

These two old people vowed to only give their daughter to a suitor who could absolutely abstain from using swearwords.[14]

One day a handsome young man came to ask for the daughter's hand in marriage. The parents answered:

"Yes, we'll give her to you, don't worry. You will work for us and you will obey us.[15] If you are capable of never using swearwords, we will allow her to marry you. We set this condition beforehand so don't blame us later that we were deceitful!"

---

14 Translator's Note: For Cambodians, the most common impulsive swearwords are curses directed to ones mother. Thus, I have chosen 'damn your mother' as a realistic translation while avoiding harsher obscenities.

15 Monod's Note: Following Cambodian custom, the groom-to-be must work for his future parents-in-law for a few months before marriage.

The young man replied:

"I can absolutely abstain from swearing. I am willing to do all that you wish and obey you totally."

"Good," said the father. "If you can refrain from swearing go now. Tomorrow morning you can begin to work for your father-in-law.

The next day the old man had his daughter prepare a meal for the beau. After the young man had eaten his fill, the father told him:

"My son, take the buffaloes and go plough the paddy field. You must plough until the rocks you see on the side of the field groan. Then you can stop and unhitch the buffaloes."

The young man went to get the buffaloes, hitched them up to a plough, and started tilling the field. He worked from dawn until mid-day, but the rocks had not made a sound. The buffaloes did not want to walk anymore, but the rocks remained silent. The young fellow was hot, hungry. He could no longer bear, and he cried out:

"Damned your mother,[16] rocks! When are you going to groan?"

As soon as he finished swearing the old man, who was hiding behind the rocks, appeared and said:

"That's enough, unhitch the buffaloes and go back to your home. I refuse you my daughter, for you cannot keep yourself from swearing."

The young man untied the animals and withdrew rather sheepishly.

Soon afterwards, another young man presented himself to the girl's parents. The old man gave him the same conditions as his predecessor. However, this time the young man was a bit more malicious.

He went to plough the rice field, taking his own packet of rice with him. After he had ploughed until the sun was at its zenith, he stopped the buffaloes, ate his lunch, and resumed his work.

---

16 See footnote 14.

Mid-day had passed yet the rocks had not yet groaned.

The buffaloes were exhausted and could no longer walk. Arriving near the rocks, the young man said:

"Dear rocks, please groan. The buffaloes can no longer bear it. Have pity on them. It is not for me as I have had something to eat; it will be no trouble for me to plough until nightfall. But these buffaloes — they are animals and they belong to my father-in-law. Have compassion for them."

Despite his pleas, the rocks did not groan. But he was careful not to swear, for he suspected that the old man was listening in hiding.

For a long time, he begged the rocks. Finally, the father saw that the buffaloes were at the end of their strength, and took pity on them because they belonged to him. Hidden behind the rocks he began to groan. Immediately the young man unhitched the animals and returned to his father-in-law's house. The old man made his daughter prepare a meal for the young man. At the end of the day, the father-in-law dismissed him:

"My dear boy, return to your home. You come back tomorrow."

The young man took leave of the old man and headed home. But after night fell he stealthily came back to hide under the old man's house to listen to what the old man would say to his wife.[17]

And here was what he had heard:

"This fellow knows how to abstain from swearing, but he has an ugly physique. He is not suitable for our daughter. Let's arrange it so he gets annoyed to the point that he swears, and then we can refuse him our daughter."

The wife replied:

"It's easy. You will get into one sack and we'll fill another sack with rice. Tomorrow morning, I will tell him that you've gone to cut wood on the

17 Translator's Note: Cambodian houses in rural areas are built on stilts. In the darkness of night a person could easily hide underneath.

mountain, and I'll tell him to carry both sacks to the mountaintop. The load will be too heavy, he will become angry and swear. You, in the sack, will hear him and then you can dismiss him."

After their conversation the girl's parents went to sleep. The young man had heard everything.

At the break of dawn, he went to resume his work for his in-laws. The old woman showed him the two sacks tied to each end of a yoke and said:

"My dear son, your father has gone to cut wood on the mountain. He told me to tell you to take these sacks of rice and follow him as fast as you can. He left before sunrise without eating. Take these sacks, climb quickly to the mountain top, and there you'll prepare lunch for your father."

The young man carried the yoke with the two sacks on his shoulder and left.

Arriving at the foot of the mountain he began to climb but the load was too heavy so he came down again.[18]

"O my dear father-in-law must be really hungry!" said the young man, while continuing to walk. "But I can't climb quickly because these sacks are really too heavy. Who could possibly carry such a load all the way to the top? If, nevertheless, my father has no pity on me and scolds me, I will accept his reprimand without saying a word."

Having said this, he put the sacks down in the middle of a field and walked away. But he soon returned without making any noise and set fire to the grass around the sacks! The old man, trapped in the sack, was surrounded by flames. He was terrified as he felt the heat and all his limbs were shaking at the thought of being burnt to death. But he could not get out.

The boy, acting as if he is returning from a distance, ran up shouting:

---

18 Translator's Note: The populated areas of Cambodia are usually flat (rice) fields with occasional hills (ca 200-600m high).

"Eh! Who set a fire that will burn my sacks? How can I get to them? They are in the middle of an inferno! I can't get near them!"

Having thus shouted, he stood outside the flames.

When the fire reached the sacks, he rushed to pull them away before they were incinerated as the old man struggled inside. The young man untied the bags to see his father-in-law in a pitiful state, covered with burns. Feigning surprise he exclaimed:

"Oh, dear father, why didn't you let me know? You could have been lost in the flames and left my dear mother-in-law a widow!"

Realizing he had been fooled, the father-in-law became quite angry, but he didn't know what to do. He got up and hobbled home without saying a word. For the rest of the day, he lay down, treating his burns and the bruises he got when he was pulled away from the flames.

At nightfall, he sent the young man away until morning. As on the previous night, the young man returned to listen to the old couple's conversation.

The husband said: "What can we do to get rid of that rascal? He's too clever, but I don't want to give him our daughter."

He told his wife about his escapade during the day and said "Find a way to send him packing!"

The wife replied:

"I've got it! Tomorrow, you will be the master and you'll order him to be the dog. You take him to hunt for turtles. If he doesn't find any, or if he runs on four legs and cannot catch up with you, we'll show him the door."

"It's a good idea, wife!" said the man. "Tomorrow, I'll follow your advice."

Having heard the old couple's plan, the young man went back to sleep. Before the rooster's crow he took several turtles and tied them, here and there, in the grass of the plain where the father-in-law had decided to hunt.

At dawn, he went to see the father-in-law who said:

"My son, we are going to hunt for turtles, but we don't have a dog. You will take its place; you will be the dog and I, your master. We will try to find one or two turtles and we return to cook them and eat here."

"Yes, sir!" said the young man.

The father grabbed a lunch-bag with rice, a bamboo tube filled with water and headed out. The young man followed him running on four legs like a dog. Arriving in the meadow, where he had tied the turtles, he dashed ahead into the grass, secretly untied a turtle, and began barking. The old man rushed towards the young man and saw him holding a turtle between his teeth. The dog searched left and right, and brought seven to eight turtles.

At mid-day, the old man got hungry. He opened his lunch-bag and started eating. The son-in-law, still acting like a dog, spotted a herd of buffaloes and ran off to bite the beasts on their legs and the buffaloes ran off into the paddy fields.

The old man chased after the dog and buffaloes to get them out of the crop.

As he did, the young man nimbly went to eat all the food his father-in-law had brought. Upon his return the old man found nothing left to eat. He was furious and chased the dog but was too exhausted to catch him. Hungry, he was forced to walk on an empty stomach. It was a long way back home. He couldn't take it out on the son-in-law because he was a dog. When he arrived home, he had his meal, and sent the young man away.

From his usual eavesdropping place that night, the lad heard the old man telling his wife about what had happened. She said to him:

"He outsmarted you playing the dog. Tomorrow do the opposite. You be the dog and he, the master. You can give him a taste of his own medicine!"

The next morning, having been told what to do, the young man took rice and water, and off he went followed by the old man who trotted on four legs. The young man walked so fast his father-in-law had trouble following him. Soon he cried out:

"What kind of a dog is this? He is always behind. Being so slow, how can he find any turtles?"

He hit the dog to make him walk ahead but the old man couldn't run through the grass. He always trailed on the path behind the son-in-law. He didn't find any turtles. The young man whipped him until he lost his breath, but the old man was too ashamed to say a word.

At mid-day, the young man stopped to have lunch and said:

"What kind of a dog is this, who can't find any turtles? Who always trails behind his master? He only knows how to eat and sleep."

The young man tucked into the rice and meat, only tossing bones to the old man who couldn't even nibble them because he has no teeth. The starving father sat and watched as his son-in-law ate. His lunch finished, the lad smacked the old man with a rattan stick and said:

"Let's go home. There is nothing more to do with such a dog." And he set off. The exhausted old man could no longer follow him on four legs as a dog so he stood up and walked behind rather shamefully.

On arriving home, the young man said:

"Mother, we have no turtles. The dog is worthless."

The old man was very annoyed. He told the young man to go home and come back in the morning.

When they retired into their bedroom, the old couple discussed the day's events. The old man related how badly he was treated by the young man and how he was deprived of food. The old woman said:

"We cannot give him our daughter, and we haven't succeeded in dismissing him."

"He is ugly", said the old man. "He is not suitable for our beautiful daughter. But all my efforts to make him angry and compel him to swear are fruitless. Think of something he cannot fulfill, something that makes him lose patience and gives us a pretext to kick him out."

"Here it is!" said the wife. "Before daybreak, you'll eat your breakfast, chew your betel nut, and then you'll hide yourself in this basket. We'll fill the other basket with salt. When this brute comes, I'll tell him that you've gone to town shopping and he should go to join you before noon. The market is too far for him to arrive on time. On the road, when he tires of carrying his load and believing he is alone, he will certainly swear."

"You're right!" said the old man, and they both went to sleep. As usual, the young man had learned about their plan.

When he presented himself at the in-laws' home in the morning, the old woman gave him two heavy baskets to carry along with the agreed upon instructions.

On his way to town, the young man thought to himself:

"This time I have to do in a way that they'll give me their daughter. I've had enough with these ordeals."

Mid-way, his put down his load saying:

"The cover of this basket is badly tied."

He then took a rope and securely tied the basket lid, trapping his father-in-law inside, and continued his trip. He arrived at a river with a wooden-bridge crossing. He put the baskets right on the edge of the bridge so that the slightest bump would make them fall into the water.

Then, he exclaimed, "Oh woe is me, time flies! My dear father-in-law will be so angry! But my load is so heavy, how could I arrive in time?

I must rest a bit under those trees, and then I'll continue my trip."

Saying this he moved away. Picking up a big log he headed back to the bridge, thumping it to imitate the heavy footsteps of an elephant. Disguising his voice, he shouted:

"Who has put these baskets in the middle of the bridge? My elephant will crush them! Somebody better move them quickly!"

While shouting he thumped heavily like steps on the bridge roadway.

Inside the basket, the old man thought that a real elephant was coming, and that it would crush him. Suddenly he felt a bump. The two baskets fell into the water as if kicked by the elephant. The poor man was suffocating, trembling, trapped in his prison thinking he was going to die.

The young man let him swallow water for a bit, having previously tied the baskets with a rattan rope to prevent them from sinking all the way to the bottom of the river. Then, he pretended to be coming from afar, shouting:

"Eh! Who dares let a passing elephant kick my belongings into the water? Woe is I! What will my father-in-law say? I am already late and now all the salt is wet."

While pulling the baskets up, he saw one of them shaking from the trembling father-in-law and said:

"Oh! Some fish have already gotten inside! Alas, everything is soaked! I'll open the baskets and dry them, but the salt will melt! I'll bring the fish to my mother-in-law who will make fish sauce for my dear father-in-law."

Having said this, he opened one of the baskets and found his father-in-law in it.

"Oh my dear father" he said, "why didn't you shout? Why didn't you let me know that you were inside? You see, you've risked being drowned. Someone rode an elephant through here, I don't know where from, and the beast shoved you into the water with his foot."

The old man listened to him without a word and returned home in furious silence. He felt duped and out of new ideas. He no longer dared set new traps so he granted his daughter to marry the young man.

We have told this story as a lesson to those who have daughters of marriageable age. If they wish to find a husband for them, they should celebrate the wedding. If they don't want them to marry, they should frankly say so. But they shouldn't emulate the trickery of this old man who wished to choose a son-in-law. First, it is not honest, and they would never have the last word between the lovers.

# Tales of Alev

## រឿងអាឡេវ

*Roeung Alev*

# Tales of Alev

# រឿងអាឡេវ

*Roeung Alev*

## How Alev Became an Orphan

Once upon a time there lived a man named Ngeh and his wife named Ngoh. They had a son named Alev,[19] At the age of seven this child, who was quite intelligent, realized that his simple-minded parents who lived in great poverty had no clue of how to improve their situation. He said to them:

"Father, mother, we are now so poor because we have no job; we don't work like others do. From now on we should grow rice during the rainy season and, in the dry season, we should grow vegetables. I will go to work in the field with father. When we need supplies — areca nut, betel or whatever — I'll return home to find the stuff we need and bring back."

19 Translator's Note: Alev means a young man with squinted eyes.

The parents agreed with his suggestion. Ngeh prepared his implements and went to work, staying in the paddy fields with Alev. After a while in the field, Alev had an urge to eat cakes.[20]

He thought to himself, "For that, I have to trick my parents!"

He said to his father:

"Father, I'll go home to get you some areca nut and betel."

Ngeh replied:

"Go ahead!"

Away Alev went. Halfway home he entered into a monastery, prostrated himself before the monks, and begged them to shave his head. Afterwards, he took leave of the monks and headed home. He covered his head, walked into the house, and pretended to be crying. Seeing him sobbing, his mother asked:

"Why are you crying like this, my son?"

Alev cried even louder. His mother rushed to pick him in her arms, lifted the *krama* covering his head, and saw that it was shaved. She was struck with anxiety, and said:

"Why is your head shaved like this, my son? What is making you cry?

"O mother, father is dead", replied Alev.

*Neang* Ngoh burst into tears and groans, remembering how sweet her life had been since she was married to her husband.

Alev said:

---

20 Translator's Note: Cambodian cakes have no equivalents in Western culture and encompass many types of sweet foods made from sticky rice, or rice and mungbean flour. They are primarily made for rituals, wedding ceremonies and Buddhist festivals.

"Mother, don't give way to despair. If you only cry, how can you prepare the funeral for father?"

"Is your father already buried?" she asked.

Alev replied:

"I have asked the neighbors to help bury him with a proper ceremony."

*Neang* Ngoh[21] immediately began to prepare pastries and cakes, and said to her son:

"My dear son, bring these sweets and make offerings on your father's grave. I have no courage to go there myself. If I go, I will see the paddy fields that your father had planted, the place where he was laid to rest, the grave people had made for him. It will be too painful for me. Go, my son, go without me."

Alev was delighted that his trick succeeded so well. He hurriedly loaded the pastries into bamboo baskets set in two *sangreik*[22] attached to the ends of a bamboo pole. He then hoisted them onto his shoulder and went off.

Halfway between his house and the fields, he set down his *sangreik*, sat beneath the shade of a mango tree, and started feasting on the cakes he was carrying.

After he had eaten his fill there were still some cakes left. He put the leftovers back in the baskets and took them to his father.

---

21 Monod's Note: *Neang* is a title used to address young women. Cambodians always address a person with a 'prefix title' before the name, e.g., *Aa* for young boys, *Mee* for young girls, *Chau* for men, *Neang* for women, *Neak* for people of higher status, etc.

22 Translator's Note: A *sangreik* is a rattan carrying frame used in Asia to carry heavy loads on the shoulder with a bamboo yoke.

Approaching Ngeh's hut, Alev again pretended to cry. Seeing him crying and his head freshly shaved, the father asked:

"What happened, my boy? Why are you crying like this? Why is your head shaved?"

"Oh! Father, mother is dead. I shaved my head to mourn her. In organizing her burial, our relatives and neighbors had made cakes for offerings. I have brought some to share with you."

Ngeh, who was a simple-minded and gullible man, believed his son and began to cry compassionately over his wife's death.

"Oh! My son, from now on your father will not return to his village on the riverbank. Your father will never leave these paddy fields. He will never want to see again the place where he had lived happily with your mother."

Pleased to have made his parents fall into his trap, Alev was rejoicing in his thought.

After a few days, Alev said to Ngeh:

"Dear father, here we are both alone. Our life is painful. There is no one to prepare meals for us, no one to make our clothes. You must take a wife with the sole aim of having someone to cook for us, to get water, to polish rice. Then we won't be so miserable."

Ngoh replied:

"Alas, my boy, it is barely one month since your mother has died! And you urge me to get married again? Don't you feel sorry for your mother? Wouldn't people despise me? People would say that my wife passed away barely a few days ago, and I already think of remarrying. I feel ashamed. I don't want to have another woman."

However, Alev continued relentlessly imploring his father.

One day, Ngeh returned from the field exhausted. Alev told him:

"Father, you are at the end of your strength because you have no wife to help and support your efforts. Do you remember the precepts our ancestors taught us? If a man without a wife goes into the forest, he neglects his house; if he cares for his house, he neglects his work outdoors. How can you earn enough to feed us? And you're exhausted. You cannot cope alone."

"And who then will ask for a woman's hand for your father?" responded Ngeh.

"Don't worry father, I'll find a woman for you. Just make preparations for the wedding."

"Do as you please", replied Ngeh.

Soon Alev got himself ready and went back to his mother, Ngoh. He stayed with her for two or three days. Then he said to her:

"Dear mother, here we are, both alone. I am only a child. I am not able to provide for us. You, you are a woman, a widow. I know a man who would like to marry you. Take him as husband if only for him to take care of us and alleviate our poverty."

*Neang* Ngoh responded:

"My child, it has been only a few days since your father passed away and you dare tell me to take another husband? It's not good. Furthermore, everyone would scornfully turn their backs on me. They would say, 'What kind of a woman is she, who has barely been widowed, and already thinks of remarrying?'"

"Mother, you are worrying about what your neighbors would say. Do they care about coming to our aid? They have money. Do they provide us with our needs?

"When I was at the paddy fields, I met a man who looked exactly like father. He loves me like his own son. He asked me 'Do you have parents?' I told him I lost my father. I have only my mother. He said to me, 'I would like to marry your mother, but will she agree? If she accepts me, I will make proper request for her hand and arrange the wedding ceremony according to our ancestral tradition.' It's up to you, Mother. If you reject him, I can't do otherwise. You will have to carry on working to provide for us both."

Finally yielding to Alev's persistent persuasion *Neang* Ngoh said:

"Do as you wish."

Alev rejoiced in his mind and thought to himself, "I will again have cakes to eat!" He promptly decorated the house and said to his mother:

"The man I was talking about wants to have the wedding without delay. I'll go through the countryside to gather chickens, ducks, fruits and vegetables. Then I'll go to ask for money from the man who wants to marry you in order to make all preparations for the wedding."

Alev went to the paddy fields and told Ngeh:

"Father, I have asked the hand of a woman to marry you. She has the face, the eyes, the height, the voice, and the complexion of Mother. I have already put her in our house. Therefore prepare everything that's needed for the wedding without delay."

Ngeh ran to his neighbors begging them to help him preparing meals, cakes, and sweets. He bought some meat, chickens, ducks, vegetables of all sorts, and fruits. Alev spent all day eating the cakes. He said to Ngeh:

"The woman I asked to marry you only agrees to the wedding at night. She does not want to marry you during the daytime."

Being naïve, Ngeh agreed to every one of Alev's suggestions. He was all prepared for his wedding at night.

When the evening came, he asked his neighbors to help carry all that he had prepared for the ceremony. Arriving at the wedding place, they began cooking rice and various dishes. Some brought fruits, others brought cakes of all sorts according to the custom.

On her side, *Neang* Ngoh asked her neighbors to prepare the reception.

Alev was preoccupied eating the cakes to satiation.

Hearing only the voice of the approaching man, but not seeing his face in the dark night, *Neang* Ngoh was wondering.

"The voice sounds exactly like my beloved husband Ngeh", she thought.

Ngeh was also perplexed when he heard the woman's voice. He thought:

"The voice of my bride is similar to that of my gentle *Neang* Ngoh."

He then climbed up to the house,[23] saw the woman who was waiting for him, and exclaimed:

"But she looks entirely like *Neang* Ngoh, my wife!"

*Neang* Ngoh exclaimed:

"But he looks like Ngeh, my husband!"

The relatives and the neighbors shouted:

"It is Ngeh!"

"It is not Ngeh!"

---

23 Translator's Note: Cambodians build their houses on stilts to protect themselves from flooding, wild animals and thieves. To enter a house, one must climb up a ladder.

"It is Ngoh!"

"It is not Ngoh!"

Meanwhile, Ngeh and Ngoh examined each other and, realizing that Alev had tricked them, felt totally embarrassed. Alev realized that his trick had been discovered and went to hide. At dawn, he went to the monastery to beg for hospitality.

Ngeh and Ngoh resumed their communal lives as husband and wife.

## How Alev Became a Matchmaker

Alev was zealously pursuing his studies in the monastery. One fine day, he said to himself:

"I will dupe some monks who have a lot of money, get some of it, and take it to my parents." He approached one young monk who was quite handsome and told him discretely:

"Venerable Sir, there is a woman who loves you. She is an extremely beautiful young lady."

Upon hearing these words the young monk felt happy and gripped with desire. He replied:

"If what you are telling me is true, I will give you one *baht*."[24]

"Venerable Sir, wait until this evening. When it is dark, I will take you to a place where I will bring the girl to you."

---

24 Translator's Note: The *baht* was a unit of ancient Cambodian currency so in Khmer one says 'one *baht* of money' or 'one *baht* of silver'. See footnote 8 for additional information.

Alev left the monk's room and went to the nearby village. He found a young Chinese merchant and asked him:

"*Choek* [25], how would you like me to find you a charming young girl?"

"Yes, certainly", said the Chinese merchant.

"If you like her, how much would you pay me to have her?"

"I will give you one silver baht."

"It's too little. If you give me two baht, I will bring you a young girl of exquisite beauty who is extremely fair of complexion."

"It's a deal!"

"Well, wait until nightfall. I will take you to her."

Alev returned to the monastery. At nightfall, when two people cannot recognize each other in the dark, Alev brought the monk into an isolated hut and told him:

"When I bring the girl in, take great care in covering your head with your robe so that she will not recognize that you are a monk with your shaved head, otherwise she will not dare come close to you."

Having said this, Alev went to the Chinese merchant's house and discreetly told him:

"I've brought the young girl I've spoken of close to here. I will bring you to her. But before going in, be sure to cover your head completely with a *krama*, for if she sees the way your pigtail is cut and braided, and your prominent cheekbones, she will recognize that you are Chinese and will reject you."

---

25 Cambodians address Chinese men as *choek* = uncle.

He accompanied the Chinese merchant to the hut where the monk was waiting.

He whispered:

"*Choek*, the girl is in there. Pay me the agreed sum now."

At the hut's door, the Chinese bent over to look and saw the monk sitting with his robe draped over his head . The Chinese didn't doubt that it was a girl. He paid two silver *baht* to Alev who wrapped them in his belt, quickly slipping away and returning to the monastery.

The monk and the Chinese merchant, left alone together in the hut each believed that the other was a woman but soon they realized that Alev had duped them. Completely embarrassed they went their separate ways.

Alev was waiting for the monk in his room at the monastery. As soon as he entered Alev asked for the money that the monk had promised.

"You cheated me and you dare ask for the money? You'll certainly get nothing from me!"

"Venerable Sir, if you don't give me my money, I will disclose to the Venerable Abbot your attempt to commit a sexual act. I will denounce you to everyone in the village and the surrounding area. You will be scorned and despised by everybody. Furthermore, you will be tried in the ecclesiastical court. It will be publicly revealed that you have hired me to provide you with a woman, that my fee was fixed at one silver *baht*, and that you refused to pay what you owed me after I fulfilled my commitment. I will not leave you in peace. I will take my complaint to the Venerable Abbot!"

Scared by Alev's threats, the monk immediately gave him one silver *baht*, but Alev did not accept it. He said:

"When we agreed to my fee you said that you would give me one *batr* of silver.[26] You will now have to fill your *batr* with silver before I accept it! If not I will tell the abbot that you slept with a woman last night.

"Knowing this, the abbot will expel you from of the monastery. Furthermore, I will lodge a complaint with the higher ecclesiastical authority who will give you a caning, defrock you from the monkhood, and make you work collecting elephant dung with your bare hands!"

Frightened, the monk begged Alev:

"Let me search for the silver. Don't say anything to the abbot or take your complaint to the ecclesiastical authorities. I will try to get the silver by selling all my loin clothes and frocks."

"Alright, then," said Alev. "Give me just enough silver to carry to my parent's home in a shoulder bag and we'll call it even!"

Entirely relieved, the monk wrapped the silver in a bag, gave it to Alev, and said:

"Take pity on me, don't soil my reputation!"

"Don't worry your grace, I will tell no one," Alev replied, taking the silver and taking leave of the monk.

---

26 Translator's note: Alev uses a play on words to his advantage here. *Baht* is an old term for a monetary unit, but the word *batr* denotes the begging bowl used by Buddhist monks. The two Khmer words are pronounced the same but have different meanings and spellings (as in the English transliteration here). Alev uses this ploy to justify asking the monk for a begging bowl full of silver.

## How Alev Taught His Father to Make Money

Alev returned to his parent's home. As he approached the house, he called to his mother:

"Mother, sew a big purse!"

"And why should I make a big purse?" asked *Neang* Ngoh.

Alev showed her what he was carrying.

Upon seeing, she called to tell her husband Ngeh that Alev was carrying a sack full of silver. Ngeh came immediately and, seeing the huge sum in the bag, forgot the anger he had with Alev's earlier practical jokes. The father and mother hugged Alev.

"Where did you get the silver?" asked Ngeh. "How did you get it?"

"How is it hard to get money? You just have to go to the market and show people your private part! Then, without fail, some people will give you one *baht*, others two or three! So, it's easy to get a lot of silver. If you want to do the same, just take a walk. Show your private part to people, one at a time, and you'll get even more money than you expected!"

Being rather thick, Ngeh the father did as Alev had said.

He went to town, stopped in front of a house and exposed himself like Alev told him to do. Offended, the residents beat him and chased him away. Ngeh went from door to door exposing himself. Every time he was chased and beaten. Frightened, Ngeh ran towards his home.

Alev was waiting mid-way. When he saw his father running back from town he spotted a Jwear [27] trader far behind him on the same road, carrying a shoulder bag filled with silk cloth, silver and gold boxes. Alev cried out to his father:

"Look out, Father! The townsmen are chasing you to beat you! Cut through the field and you'll escape!"

Looking back, Ngeh saw a man walking in his direction with a bamboo pole on his shoulder. He really thought that a townsman was after him so, filled with fear, he ran into the field as Alev advised.

Alev then waited for the *Jwear* with a plan to trick him, too. He told the *Jwear*:

"Big brother, that man is chasing a deer with a broken leg, but alone he won't be able to catch it. If you go to help him you'll both be able to catch it and we will share the meat!"

Looking in the direction Alev pointed the *Jwear* saw a man running and believed he was really chasing a deer. Thus, he left his bag with Alev and ran to help Ngeh. While running, Ngeh looked back and saw the man running after him. Thinking he was being chased he tried to run even faster.

---

27 Translator's Note: While Monod called the traders "Cham" in the original text, Cambodians call them Jwear, meaning Javanese people. In the 1940s, I saw individual traders on foot carrying shoulder bags and a wooden stick walking from village to village selling small goods. One Jwear and his family regularly sailed from the Gulf of Siam up the river to dock in my hometown for weeks at a time. From there, he walked to nearby villages to trade with his shoulder bag and wooden stick. His sailing boat was similar to the traditional Indonesian vessels. Chams, on the other hand, generally pursued different professions. When Champa was conquored by the Vietnamese, the Cham people fled into Cambodia. As a child, I remember Cham living near my home but they were either butchers (beef only) or fishermen. While Cambodians differentiate between Chams and Malay I noted that Monod used the word 'Malais' and 'Cham' interchangeably.

Alev, meanwhile, took the *Jwear*'s bag to his mother to stash it away and then Alev quickly left the area.

Realizing that he had been duped, the *Jwear* rushed back to the road to look for his goods. But Alev had vanished. Regretting the loss of his possessions, but unable to find anyone, he set out to search for Alev.

## How Alev Took a Bride

Alev ran away. He arrived in a distant village where he met an elderly woman who, assisted by her granddaughter, was loading her modest belongings into a sampan. They were moving to another village nearer her friends and relatives because her adolescent granddaughter was reaching a marriageable age.

Alev fell in love with the young girl and began helping them load things into the sampan. Seeing Alev being so goodhearted, the old woman asked: "*Chau*,[28] where are you going?"

Alev replied:

"I request permission to go with you."

"What is your name?" the lady asked.

---

28 Translator's Note: In all social interactions, Cambodians rarely address a person by name. Depending on the relative age of the conversation partners, they always use appellative words like *bang* (big brother/big sister), *p'aun* or *aun* (little brother/little sister), *poo/meeing* (young uncle/aunt), *oum* (old uncle/aunt), *yeay* (grand-mother/grand-father), etc. These words do not denote actual familial relationships. *Chau* literally means grandson, but in the context of the Khmer conversation, it means 'young man.' Furthermore, the word *k'nhom* = I is rarely used.

Alev answered:"My name is *Chee chau prâsa.*[29] Wherever *Yeay*[30] is going, allow me to follow you."

The old woman rejoiced in her heart, thinking that Alev can help row the sampan.

After everything was loaded onto the sampan, Alev went to the back of the boat to row. The grandmother helped by paddling at the front. The granddaughter sat in the middle, smiling, sometimes looking at the grandmother and sometimes looking at Alev.

After rowing a short distance, Alev pretended to have forgotten his machete and said to the woman:

"Oh *Yeay*! I forgot my machete on the riverbank while I was busy loading your belongings. This machete is a valuable inheritance from my ancestors. Please allow me to turn back the boat to get it."

The old woman agreed to let Alev turn the boat back. When it reached the quay, Alev said:

"*Yeay*, could you kindly go to get my machete, I left it against the tree on the river bank near the path where we were loading your belongings."

As soon as the old woman walked up far enough on the bank out of sight, Alev reversed the boat in a hurry and rowed vigorously downstream. Not being able to find the machete, the old woman returned to the boat, but found neither the boat, nor Alev, nor her granddaughter. She looked down the river and saw Alev paddling the

---

29 Translator's Note: Here Alev makes a pun. *Chee* is a friendly term used by an older person to address someone who has just left the monkhood, or a younger man. *Chau prâsa* means grandson or granddaughter in-law. To the ordinary people, *chee chau prâsa* = grandson-in-law. Alev cleverly took advantage of this to introduce the idea of him marrying the granddaughter.

30 See footnote 28.

boat with full force. She beat her chest crying in despair, and ran after the boat shouting for help:

"Help me! *Chee chau prâsa* has kidnapped my granddaughter! Help me! *Chee chau prâsa* has kidnapped my granddaughter!"

Hearing her cries, the riverfolk all responded:

"If the husband kidnaps his wife there is nothing we can do! A man is allowed to kidnap his wife if it pleases him!"

Everyone thought that the granddaughter was Alev's wife and Alev was the grandson-in-law. No one helped the old woman and the sampan disappeared down the river.

Finally, she explained to the riverfolk:

"The name of the creep who kidnapped my granddaughter is *Chee chau prâsa!* But he is not married to my girl. He stole my granddaughter and he stole all my possessions!"

The villagers understood too late that Alev had duped the old woman, kidnapped her granddaughter and stolen her possessions. Alev had already gotten a good lead and it was too late to catch him.

During this time, Alev continued to row. At nightfall, he gently said to the girl:

"The reason *Bang* abducted you is because *Bang* loves you very much. *Bang* wants to marry you."

But the girl did nothing but sob uncontrollably, missing her grandmother with whom she had lived her entire life.

"My grandmother will be searching for me," she said. "She won't find me. What if she jumps in the water to drown her despair? How will I know? Or what if she misses me so much, she starves herself to death? I beg you to take me back to my *Yeay*. If not I will jump in the water and kill myself before your eyes!"

Steering the sampan into the quiet woods Alev spoke tenderly to the girl:

"If *bang* abducted you it's for love, because *bang* wants you to be his wife. If you jump into the water and drown, who then could be my wife?"

The maiden replied:

"If you love me, why didn't you ask for my hand according to the custom?"

Alev replied:

"Ô *Neang*, my heart is impatient! How can I bear the waiting, if I ask for your hand according to the custom?. It's well and good if I succeed, but if I am refused, I would be wasting my time. Therefore, I abducted you to take you to the land of my parents and my ancestors where we can have a proper wedding according to tradition. Don't be sad, my love. *Bang* will soon take you to see your grandmother. Don't worry."

With the power of his sweet words, Alev calmed the heart of the young girl who fell asleep at his side.

❦

## How Alev Fought the Pirates

The next morning, Alev continued the trip.

As they floated downstream, they ran into the midst of five hundred pirates waiting to ambush and rob travelers on the river!

Realizing there was no way to evade them, Alev rowed the sampan straight into the middle of them and went to talk to the group leader:

"Despite your great number, you dare to only rob merchants travelling *alone* in small isolated boats far from villages, and you only get small rewards. As for me, I never attack small prey! I pillage cities and kingdoms, attacking important groups. I do it alone to become master of their capitals and provinces!

"It is because I know all types of magic spells that render me invulnerable and invincible! These incantations make it so swords can't cut me and fire can't burn me. I've just come from pillaging a city where I kidnapped this young girl after sacking the entire town! If you don't believe me, ask the girl."

The pirates, hearing Alev boasting about the power he gained from his magical incantations, wanted to learn more from him, and so they said:

"We want you to teach us all the magical formulas! Agree to be our teacher, and we will work together."

Alev replied "If you all want to learn, I will teach you my art. The only difficulty is that we need an appropriate place to train where no one will find us. We must therefore find an isolated island, far from the shore, where we can work without risk."

Alev and the pirates began searching for an isolated island in the middle of the sea. They found one with a nice sandy beach. Alev went ashore and found a spot out of sight from where they anchored the ship. Alev said to the pirates:

"Now, if you want me to teach you the magical formulas that will give you unlimited power, it is essential that you instantly follow my instructions and do exactly as I say. This is the only condition to make my magic spells work for you!"

All the pirates agreed to obey him precisely.

Alev then ordered them to build a platform supporting an altar decorated with vines, flowers, incense sticks, and a seven-stage ritual parasol. Then, he asked the pirates to dig a large pond in the sand deep enough to submerge a man over his head.

With best preparations complete, Alev ordered all five hundred pirates to shave their heads and then he said to them:

"To give power to the spell that I will teach, you must remove all your clothes and put them in the junk. Then, you must all submerge yourselves completely under the water and, without returning to the surface while holding your breath, recite the formula seven times. You must all do this precisely without changing anything in the incantation or it will lose its power for everyone. Now get yourselves ready while I go into the forest to prepare."

Alev waited until the pirates returned from the junk without their clothes, then he went to where the ship was anchored and whispered to his wife:

"Listen carefully to what I'm about to tell you. Pull the anchor rope shorter, hold it tight, and be prepared. When you see me coming down the bank towards the boat, you must pull up the anchor as fast as you can."

He then made a detour into the forest and returned to the pirates.

He taught them a long, meaningless incantation that he made them repeat many times until they could do it without mistakes.

Night fell and he said to them:

"You must all dive together at the exact same time, and you must return to the surface at the same time for the incantations to be effective and powerful. Are you ready? Dive!"

When the pirates all submerged at once, Alev rushed down towards the junk, pulled up the anchor, and set sail.

When the five hundred pirates returned to the surface they searched for Alev but didn't see him anywhere, and they asked each other:

"Where is our venerable teacher?"

They searched the ritual platform, but didn't find him. They called for him, but he didn't respond. Finally, they went down to the mooring site where they didn't find Alev but they did see that their junk had disappeared. That's when they realized that they had been fooled! But they had no means on the island to pursue Alev.

The five hundred pirates then hastily began cutting bamboo in the forest to build a raft that would get them back to the mainland.

## How Alev Saved the Pirate Village from Ghosts

Alev and his wife swiftly sailed away in the luxury of the pirates' junk, taking along all the treasures of five hundred thieves. They sailed throughout the night, for an entire day, and by evening they arrived at a village. But Alev discovered that, in this village, there were no men, only women and children. He immediately suspected that this was the village of the pirates whom he had fooled. He dropped his anchor and entered the village.

The wives of the pirates didn't recognize the junk that had belonged to their husbands because when they left the village they were empty-handed. It was much later that the pirates encountered this junk, which they plundered and captured.

After anchoring the boat, Alev took a piece of chalk and a writing-slate, came ashore, and drew some magical signs acting as if he was calculating something.

The women and children of the pirates gathered around him and, seeing the different symbols he inscribed, truly believed that Alev really knew how to tell fortunes. They asked him:

"Kind Sir, you know divination. Can you use your art to tell us the fate of our husbands and fathers? It has been many months since they left and we have received no news."

Now certain these women were the wives of the pirates, Alev replied:

"That will be no problem if it will please you! Don't tell me anything. I will make my calculations, align the signs and I will know all. To learn whatever you want to know, you must only bring me candles, incense, betel and areca nuts. Then you must maintain complete silence as I consult the signs and make offerings to my mystical master."

The wives of the pirates rushed to all the homes to alert their companions. Soon, they all came with candles, incense sticks, flowers, areca nuts, betel leaves, banana and sugarcane to offer to Master Alev.

After receiving the offerings, Alev took his slate-board and chalk and acted like he was consulting the spirits. In fact, he was calculating the probable time that the pirates would return to their village. He told the women:

"All your husbands will return the day after tomorrow. But before that a danger will menace you! Tomorrow night, naked, bald-headed ghosts will come into your village, looking for a way into your homes to spread a terrible epidemic of smallpox! It is essential that you take measures to prevent this plague!"

The frightened wives of the pirates asked Alev how they could possibly avoid this sickness.

"It's very easy," responded Alev. "At nightfall, all of you, women and children, must wait at the door of each house carrying heavy wooden sticks. When you see the nude, bald-headed phantoms, beat them to prevent them from getting in. Don't let a single one get into your homes!"

The next day, the pirates reached the coast and drew close to their village. But, not having any clothes, they hid in the woods until dark before going to their homes. After dark, the pirates walked into their individual homes. But their wives and children, all on watch for the phantoms, were waiting at the doors. Upon seeing nude, bald-headed men entering their homes they began beating them with all their might until some were injured or even unconscious. Some suffered broken bones while others fled.

Finally, the women recognized their husbands and the children recognized their fathers. In tears, they told the pirates about what had happened. Upon hearing their description, the pirates quickly recognized Alev but they could do nothing. They were all bruised and badly wounded from the beatings and they did not know in which direction Alev went.

Meanwhile, Alev was hiding quite near the village. He heard the return of the pirates, the shouting of the wives, the beatings and the shouts of the husbands. So he hastily returned to the junk, unfurled the sails and headed toward his wife's village.

ꟈ ❀ ꟈ

## How Alev Became Wealthy

When they arrived at the village Alev and his wife went to meet the grandmother. On finding her, Alev prostrated himself before her, begging for her forgiveness and offering her all the treasure in the junk. Upon seeing those riches the grandmother forgave him, really liked Alev now, and fully accepted him as her grandson-in-law. Alev built a house and hired several servants to look after his grandmother-in-law and his wife.

After some time Alev took leave of his grandmother and his wife saying that he wanted to go visit his parents. The grandmother loved her grandson by marriage with all her heart but didn't dare stop him from visiting his father and his mother.

"Don't stay away too long!" she implored. "Come back soon because we're all alone with no one to care for us."

Alev's wife wanted to go with him and said:

"I want to go with you to meet your mother, your father and all your relatives in your village. Furthermore, I don't want to be apart from you. It's a sad situation for a wife to be far from her husband. She has no one to defend her, to guard her. People will look at me as a widow and ridicule me. I want to go with you, my husband."

"My darling, *bang* also wants to take you with him. But think of grandmother, who is very old, who may fall ill. Day and night she would be alone, with no one to care for her, to entertain her, to find her medicines. When we ran away together, she suffered so much but now she is happy. But if both of us leave her again, she'll certainly die. We already made that big mistake once, we shouldn't repeat it again."

His wife, filled with compassion for her grandmother, agreed to let Alev go alone. She prepared his baggage with food supplies for the road, and asked:

"How many servants and oxcarts do you want to take with you?"

Alev replied:

"I won't take any. Your *bang* will go alone."

Alev did not want to bring any servants because he had the wicked intention of having more wives on the road. If he had servants with him, people would think that he is already married so he wouldn't succeed in asking for another girl's hand. He said to his wife:

"*Bang* is used to travelling alone. If I take servants, oxcarts, cows and water buffaloes my trip will be slower and I won't be able to return to my love as quickly as I wish."

Alev packed in his bag only money and enough food supplies for the road. The grandmother repeatedly said to Alev:

"When you arrive and see that your parents are well, do return quickly, dear grandson."

Alev said goodbye to his wife and grandmother and left.

When he arrived at the house of his father Ngeh and his mother *Neang* Ngoh, he gave them the money he brought. His parents were delighted and asked:

"Where have you been for so long? Your mother only looked to the road every day, hoping to see her son!"

"I went to find work because you, mother and father, don't think of making a living as other people."

His parents replied:

"Do as your heart desires my son! As for your mother and father, we work just to survive and to preserve our possessions for you in the future. Now, you look after yourself and make your own living as you please."

Alev stayed with his parents for a few days and left again.

He arrived in a grand city filled with people. He visited the royal palace, where he took a close look at the houses of dignitaries and wealthy people. He noticed one large manor with a tall roof that was filled with splendid treasures.

The mansion had stables with cattle, buffaloes, elephants, horses, and ox carts. Many servants were busy working everywhere. There were magnificent orchards and gardens with flowers of all types and all colors in pots arranged in rows. There were ponds with fish of silver and gold playing beneath white lotus, red lotus, and all types of water lilies. And finally he saw a beautiful young girl.

Alev instantly fell in love and was overcome with desire for the girl. He went in to present himself to the master of the house, a *sethei*[31] of great renown. Alev petitioned the *sethei* to be accepted as a *nephew*[32]

---

31 Translator's Note: *Sethei* is a Khmer word used in classic Cambodian literature and still in use today. In olden times it referred to a very wealthy, powerful man who had received a title awarded by the king in the form of a certificate or a white parasol. The word *sethei* is used throughout the story instead of "wealthy man."

32 Translator's Note: Monod translated the Cambodian term "*neveu*" using the word "client." In ancient Roman society, a client (Latin, *cliens*) was a commoner (plebeian) who was sponsored by a patron benefactor (*patronus*). The patron assisted his client with his protection and regular gifts; the client dedicated his vote whenever the patron or his associate was up for election.

In Cambodia, a young stranger who volunteers to be a servant (not in bondage) in a family richer than his/her own is called nephew/niece (literal translation). The person lives with the new family and is provided with food, clothing and perhaps business opportunities in the future.

in the family. The *sethei* was sympathetic and had a liking for Alev so he asked:

"Where are you from? Where are your parents?"

Alev answered:

"Sir, I come from far away. My father and my mother once possessed great wealth, numerous servants, cattle, buffaloes, elephants, horses, and a beautiful manor as you have. But both of them fell ill and died. My heart was broken and I could not bear to stay there alone because I was used to living with my parents. I left my home, my wealth, and now after a long voyage I am here to ask that I may live with you. Sir, if you accept me I will do anything you tell me to."

The *sethei* agreed to take Alev into his household.

Every day Alev got up early, cleaned the house, looked after all the valuable object, and arranged them in their proper places, as if they were his own. Seeing how diligent and careful Alev was in caring for his property, the *sethei* became quite fond of him and gave him authority over the entire household.

Whenever the *sethei* went for the audience with the king, he brought Alev along. After accompanying the *sethei* so often, he soon got to know all the dignitaries, senior ministers, judges, privy councilors, administrators of all ranks and their relatives.

In public, Alev always played dumb. When asked his name, he replied, "Alev Tev,"[33] which opened him up to much teasing and many insults, even from the servants of the powerful people. Whenever

---

33 Translator's Note: *Alev* = a young man with squinted eyes. *Tev* = warped, crooked. *Alev Tev* is therefore a common Cambodian insult to mock someone who looks retarded, dumb or unusual.

anyone saw Alev coming, they called him Alev Tev. But Alev never reacted to anyone's insults, and he never showed any sign of anger.

Alev frequently visited the Courthouse, listening to the court proceedings, and thus learning civil law and customs. He also took a special interest in collecting papers and letters that people threw away, especially when those papers bore the seals of privy councilors, high court judges, and ministers who had great wealth.[34] Alev had a plan.

He used wax to copy the various seals creating counterfeits in the exact shapes and sizes of the originals. Then, he wrote notes of debt using the names of the high officials acknowledging that they had borrowed money from him: some for 100 *nein*,[35] some for 200 *nein*, and some for 500 *nein*. He added the corresponding seals to the letters, folded them and put them in a box.

Soon, Alev began leaving the box with the *sethei*'s wife each time he left the house. It became a regular part of the day for Alev to go to the *sethei*'s wife to say:

"Madame, I come again to ask you to please take great care of my box and please do not let anyone open it."

After many weeks, the *sethei*'s wife became more and more curious. One day, she decided to peek into the box to find it was full of papers. She closed the box.

But after another week went by and her curiosity grew again. What type of papers could the young Alev have that were so important?

---

34 Monod's Note: In ancient times, Cambodian officials never signed documents, instead they stamped official letters with distinctive seals for authentication.

35 A silver bar ressembling a miniature hog trough weighing approx. 375. g. It was used from the late 18th century until the French introduced the silver piaster in late 19th century.

Again the *sethei*'s wife opened the box but this time she began reading the documents inside. She quickly discovered that almost every high official and dignitary in the land owed Alev a great deal of money! The total amounted to a huge sum and every document was stamped with the appropriate official seal. Too surprised to keep the secret to herself she took the box to show her husband. Having examined the papers, the *sethei* said to his wife:

"When Alev first came, I asked about his parents. He told me they were dead, but that when they were alive they were as wealthy as we are. Now seeing all these papers proving that the court officials owe him so much money, I realize that he had certainly told me the truth. His intelligence and character show that he is from a good family. Furthermore, he cares for our property well. He knows what is missing, what needs repair, and what needs to be done. He is like our son.

"Now our daughter has reached her marrying age. Many princes and court officials have already come to ask for her hand. But none of them won a place in our hearts so we haven't agreed for her to accept. I would gladly give her to Alev, but if we do we will be ridiculed because he is an orphan here without anyone knowing his family background. It will be a shame if we don't give her to Alev because his character and behavior are perfect. He cares about our business as if it were his own. I've considered this problem but it's difficult to resolve."

"It's easy to avoid being ridiculed!" the *sethei*'s wife replied. "We will marry them at night with a simple ceremony — just large enough to avoid making the forest spirits angry. The young couple will then be married, but secretly. If people learn about the marriage later, who would mock us? Most of them owe Alev money anyway."

The *sethei* agreed to his wife's suggestion believing it was his daughter's destiny to become Alev's wife. He called Alev and said:

"Since you came to live in my house, I have seen your actions, your passion, and your care for my work, acting as if you were my own son. To reward you, I will give my daughter to you in marriage."

Alev was filled with delight.

The *sethei* called his daughter and together they all made ritual offerings to the ancestors and spirits according to the ancient traditions of marriage.

A few days after the wedding, Alev's wife told him that she wanted to go have an audience with the king. Alev said to her:

"I will wait at the courthouse.[36] When you pass in front, if you see me wave to you with my hand, you must bring betel on a gold platter and knee down to present it to me. After I take the tray, you must bow to me and then we will leave together."

Having thus instructed his wife, Alev dressed himself with an old *sampot* and vest and went to sit in the courthouse. All the dignitaries, high officials and judges were there with their servants, having arrived by elephant, horse and carriage.

Upon seeing Alev in his miserable clothes they began to mock him. Some tapped his head, some poked his back, others tugged on his arms asking him to clown around, as he often did when they asked him. Alev was so skillful acting like a fool that no one knew how intelligent he really was. They all assumed he was a pitiful pauper, living on alms, which is why they all made fun of him.

Soon, the *sethei*'s daughter passed by the courthouse on her palanquin, accompanied by maids and servants carrying silver and

---

36 Monod's Note: Cambodian Courthouses (*sala choum noum*) were built on short stilts and had no walls, only bare columns supporting the roof above the floor. Everyone outside can clearly see what happens inside and vice-versa.

gold boxes and marching in procession towards the royal palace. She looked towards Alev who never made a sign so she proceeded on towards the palace. Upon seeing her pass, the dignitaries said:

"The *sethei*'s daughter is the most beautiful of all!"

"The sons of princes themselves have been unable to obtain her hand in marriage!"

"Happy will be the man who weds that woman!"

Each one elaborated on what the others said. Having heard the discussion, Alev said to the officials:

"You said, gentlemen, that all the highest officials have asked for the *sethei*'s daughter in marriage without success. Just wait, gentlemen, for her to come out the palace. I will call her and she will bring me betel nut to chew! Dare you make a bet?"

Because Alev only acted crazy in their presence, the officials thought this bragging was just another example of his buffoonery. They mocked him, entirely unaware that Alev was far from crazy, and never suspecting how clever he really was. The officials replied, "We'll happily make the bet that the *sethei*'s daughter will not respond to your request! But what will you bet? You have nothing to gamble."

"Don't worry about that, gentlemen. If I lose the bet, I will write a note guaranteeing to be your slave for life. I will do everything you order me to."

The dignitaries and officials were delighted by his offer. He was so amusing that they all wanted to have him as their slave.

"He's lost his mind," they said "if he thinks that the *sethei*'s daughter would respond to his request! Let's take the bet with him. He'll be a slave to all of us, and we'll take turns being entertained. We'll make him write down all the silver and gold he wants for the bet and keep a record on paper."

After drafting the terms of the bet in letters the officials said to Alev:

"How much money do you want? Elephants with howdahs, horses with saddles and harnesses — you must write down everything you want."

On every one of the dignitaries betting letters Alev listed all the silver, gold, elephants and horses he wanted. Then he had them all put their seals on the letters and he tucked the papers in a bag wrapped around his waist. He wrote his own agreement to be a slave for life to the winner if he lost, and deposited that letter at the palace ministry. The preparations complete, he sat and waited at the courthouse entrance.

A short time later the *sethei*'s daughter came out of the palace. As she approached, Alev waved to her and called out:

"*Neang*, bring *bang* some betel nut to chew!"

The *sethei*'s daughter quickly got down from her palanquin, carefully placed betel nuts on a gold platter and walked to Alev, bowing to offer the platter.

Alev then took his wife's hand and led her to the most elegantly fitted elephant he had just won. He motioned for his servants to mount the other elephants and horses waiting before the courthouse and headed towards his father-in-law's house.

The dignitaries and officials who lost the bet stared speechless. Tears welled up in their eyes as they realized their favorite mounts, saddled with gold and silver, were now lost.

His in-laws were astonished to see Alev and their daughter returning home with a magnificent entourage of elephants and horses richly fitted with gold and silver howdahs and saddles. All the servants in the home leaned out the windows to gaze in amazement at the newlyweds.

The *sethei* asked Alev how this was possible.

"I have begun to collect the debts owed to me." answered the young man.

His heart filled with joy, the father-in-law said: "Truly no one can look down on us now!"

From then on, the *sethei* and his wife loved Alev even more. Alev regularly went to collect the balance of the money the officials owed for losing the bet. Little by little, he began managing all his in-laws' business to relieve them of any worries.

Years later, when the *sethei* passed away of old age, Alev became the principle merchant in the capital.

We have told the story of Alev as it was told from generation to generation. For those who read it, don't make fun of us if you don't believe it!

# Kung the Courageous

# រឿងគង់ហ៊ាន

*Kung Hean*

# Kung the Courageous

# រឿងគង់ហាន

*KUNG HEAN*

A long time ago, there lived a man who had two wives. His name was Kung and his two wives were *Neang* Am and *Neang* Kom.

One day Kung took his two wives on a trip to visit their parents in a far away province. Once there, they found the region lived in fear of a tiger that constantly came to attack the people and animals there.

Kung arrived at a dense forest near the village he was visiting. The tiger was in the woods. When it saw Kung from a distance, it jumped out with a terrible roar. Kung, his arms and legs trembling, ran to hide in a hollow tree, nearly fainting from fear. As he did this *Neang* Am and *Neang* Kom joined forces and, with strokes of a club, beat the big cat to death. Seeing that the tiger was dead, Kung came out of hiding, took a stick and began beating the tiger corpse with all his might. His indignant wives said:

"You're not a man! You're are a wimp! And you are a coward to beat this tiger that is already dead."

Kung was furious and insulted his wives by saying:

"No one has ever seen a woman killing a tiger! Only men have such courage!"

Kung cut a piece of creeper vine, tied up the dead tiger, and brought it to the village with the help of his two wives. Seeing such a wonderful sight, all the village people were delighted and asked:

"How could you kill this beast? It is ferocious. Do you know how many men, buffaloes and cattle it had devoured? You did us an immense service."

"Kung saw the tiger and ran to hide in a hollow tree!" the two women shouted. "The two of us, women, succeeded in killing the ferocious beast."

Hearing these words, Kung hurled abuse at his wives.

"Never," Kung cried, "has a woman had the audacity or strength to kill a tiger! All you people of this village know this well!"

And, full of conceit, he told his story:

"The tiger was there, I found myself here. I took a club like this and beat the tiger. It fell dead right there!"

As he spoke, Kung mimed his arm movements, jumping right and left, waving his club and shouting to impress the village people. All the people there were filled with respect for him and unanimously decided to call him "Kung the Courageous."

His reputation as a valiant man reached the king who raised him to the rank of government officer. It so happened that a formidable crocodile came to settle in the river that flowed through the capital city. Every day it caught and swallowed one of the king's subjects.

Soon, no one dared to go near the river; commerce was interrupted; ships swayed empty in their moorings; the whole country was desolate.

The king, informed of the situation, gave the order for Kung the Courageous to go and capture the crocodile. Kung was overwhelmed with fear.

But how could he argue with an order from the king? He replied:

"May Your Majesty worry not. I am at your service!"

He returned home crying and told his wives:

"O my dearest ones, I must bid you goodbye! The king has ordered me to catch a terribly vicious crocodile that is haunting the river. It's certain that I will lose this time. That cursed beast will devour me. When I fought the tiger, it was on dry land; I had all the means. But this time, what force will I have under water? I cannot even see the beast. But it's an order from the king so I can only obey. I can do nothing but jump into the river and let myself be eaten."

Kung called together his children, his relatives and neighbors to bid farewell. He was pale with fear, his teeth were chattering. Then he was on his way. He could hardly walk because his legs wobbled so badly. A cold sweat ran down his spine. He staggered with fear.

Arriving at the river, he saw the huge crocodile floating asleep close to the shore. Having heard that Kung the Courageous was coming to kill the monster, the people from the city gathered on the riverbank to watch.

At the water's edge, Kung noticed two tree trunks that grew out from the same stump in the shape of a fork. He sat down for a while gathering his thoughts. The sleeping crocodile floated on the surface just two meters away from him. At the sight of the beast, Kung was seized with fear; he could not breathe and his hair stood on end. Suddenly he stood up, unable to bear the tension any longer. He wanted to finish the situation at any cost. Closing his eyes, he dove into the stream!

Awakened by surprise, the crocodile made a tremendous effort to jump onto the bank. Fate, however, brought the beast to fall in the fork of the two tree trunks. The crocodile was caught in between the branches like in a vice, unable to move forward or backward.

Kung the Courageous emerged to the surface, counting the seconds he had left to live, but then opened his eyes to see the crocodile caught between the trees. He shouted to his children to bring a spear and strike it. Kung only dared come close to the animal when it was really dead.

"Look!" he said. "What strength and courage I have! I swam under water to get to this terrible beast and I threw it towards the bank with such skill as to catch it caught between the trees.

The spectators all thought he told the truth and lauded him with praise. He returned to the city to report the story of his great achievement to the king. For his distinguished service the king awarded him with a new official title even higher than the previous one.

From then on, the reputation of Kung the Courageous was incontestable.

Sometime later a war broke out; an ambitious neighbor invaded the king's territory. The king entrusted the command of all of his armies to Kung.

Kung the Courageous was shattered. He returned home and crawled onto his mat.[37] He did not eat; he was unable to utter a word; his eyes rolled upwards with fear.

His two wives approached him and asked:

---

37 Translator's Note: In ancient times, Cambodians had no beds and slept on woven mats laid on the floor.

"*Bang*, why are you lying down like this without eating? What happened to put you in such a pitiful state?"

Kung tried to gather all his strength to reply:

"The king put your *bang* at the head of his armies to go and fight the war. *Bang* is shaking with fright. *Bang* doesn't know how to avoid obeying orders, yet he does not want to go into battle."

"Don't be frightened like this," his wives said. "We will accompany you.

"We will help you, we promise. Get up and eat your meal. Take your bath as usual, and calm down."

Cheered up by his wives, Kung the Courageous got up, took a bath, and had a meal. Then he made his preparations to go fight the enemy.

When the time came, he took leave of the king and went to war accompanied by his two wives. Kung sat astride an elephant's neck. *Neang* Am and *Neang* Kom sat behind him. He was surrounded on all sides by his army, his troops marching in formation with musicians in front and banners fluttering in the wind.

When the enemy troops were in sight, Kung was blinded with fear.

In his panic, he hit the elephant's head with his mahout hook. At the same time Kung lost control of his bladder and bowels and began soiling the elephant's neck. Thinking that its rider was urging it to run, the elephant went hurtling past all the troops and tore into the enemy ranks. Seeing Kung the Courageous dashing into the middle of their formation, the attacking enemy forces believed that any man who dared to expose himself to such danger must be endowed with supernatural powers. The enemy ran for their lives in disarray, leaving their animals, and throwing away their weapons and equipment.

Having achieved such an astounding victory, Kung the Courageous regained his confidence. He convened his officers to boast about his audacity. Some were skeptical, for they saw the pungent proof of Kung's panic running down the neck of the elephant and said:

"What kind of a commander craps his pants at the sight of the enemy?"

"Eh!" Kung replied, "What does that prove? Does one stop in the heat of battle to go to the restroom? The enemy would have easily killed us all. Real courage is to think of nothing but victory when facing the enemy!"

The whole army listened to Kung's speech. Some—those with intelligence—knew the truth about Kung's lack of bravery. But the majority lacked perspective and gave Kung a standing ovation.

Kung the Courageous returned to the capital as a triumphant victor. He went to greet the king and reported how the enemies ran in disarray as he charged towards them.

The king rejoiced with all his heart. He lavished Kung with honors and made him the First Officer of the kingdom. He decorated him with the highest award and offered him magnificent gifts.

Kung was even more full of himself about his strength and valor than even before.

This story was told to us by the old people who learned from their ancestors. For any curious people who read it, do not question us because we retell it in the same way our predecessors did.

# The Tale of the Female Partridge and the Male Partridge

## រឿងទទាញីឈ្មោល

*Roeung Totea nhee, chmaol*

# The Tale of the Female Partridge and the Male Partridge

## រឿងទទាញីឈ្មោល

*Roeung Totea nhee, chmaol*

Once upon a time, there were two partridges, one female and one male, that lived in a forest. They were husband and wife and one day the female partridge became pregnant.

When her gestation period was nearing the end, the two birds built a nest of straw and leaves, hidden within deep foliage clumps to avoid predators. The female then laid two eggs which she incubated with the greatest of care.

Two chicks soon hatched from the eggs: a female and a male. The mother cared for them and kept them warm beneath her wings. If she had to leave the nest, her husband would take her place. They took turn continuously and never left the chicks alone at anytime.

When the chicks began to grow feathers, the mother's affection grew even stronger. Nothing was dearer to her than her chicks.

That year, it happened that the dry season lasted longer than usual. Grasses were scorched and dry tree leaves littered the ground.

One day, a hunter took his crossbow and went hunting on the plain. Seeing the dry grass, he set a fire to drive the animals inside out so that he could shoot them. The fire spread rapidly and reached the forest; the whole sky was darkened by the smoke. Trees and bamboo bushes were engulfed in flames that rose high into the air. The burning fire raged, sounding like a violent thunderstorm.

Hearing the commotion, the male partridge flew out of their nest to soar high above the forest canopy to see what was happening. He saw the forest burning and the fire, whipped by a violent wind, was spreading rapidly towards the nest. He shouted with all his strength:

"My darling partridge! Leave the chicks and fly to me immediately. Look how the forest burns! Look at the flames rising high into the sky!"

The female flew up to see what was happening. The fire was spreading quickly and she thought only of her chicks.

"Oh my dear chicks!" she lamented. "You were just born into this world so you cannot yet fly! You will helplessly be consumed by fire with no chance of saving yourselves. Your mother is desperate! She has no hands to carry you with her. But she will not leave you; she will be consumed by the fire with her little ones!"

Turning to her husband she said:

"Soon, the fire will reach our nest. My babies will die! I do not want to leave them alone in their suffering. I will die with them. As for you, what do you want to do?"

"I will also stay with our children and die with them!" said the male partridge.

Both birds flew down to their nest and the flames raced closer and closer. The mother partridge shielded her chicks with her wings. The father partridge wrapped the mother with his wing. Both birds were terrified and shook all over. The heat was intolerable. No longer able to bear the heat, the male partridge suddenly took flight into the air. The female lifted her head and saw her husband deserting her and her chicks. She thought to herself:

"Men's words can never be trusted. When I am reborn,[38] in whatever form, I wish that I never have anything to do with a male. In my new life, I pray that I will not become the wife of a man who does not keep his promises."

As soon as she finished this thoughts, the fire reached the nest and killed the female partridge and her chicks.

Hovering high above the nest, the male saw his wife and children perish in the flames. He thought:

"Oh, how faithful my wife was to her words. She said she would choose to perish with her children. There she is, really dead. It is not right that I alone survive, after betraying my own promise. It is only correct that I, too, should sacrifice my life.

"When my wife is born again, whatever her new existence is, I want to be reborn in the same status and become her husband in that life, and for all my future lives."

Having made this wish, he let himself fall onto his wife's body and be burned to death.

---

38 Monod's Note: The Cambodian cosmogony believes in the migration of the soul. Each sentient being has a soul that after death, may go to *Sthan Suor* (Sanskrit: *Sthana Svur* or *Svarga* = paradise), or descend to *Sthan Norok* (Sanskrit: *Sthana Naraka* = hell) where it (soul) is reborn as a new life form in a new *jeat* (*jata*) = existence. The souls may successively take life forms as animals or humans.

Translator's Note: The future life form of an individual sentient being depends on the deeds committed in the current life.

## The Princess Who Would Speak To No Man

So it came to pass that this male partridge — who broke his promise to his wife — was reborn as a son of a very poor man who lived in the kingdom of Peareanasey[39], situated on the outer edge of the world.

He was an ugly boy. His body was covered with warts and cysts as big as a thumb. He was devoid of intelligence. For this reason, his father called him Turpolpheap.[40]

The female partridge — who had kept her word — was reborn as the daughter of *Neang* Nanteartevi, the principal queen of King Promtoatt in the kingdom of Peareanasey. She came into this world in the form of an exceptionally beautiful girl. In the entire world, one could find no girl who compared to her beauty. Thus, her parents gave her the name of Chonbatkalyani.[41]

When she was old enough to speak, she spoke only to women, never to men. Even to her father, the king, she never said a single word.

As she grew up, she became more and more beautiful. If a man saw her, he would stand still just to admire her and couldn't take his eyes away.

Her mind was as bright as her beauty. She was literate, and became familiar with religious works and traditional precepts. She knew how to solve all the enigmas. Few could equal her intelligence.

---

39 Translator's Note: In Cambodian folktales, *Peareanasey* was referred to as Baranasi, the present day Varanasi in Uttar Pradesh, India. Being far away from the Himalayas (regarded as Mount Meru, the center of the universe in Hindu-Khmer mythology), it is thought of as the edge of the world in Cambodian tales.

40 Monod's Note: *Turpol* (Sanskrit: *durbala*) = weak, feeble, sickly. *Pheap* (Sanskrit: *bhava*) = condition, state.

41 Monod's Note: *Chonbatkalyani*: equivalent to Sanskrit, *Janapadakalyani*; *jana* = human being; *pada* = sign; *kalyani* = beautiful, pleasant.

Her father, the king, seeing that his daughter would never talk to any man, had no idea how he could convince her to marry.

After pondering this problem at length, he decided to have a tower built in front of his palace, surrounded by beautiful gardens. He gave this tower to his daughter as her residence. Then, he made announcements to the whole kingdom as well as foreign countries, large and small, that his daughter lived in this tower. He invited kings, dignitaries, and even ordinary men to come stroll in the gardens, declaring that he would wed his daughter and bestow the title *Obbarach*[42] upon any man capable of inspiring Chonbatkalyani to speak only five times. If this happened, loud drums and gongs would immediately announce the event with great fanfare. The man who succeeded in making the princess speak would be presented to the king who would receive him as his son-in-law.

Everyone was free to come and try his luck. The only condition was that, men were forbidden to enter the tower, or frighten the princess, or use force to make her talk. The king's proclamation was announced throughout the country and beyond. Countless men came to the gardens.

To attract the princess' attention, some men dressed in magnificent outfits, some displayed sword fighting, while others displayed boxing, riding, or racing carts, each trying to impress the princess in his own way.

42 Monod's Note: The title of *Obbarach* (that has been wrongly translated to French as 'Second king', which has no corresponding reality) is a title given to the first prince of the Cambodian court.

Translator's Note: According to the Cambodian dictionary, *Obbarach* is a royal title of a prince or high official appointed by the reigning king as his immediate deputy.

The princess watched the endless displays from the tower, but she neither smiled, nor uttered a word.

## The Brilliance of Stupidity

When the king's proclamation reached Turpolpheap's ears he said to his mother:

"Oh mother, they say that the king's daughter never speaks to any man and that His Majesty has established a competition for all men to come and try their luck. If anyone succeeds in making the princess speak, he will become her spouse. I would like to go and watch to see who wins the princess' hand. Please give me two bowls of rice and a pot and I'll go to the tower."

"Oh my dear son, you are ugly and very poor; you own only the single *sampot*[43] that you are now wearing. All those who go to the tower are handsome young men with splendid attire. Don't go. You will embarrass yourself. It is not you that the princess will fall for!"

"I do not wish to have Chonbatkalyani's hand. I want only to see the entertainments. Since I was born, I have never seen any festive gathering. Please, kindly let me go to see it!" pleaded Turpolpheap.

Feeling sorry for the boy, his mother gave him a bag of rice, three dried fish, some salt, some *prahok*,[44] one pot and two bowls, and said to him:

---

43 Translator's Note: A *sampot* is a traditional Cambodian garment consisting of a rectangular piece of cloth about 2m long, worn by wrapping around the waist; the two ends of the cloth are rolled, pushed between the legs and hooked behind the waist; similar to Mahatma Gandhi's *dhoti*.

44 Monod's Note: *Prahok* is fermented salty fish that is a major traditional source of proteins for Cambodians.

"Now you can go, my child, but come back soon. You have never been to a big city, don't stay too long."

Turpolpheap took his rations and went off with the crowd.

Suddenly, a heavy rain came and he was soaked, wet and shivering. He looked for shelter, but the people in the various royal halls prevented him from entering. They pointed to him a garden pavilion at the foot of the tower. Chilled to the bone, Turpolpheap ran to take shelter in the pavilion.

When the rain stopped, he tried to make fire to warm himself up. He took a single stick of wood and, as much as he tried, he could not get it to ignite. Even if the fire looked as though it would start it went out immediately. Turpolpheap said to himself:

"I don't understand why this fire is afraid of the wood!"

Watching from the tower, Princess Chonbatkalyani said:

"Is this boy crazy trying to light a fire with a single stick of wood? How can it stay lit? He only needs to cross a few pieces of wood together, then his fire will burn!"

Turpolpheap looked up and saw the princess. He went to gather an armful of dry wood, lit the fire, and blew on it to make a nice big flame. He sat near the fire to get warm. To dry his wet clothes, he moved closer to the fire until he got burned. He jumped backwards, bumped against the wall and was thrown forward into the fire and got burned again. Princess Chonbatkalyani said:

"He really is crazy! Why doesn't he dry his *krama*[45] first and then put it on as he dries his *sampot*?"

45 Translator's Note: The ubiquitous Cambodian shawl.

Without looking up Turpolpheap began drying his *krama* over the fire. When it was dry, he put it on to dry his wet *sampot*. Then, he changed back into his dry *sampot*.

By the time Turpolpheap dressed himself with dry clothes he was hungry and began preparing a meal. He cut a tree branch to make two pegs that he pushed into the ground on either side of his fire. Then he went to the pond to get water with his cooking pot.

The pond, however, was covered with duckweed. So Turpolpheap left his pot on the bank and waded into the pond, clearing the duckweed with his hands to get to the water. Then he turned around to take the pot but as he did the duckweed spread back to fill the space he had just cleared. Turpolpheap went back to the bank, set his pot down, and returned to the water to clear the duckweed again. And again the duckweed drifted back before he could dip his pot to get clean water. He repeated the same attempts many times without succeeding to get the clean water.

Observing all this from the edge of her balcony the princess became thoroughly annoyed, and said:

"This guy is really nuts! How will he ever get clean water acting like that? He only needs to hold the pot in one hand and sweep the floating duckweed with the other, and he will get to the clear water easily!"

For a third time Turpolpheap heard the princess clearly and followed her suggestion. He filled his cooking pot with water, poured in his rice, and set the pot on the two pegs that he had prepared over the fire. As soon as he took his hands away, the pot tipped over and extinguished the fire.

Undaunted, Turpolpheap rebuilt the fire, returned to the pond to get water, put rice in the pot and placed it on his two pegs again. Once again the pot tipped over. As before, he repeated his rice-cooking attempt without success.

Princess Chonbatkalyani grew more and more impatient as she watched Turpolpheap's merry-go-round act, and finally said:

"Truly, this boy is completely mad! Who on earth would think of putting a cooking pot on two pegs? He only has to push three pegs in the ground, as everybody in the world does, and his pot will never tip over!"

Once again, Turpolpheap listened to the princess's advice, added a third peg in the ground and began cooking his rice. He stirred the rice with a wooden spoon then tucked it into his belt. When the water was boiled sufficiently, he searched for his spoon to stir the rice, but had forgotten where he put it! He searched all over the area, but couldn't find it. Talking to himself he shouted:

"Where have I put the spoon? If I don't find it, my rice will be burned!"

On hearing this the princess rolled her eyes upwards and said:

"Oh my! He tucked his spoon in his belt and now he's searching for it everywhere!"

Hearing these words, Turpolpheap found his spoon, stirred his rice and drained it to prepare to eat. Now that his rice was cooked, he took his meal and put his pot back in his bag.

Soon after, a provincial governor approached with a pair of oxen and a racing oxcart. The governor had just taken part in the daily race in the royal gardens and he called to Turpolpheap to ask:

"Do you have horses or oxen young man?"

"No sir, I have none," Turpolpheap replied.

"Well then hitch up my oxen to my cart and take them for a tour of the gardens!"

"Sir, I have never driven a cart before," Turpolpheap protested.

"Go ahead and drive it anyway! Even if you break the cart, never mind, I won't make you pay for it!"

Excited by the idea, Turpolpheap positioned the cart and then began putting the yoke on one ox's neck. He then attached the yoke to the second ox, but he mistakenly harnessed one ox facing forwards along the cart shaft and the other facing backwards! Then he tried to drive the cart, but the oxen could not move.

Turpolpheap used a goad to poke the head of one ox and the rump of the other. The two oxen jumped wildly. All the men around burst out laughing. Turpolpheap had certainly not acted this way as a ruse, but purely out of stupidity.

From her tower balcony Princess Chonbatkalyani began laughing too, and said:

"This boy is unbelievably foolish! Everyone knows to attach both oxen under the yoke with their heads facing forwards along the shaft! That is the only way they can pull the cart!"

The princess had barely finished speaking these words when the sudden sound of drums and gongs startled her from her reverie! She never thought that she had spoken aloud to Turpolpheap. Convinced that she had only been talking to herself she thought:

"Why are they beating the drums and the gongs? I didn't speak to anyone!"

Meanwhile, the ladies in waiting and the palace secretaries in charge of noting the princess' utterances ran to prostrate themselves at the feet of King Promtoatt, and told him:

"Since the beginning of these festivals, Your Majesty's august daughter never said a single word to any of the men. Then, she suddenly spoke several times to an ugly individual, covered with warts! Our hearts were broken! We did not want to note down her words, nor did we want to beat the drums and gongs...but when she addressed that man five times we had to act! Your Majesty's orders were explicit!"

The king replied:

"If that is the case, go get the man. No matter how ugly he is, the princess has spoken to him and he shall be her husband. A king must be true to his word."

The palace officials ran to Turpolpheap and told him:

"His Majesty orders that you go to the palace to present yourself to him."

Turpolpheap was frightened and all his limbs began to tremble. He prostrated himself before the officials and asked:

"My Lords, why does the king ask for me? What horrible thing have I done?"

"We don't know anything. Come quickly!" they replied.

Turpolpheap was brought before the king. His Majesty was filled with sadness to see him, but the king could not retract his vow. He ordered his staff to take Turpolpheap to bathe him, dress him with sumptuous clothes from the royal wardrobe, and bring him back before the throne.

This turn of events was closely watched by the greatest *devata*,[46] who Indra[47] himself put in charge of protecting the royal palace.

"This man was afflicted with repulsive looks because he did not have a trustworthy heart at the end of his previous life," the *devata* deduced. "His ugliness was a punishment inflicted on him until he acquired resolution and strength. His ordeals have lasted long enough. I will go to heaven to find an elixir to sprinkle upon him to cure his woes."

The *devata* returned from heaven with a gold cruet filled with a magical elixir. As the officials took Turpolpheap to bathe him, the *devata* poured the elixir over his body. Instantly, his warts vanished and his complexion assumed a golden hue. Suddenly he was more handsome than all other men, in fact even as handsome as a heavenly *devata*!

The officials were astonished. They said to themselves:

"The man we brought in was hideous. We merely immersed him in water and he became exceptionally handsome! All his flaws

---

46 Monod's Note: In Sanskrit, *deva* are celestial beings. It is incorrect to translate *devata* as Gods because Buddhism is monotheist.

Translator's Note: In the Hindu pantheon, *devata* is a singular or plural term for male or female semi-divine beings similar to angels. Regarding Buddhism, Monod should not have considered Buddhism as monotheism because Buddha is not worshipped as a god. Buddhism a philosophy more than a religion — it has no God in the style of Western religions like Christianity, Judaism, or Islam.

47 Translator's Note: Ancient Cambodian mythology, based on Hinduism, held Indra as the supreme leader of all *devata*, who were less powerful celestial beings. In Indra's heaven, one group of female *devata*, called *apsaras*, danced to entertain the gods while their male companions, called *ghandharvas*, played music. Readers should note that there are many different kinds of *devata*: *apsaras* and *gandharvas* are only two varieties. *Devata* also include divine guardians such as nature spirits, Lokapalas (Guardians of the Directions), village spirits (*gramadevata*), rice spirits, weather spirits, and many more. Even the *neakta* we read of in the first of Monod's tales can be seen as a type of *devata*.

disappeared! This is incredible! Is this man really Turpolpheap, or has another taken his place?"

"I am really Turpolpheap," said the young man.

The officials could not believe him and they anxiously discussed the matter among themselves.

When they dressed the young man in exquisite clothes his look was even more attractive. All the women who saw him felt their hearts fluttering. The officials themselves acknowledged his strikingly handsome appearance.

The officials took Turpolpheap and reported to the king:

"Your Majesty, here is the man we brought to the bath. When he came out, he became the man who is before your Majesty now. We cannot explain this miracle."

As the king looked at Turpolpheap his heart filled with joy. But his astonishment was so great that he suspected that his officials contrived to get rid of Turpolpheap and substitute another man. Consequently, the king decided that the young man must be taken back to the tower and tested again. If the princess again speaks to him the required three times the wedding would take place!

As the king meditated on this the *devata* who guarded the king, the sacred sword, the royal crown, and the different parts of the palace joined together for a discussion:

"Turpolpheap is now physically attractive but he still has no intelligence. Let us grant him the power that will enable him to entice Princess Chonbatkalyani to speak!"

One of the *devata* then said, "I will enter Turpolpheap's heart and become his intelligence!"

A second *devata* said, "I will enter the stairs of the tower!"

"And me, I will enter the mat that the princess sits on," said another.

"And I, into the silk cushion that sits at her side," said a fourth.

Another volunteered, "Her gold bowl shall be my place."

"I shall enter the princess's engraved silver pedestal tray," said a sixth.

"And I shall enter her gold hairpin," said a seventh *devata*.

"And working together we'll use our sharp minds to make Princess Chonbatkalyani speak to Turpolpheap!" declared all the *devata* in unison!

The *devata* quickly infused themselves in all the places and objects as they had agreed. As celestial beings they were invisible to human eyes.

As the *devata* initiated their plan, the King put his idea into action.

"Turpolpheap," said the king. "I want you to go test my daughter once more. I myself shall go to the tower listen, but you will not see me. If the princess replies to you — if she speaks just three times — I shall give her hand to you as your bride."

The *devata* who had entered the young man's mind and given him an aptitude for reasoning replied:

"I beg your Majesty's pardon. Your humble servant has heard your order, but it is not proper for me, an ordinary countryman, to go to test the princess, or even to talk to her. That would be disrespectful of her royal blood!"

"I give you the permission to speak to her as you like," replied the King. "You must only refrain from using force!"

Turpolpheap took leave of the king and went to the tower that was now surrounded by a crowd of dignitaries eager to witness the second test. He stopped in front of the steps and said loudly to himself:

"I know the etiquette; one should not enter a house uninvited, therefore I cannot go into the tower. If someone invites me, I'll go in!"

The *devata* in the stairs replied:

"My Lord, I invite you to climb up to the tower. I, the stairs, beg you to walk upon me without hesitation."

Turpolpheap climbed up and stepped inside the tower, where he stopped and said:

"I do not know where to sit, without being invited!"

The *devata* in the princess's mat replied:

"My Lord, I invite you to come here, to sit down upon me, the princess's beautiful mat."

Turpolpheap sat near the princess, but she turned away from him.

After a while, Turpolpheap said:

"I really wish to chew betel-nut, but no one offers it to me."

The *devata* in the engraved silver pedestal tray pushed the tray gently over the mat to Turpolpheap and said: "I beg, Lord, to chew the prepared betel that I hold."

Chewing betel, Turpolpheap said:

"I can tell many wondrous tales, if only someone would ask to hear them!"

"I am most interested, My Lord!" replied the *devata* in the silk cushion. "I beg you to share a story!"

Satisfied, Turpolpheap started his tale...

ꕥ ❀ ꕥ

## The Princess and the Four Magicians

"Once upon a time, a very long long time ago, there lived four men in the Khmer land who wished to become magicians.

"One day, they set out together to seek a famous *achar*[48] to study magical formulas and incantations. The *achar* lived in the Kingdom of Savothi, known in the present day as Burma.

"After their long journey the *achar* accepted the four men as students and each one of them adopted a magical specialty.

"One man studied a magical formula to guide arrows; the second man studied the art of the *hora*, the ancient Indian system of astrology that foresees the past and the future in the stars; the third man gained the power to live under water; and the fourth man acquired the power to revive the dead.

"The man who studied the technique of guiding arrows could always shoot and hit the target, even when it was beyond his sight!

"The man who studied the *hora* could see events in the past and future as clearly as if they were happening right before his eyes. Not only could he see things on the surface of the Earth, but even things buried in the ground since antiquity. Through his calculations he could see anything and nothing was hidden from him.

"The man who learned the skill of living under water could stay submerged for an entire day without difficulty.

---

48 Monod's Note: Sanskrit, *Acharya* = Teacher; one who gives lessons.
Translator's Note: Cambodians would normally refer to a *Moha reussey/reussei* (*rishi*), a hermit with magical powers, as a teacher for magic and incantations.

"Finally, the man who learned how to revive the dead could bring both men and animals back to life for up to three days after their demise.

"When the four men completed their studies, they took leave of the *achar* and returned to the Khmer land.

"During their journey they arrived one day at an ocean and stopped to have their meal on the shore. One of them asked the astrologer:

" 'What will we encounter today?'

"The astrologer did some calculations then said:

" 'By mid-day, we will meet an *intri*.[49] It will fly high in the air and, in its beak, it will be carrying the daughter of a king. The young princess will be dead!'

"The man with the power to guide arrows said:

" 'If this prediction is correct, I will shoot down the *intri*!'

" 'If it then falls into the sea, I will go into get them both!' said the man who could live in the water.

" 'If the princess is dead, I shall bring her back to life!' said the fourth man.

"Later that day, when the sun had reached its zenith, the group saw a dark spot, moving quickly high in the sky. As the object moved closer they saw it was an *intri*, now appearing to be as large as the palm of a hand.

"The archer quickly drew the string of his bow and released an arrow that soared high in the sky. On reaching its target the arrow pierced the *intri*'s chest and the giant bird fell towards the sea. As it

49 Monod's Note: An *intri* is a mythical eagle.

fell the men now saw the form of a women in its beak. The man who could live under water immediately dove into the ocean and swam towards the falling bird.

Soon, they saw him swimming back to shore, a beautiful young girl in his arms. When he came back to the beach they all saw that the girl was already dead. The forth man rushed to her body, whispered his incantations of revival, and her chest heaved as she came back to life.

"All four partners were smitten with her beauty. Each man claimed that he deserved to have the princess as his wife and they began to quarrel."

Pausing, Turpolpheap asked the silk cushion:

"Cushion, you asked for the story. Tell me, which of the four men had the right to claim the princess?"

The *devata* concealed in the cushion deliberately gave a wrong answer by saying:

"In my opinion, the young lady should belong to the man who revived her!"

Hearing the cushion at her side make such an unjust remark, Princess Chonbatkalyani smacked the cushion hard with the palm of her hand, and shouted:

"That's wrong! The young lady should be given to the diver, for he was the first man to take her in his arms and had seen her nude body. The man who shot the arrow should be considered as her father, for he saved her from destruction. The man who revived her is like her mother, for it is the mother who gives life to a child. As for the astrologer, he is like the princess's brother, for only he knew of her whereabouts, but he did nothing else for her!"

Princess Chonbatkalyani had certainly rendered her judgement in accord with fairness. When she answered the question posed by Turbolpheap the secretaries recorded it as one utterance.

## The Man Who Swallowed His Wife

"I would like to tell another tale of ancient times," Turpolpheap continued, "but I don't know if anyone is interested to hear it?"

At that moment, the engraved designs on the silver tray at the princess's side flashed in the light of a flickering candle. The *devata* inside spoke and said:

"I would very much like to hear your story! Please, tell it my Lord!"

And so Turpolpheap continued....

"A very long time ago, there lived a husband who was extremely jealous. He was so jealous that he took his wife into a dense forest atop a mountain to live. He cleared a patch of land for them to grow their crops and the couple stayed there, completely isolated from the world.

"After some time, his wife gave birth to a baby girl who grew up to become a beautiful maiden. One day a young hunter from a nearby mountain passed by, saw the girl, and fell in love. Liking the look of the young man, and sympathetic to her daughter's situation, the mother allowed the hunter to secretly court her daughter. Finally, he convinced the daughter to become his mistress. Not only that, the young man also courted the mother until she, too, became his lover.

"Mother and daughter both knew each other's secret and that they were mistresses to the same man. However, realizing the seriousness of their wrongdoings they dared not blame each other. The jealous husband knew nothing and they had to keep it that way.

"Nevertheless, he became suspicious one day when he noticed that his daughter was pregnant. He did not know what to do. The jealous husband was quite agitated by the situation. He couldn't bear staying at home so, every day, he went out hunting in the forests from dawn until after dark.

"At the same time, in the same region, lived yet another extremely jealous man. This other man had learned from an *achar* a magical spell that gave him the power to swallow a person whole, and hold them alive inside of him. Wherever he went, this husband took his wife by swallowing her, thereby preventing anyone else from seducing her.

"One day his wife asked:

" 'My husband, how is it possible for you to swallow me whole as you do?'

" 'I know a powerful magical formula,' he replied.

"And the wife said:

" 'I would like to learn it too.'

" 'Why do you want to learn it?' asked the husband.

" 'Because I do. And if you don't teach me, I'll hang myself!' retorted his wife.

"Because the man loved his wife, he began teaching her the magical formula. She studied and studied and finally remembered the incantation perfectly.

"The woman could now swallow a man alive and, on that very day, she took a lover. From then on, her lover spent the days with her while her husband worked in his fields. She would then swallow her lover as soon as her husband returned home from his work. The husband suspected nothing.

"One day the husband told his wife: 'Tomorrow at dawn, I need you to cook a large portion of rice and pack it carefully to travel. We are going off the mountain tomorrow to visit my mother since she has never met you.'

"Having said this, he went to sleep. In the morning, he packed the provisions into his shoulder bag, he swallowed his wife, and then set off for his mother's village.

"By mid-day, he reached a lake in the middle of an uninhabited forest. He stopped beneath the shade of a tree, spit out his wife from his belly, and was preparing to have the meal together with her. Before eating, however, he decided to go bathe in the lake. The water was very shallow near the shore, so he went farther and farther from the bank to search for deeper water.

"While he was wading deeper into the lake his wife spit out her lover from her belly and made love to him. Then, she quickly fed her lover some of the food and swallowed him back as soon as she saw her husband returning from his bath in the lake. Upon his return, the husband ate his meal with his wife, swallowed her, and then set off again towards his mother's village.

"By coincidence, the other jealous man — who was hunting to forget his suspicions about his pregnant daughter — came to the exact same lake at the exact same time as the other jealous man.

"And as he hid in a bush he saw the other jealous husband spit out his wife and go to bath in the lake. Then, he saw the wife spit out her lover in turn, make love to him, feed him, and swallow him again upon the return of her husband!

"Now the jealous man said to himself:

" 'Here is a man who can swallow his wife to guard her from others. Yet despite this, she still has a lover. So how can I, a man who leaves his wife and daughter alone all day, every day, how can I be sure that they are faithful?'

"From his hiding place the hunter saw the other jealous husband return from the lake, eat with his wife, swallow her again, and head off on his voyage. The hunter decided to reveal himself to meet the man face to face, and when he did he asked:

" 'Where are you going?'

" 'I am going to visit my mother,' answered the man.

"The hunter then said, 'Let our meeting in the forest be the beginning of a lasting friendship. Friend, take a break from your journey and come to rest for a while in my house.'

"The hunter led the other jealous husband back to his house, where they were met by his wife and his pregnant daughter. The hunter told them:

" 'Put rice to boil on the fire quickly. I brought a friend with me. As soon as rice is cooked, bring it so we can eat together.'

"The hunter's wife and daughter prepared the meal and then the wife set four places: one for the guest, one for her husband, one for her daughter, and one for herself.

"The hunter said:

" 'Wife, there are not enough places set here tonight. You must add more places for whoever is in my friend's stomach! My friend, spit her out! We will all eat together."

"His new friend was quite surprised. How could he possibly know about his magical ability to swallow his wife? Nonetheless, the friend spat his wife out from his stomach. The hunter's daughter brought one more bowl.

" 'But we need yet one more bowl!' said the hunter looking directly at his friend's wife. "Madame, is it not true that you also have a man in your stomach? Do spit him out so that he may eat with us, too!"

"The woman was shocked and confused, but she could not deny the truth. Her face turned red, she coughed three times and out came her lover right in front of her husband!

"Realizing that he had been cuckolded by his wife and her lover the man no longer wanted to live. He held his breath until he died. Overwhelmed by deep remorse and guilt at her husband's death, the unfaithful wife also held her breath until she died. Her lover, blaming himself for causing the deaths of two people, decided that he could live no longer either.

He, in turn, stopped breathing until he died.

"Due to the horrific events that unfolded because he revealed what he had seen, the hunter stopped breathing and died. Seeing this, his wife and daughter realized that the meal they prepared had drawn all these victims to their death, and they stopped breathing also. At that moment, the lover of the two women arrived and, finding his lovers dead, also held his breath until he expired."[50]

50 Translator's Note: While this reads well as a story, it does not consider the moral value of the events. Everyone commits suicide out of remorse for their guilt. The women's lover killed himself because he caused of death of the women's husband and father.

Turpolpheap then said, "I would now like to ask a question of the silver tray. Of all the people in the story, who is responsible for this tragedy?"

The silver tray, making sure to give the wrong answer, said:

"In this case, the hunter is clearly the one who was responsible! Instead of keeping the secret of the wife's infidelity that he witnessed, he revealed it in broad daylight and to the husband himself! He caused anger and confusion. The death of all the people should be attributed to him."

Hearing the silver tray's answer, which was contrary to jurisprudence, Princess Chonbatkalyani grabbed the tray, flung it across the tower chamber and shouted:

"Certainly not! The responsibility falls on the women! They cheated their husbands by having lovers! They caused their husbands' deaths, and it must be regarded as if they had killed them!"

While the princess' judgment was perfectly fair and accurate, the royal secretaries noted her second speech.

## The Four Women of Siam

Turpolpheap and the princess sat in the stillness of the tower chamber. Momentarily, he asked if anyone wished to listen to one more story.

As he spoke the gold bowl on the matt before him vibrated, causing the water inside to shimmer and dance. The *devata* in the gold bowl then said:

"Please do share another tale with us, sir!"

Turpolpheap thus continued as follows:

"Once upon a time, long, long ago there were four women who lived in Siam. They came together with the goal of finding intelligent men to marry. One day, they met a man of reasonable character who asked them:

" 'Where are you four ladies going?'

"The women answered:

" 'We are looking for intelligent men to marry.'

"The man responded:

" 'Well, I am looking for an intelligent woman to be my wife. We happen to meet like this — perhaps it is our destiny to be married together!'

"All four women replied:

" 'We will all accept you as our husband, but first you must go and look for us in our homes.'

" 'Where are your homes?' asked the man.

"In a cryptic reply, one woman showed him her hair, the second woman pointed to her eyebrows, the third opened her blouse to show her breasts, and the fourth gestured to her *sampot.* And then the women all stood up and walked away.

"Puzzled, the man continued sitting there trying to solve the women's riddles without success. In vain, he began searching for their homes, but he couldn't find a single one. In his quest, he happened to pass a convicted criminal being crucified. The condemned man was in terrible pain and cried pitifully. The tortured prisoner begged:

" 'O Lord, I am so very thirsty, kindly give me some water please.'

"To which the man replied:

" 'I am too preoccupied now. I cannot go to find water for you. I am busy searching for solutions to mysteries that I have not yet solved.'

" 'Don't worry about your puzzles!' the convict said. 'I'm sure I can solve your riddles if you just give me some water to drink.'

"Intrigued by that possibility, the man went to get water. On his return the convict drank deeply and then asked what the puzzles were.

"The man described the clues that the women showed him when he asked where they lived. The tortured convict said:

" 'The woman who showed you her hair meant that she lives in the house where they spin silk. There is only one house here where this work is done. It is easy for you to find it. The woman who showed you her eyebrows was telling you that her house has a thick hedge in front. The woman who showed you her breasts has planted in her garden one pumpkin plant that bears two fruits. And the woman who showed you her *sampot*, lives at the weaver's house.'

"Encouraged by this information, the man set out to search for the women's houses. When he easily found them all the women asked him:

" 'Did you solve our puzzles yourself or did someone help you?'

" 'The convicted man on the cross helped me,' the man confessed.

"The four women then said:

" 'If that is so, it is the tortured man who is intelligent. Let us go to ask that he be released and we will take care of him. As for this man, he is an idiot and we cannot take him as husband.'

"The women petitioned the court for permission to take the convict down from his cross so they could care for him. One woman went into the forest to collect medicinal herbs. The second went to ask the neighbors for rice and fish to feed the unfortunate convict. The third woman cooked for him. The fourth treated his wounds and looked after him.

"Every day the four women took care of the man until he finally recovered completely. Then, the women quarreled among themselves over the man they cared for — each of them wanting to have him as a husband!

"The first woman said:

" 'If I had not gone to collect the herbs, how could we have treated his wounds?'

"The second women then said:

" 'But if I did not provide rice and all the other foods he would have starved, and then what good would the drugs have done?'

"The third woman raised her voice for all to hear saying 'It's nice to have all the food supplies. But if I had not cooked them they would have had no use!'

" 'Well!' said the forth woman, "If I didn't wash his wounds with warm water and if I didn't rub medicinal anointments on his body, all your efforts would have been for nothing.'

"The four women continued squabbling over the man. Finally, they decided to bring their case to the court. Turpolapheap paused and then said:

"But I didn't know how the court decided. Gold bowl, do you know who of the four women should have the man as her husband?"

The gold bowl answered quickly:

"It should be the woman who cooked the food! The convict could not have fed himself and without her he could not have survived!"

Princess Chobatkalyani's eyes widened as she glared at the bowl saying:

"Golden bowl! Your judgment is unfair! The man should be given as a husband to the woman who washed him and dressed his wounds, for she had seen and touched his body. The woman who cooked for him should be considered as his mother, for this is how a mother cares for a child. The woman who gathered medicinal herbs should be regarded as his father, for when a child is ill, it is the father who goes out to look for medicine and calls a doctor. Finally, the woman who found his foodstuffs should be thought of as his older sister, for when the parents are in difficulty, it is the older sister who is in charge of providing for the younger brother."[51]

Princess Chonbatkalyani pronounced her judgment in perfect harmony with the justice of the land. And as she did, the secretaries and her father in the shadows all noted her third speech.

## Turpolpheap and the Secret of the Soul

Turpolpheap realized that he had again succeeded in the challenge, but he continued nonetheless:

51 Monod's Note: Three versions of the story of four women looking for husbands were recorded by A. Leclère: Twice in *Laotian tales* (1 vol., Ed. E. Leroux, 1903) under the title "*The Thief and the Four Women*", p 90, and "*The Tortured and the Four Prostitutes*", p 164; and in "*Cambodge, contes et légendes*", Librairie Bouillon, 1885. These variations did not convey the full depth of the story..

"I have a final question that I would like to resolve. If someone is intelligent enough to solve it, please explain it to me, for this mystery worries me a great deal."

At Turpolpheap's statement the princess's gold hairpin glittered in her thick, black hair and the *devata* inside the pin said "Do not hesitate to ask me! I can solve all mysteries without fail!"

Turpolpheap then said, "This is a serious question relating to death. When a person dies, what happens to the soul? Is it true that it reincarnates and lives a new life?"

The gold hairpin replied:

"When a person dies, he is completely dead; he is not reborn anywhere and my answer is easy to verify. Who has ever seen a dead man reborn? One can ask everyone in the whole world, and not one can reply: 'In my previous life, I was in such and such form, living in such and such country. When I left my body in previous life, I came to reincarnate here in the present form.' Certainly no human being can pretend to have such memory. I conclude that death destroys us all completely!"

Outraged by this answer, Princess Chonbatkalyani angrily pulled off her hairpin, threw it on the mat and exclaimed:

"Gold hairpin, you are extremely stupid! Saying something like this is a great sin! Our Master the Buddha said that our physical form on this earth is the result of an infinite series of successive reincarnations. The instant we take a new life in our mother's womb, we entirely forget our past.

We know not where we came from and our memory is absolutely empty. The moment our earthly body dies and frees our soul, the latter again loses all memories of its previous life. As long as we reincarnate in successive lives, we cannot preserve the memory from one life form to the next. If one day we reach the supreme knowledge of the Buddha, then we will be able to recall all our successive lives.

"Lord Buddha prescribes that during our life as humans we should be altruistic and charitable. Being charitable means that one should contribute to the building of monasteries, create images of the Buddha, make offerings to the monks, or perform other religious acts. Being charitable also means helping to alleviate the suffering of others, ending people's misery, looking after the sick, and helping convicts. Being charitable means giving to the poor.

"He who has devoted his life to charitable acts will reincarnate in an attractive body in a respectable family, gifted with intelligence, and having authority over men, for he is apt to be their leader. He enjoys people's praise and respect.

"All around us, we see people who are human beings like us. How do you explain that some are powerful, others are wealthy, some are blessed with good physical qualities, whereas others are poor or ugly to behold? It is the consequence of their previous lives that people are rewarded or punished in their current ones!"

The widespread sounds of drums and gongs interrupted Princess Chonbatkalyani's talk because earlier, when she had spoken for the third time, her father the king had sent one of the secretaries to the court to begin preparations for a royal announcement.

Turpolpheap then faced the princess and addressed her directly:

"O Princess Chonbatkalyani, most beautiful of all princesses, I have come to visit you in your residence but you have not said a single courteous word to me. Your stairs, your mat, your silk cushion, your silver pedestal tray, your gold bowl and even your hairpin —

which are merely inanimate objects — all graciously welcomed me. But you, princess, you have not shown the slightest regard for me. Nevertheless, I am the one that destiny has favored over all other men. But since you neglect me, I request your permission to leave."

Having said these words, Turpolpheap stood up and headed for the door, but Princess Chonbatkalyani stopped him by saying:

"Wait! Do not leave. I will talk to you."

As the sounds of drums and gongs continued outside the tower, King Promtoatt was delighted that his daughter would finally be wed. The entire kingdom celebrated the marriage of Princess Chonbatkalyani and Turpolpheap with magnificent festivities. The king gave Turpolpheap a new name of Sovanbotum[52] as well as the title of Obbarach.

Several years later Sovanbotum succeeded his father-in-law to the throne of Peareanasey.[53]

Undoubtedly, one could ask the question: Is it possible that Turpolpheap, for having kept his word just a single time, could have earned such a merit to be awarded the throne?

We reply: Certainly not.

But Sovanbotum and Chonbatkalyani, who were husband and wife, performed much charitable work and many good deeds during a great number of previous incarnations. When they reach the end

---

52 Monod's Note: Gold lotus.

53 Monod's Note: The story of the silent princess was repeated by A. Leclère in his short story *Neang Pancha Kalyaney* with quite significant variations *(Laotian Tales*, p.160 and p.167). In this Laotian tale, the suitor is a prince. He blamed the young girl for not replying: "I am the son of a ruling king. She did not reply to what I have said, only her betel box did! — The princess rushed towards the prince, embraced him in her arms and said very wise and pleasant words to him". The behavior of the princess is presented far better in the Cambodian tale.

of the series of lives yet to come, it is certain that they will become Buddhas in their turn.

But, one may further ask: How is it that these two beings were reincarnated as partridges?

Here is the reason:

In a previous existence, they were humans, husband and wife, living in Langka.[54] There was a famine and the two spouses went to search for roots in the forest. The forest was very dense, almost impenetrable. They set fire to the forest causing a pair of turtledoves and their two chicks to burn to death. Sovanbotum and Chonbatkalyani were thus reincarnated as partridges while the turtledoves were reborn as the hunters who set the forest fire that killed the partridges. The punishment for our bad actions does not occur in just one reincarnation, but takes place during hundreds and hundreds of our successive lives.

54 Translator's Notes: Monod identified this as Ceylon, present day Sri Lanka.

# The Foundation of Angkor

# រឿងស្ថាបនាប្រាសាទអង្គរ វត្ត

# The Foundation of Angkor

# រឿងស្ថាបនាប្រាសាទអង្គរ វត្ត

In year 600 of the Buddhist era,[55] there lived a man named Lim Seng in the province of Shanghai, China.

Lim Seng was fifty years old and lived in great poverty. After borrowing six silver bars from a merchant, he got himself into debt bondage to his creditor who assigned him to clear and cultivate a piece of land along a riverbank. During the season when all types of flowers bloomed, Lim Seng made an ample harvest for his master each day.

One day, five *apsaras*,[56] celestial nymphs living in the palace of Indra, took a flight and came frolicking on the earth. They saw Lim Seng's garden in full bloom and went in. One *apsara*, named Dibsotachan,[57] picked six flowers whose fragrance enchanted her. Her nymph sisters wandered about the garden without picking

55 Translator's Note: This is the Gregorian calendar year 57 A.D.

56 Translator's Note: In Khmer *Tepthida* = celestial nymph. In Sanskrit they are called *apsaras*.

57 Translator's Note: The name of this celestial woman does not match any *apsara* names from Hindu literature but names in Khmer legends may come from Sanskrit, Pali,  In Khmer manuscripts dating back to 1878 (collected by E. Aymonier), Dibsotachan is spelled *Tibvsutacn*. Khing Hoc Dy (1990) translates this as 'the moon's divine daughter', while others suggest "divine moon angel with magical hearing" as described below.

any flowers for their pleasure. Upon their return to their celestial residence, they revealed Dibsotachan's petty theft to Indra. The great god interrogated the culprit and condemned her to descend to earth to live as a human for six years, and as Lim Seng's wife.

Dibsotachan, ashamed and in despair over her fate, took flight and descended to earth to see Lim Seng. She admitted to him that she had stolen six flowers and told him:

"As punishment, Indra ordered me to be your wife for six years."

"I live in extreme poverty," Lim Seng replied. "I cannot take you as my wife. My master is very mean. He barely gives me enough food to survive."

"Never mind," Dibsotachan replied, "I will help you! I will teach you the knowledge of unknown arts that no one can emulate. If you don't take me as your wife, how can I fulfill Indra's sentence? Please have pity upon me."

Lim Seng received Dibsotachan in his home. He was proud of this *apsara*, more beautiful than any woman on earth. Soon he fell deeply in love with her.

After living with Lim Seng a few months, Dibsotachan saw his honesty and his difficult life, took pity on him and asked :

---

*Tipv* (Khmer) = *divya* (Sanskrit) or *dibba* (Pali) means "divine, heavenly, magical." In Khmer, the first *b* remains but the second '*b*' is replaced by '*v*' (*dibva*). A derivative Pali-Khmer word is *devataa* or *debtaa* in which the '*i*' becomes an '*e*'.

*srotra* (Sanskrit) or *sota* (Pali) means "ear". Combined with the first term *dibba-sota* means "divine ear", i.e. claraudience, one of six higher powers (*chalabhiññã*) described in the Pali Canon.

*chant* (Khmer) = *candra or canda* (Sanskrit & Pali) means "the moon", an association the Khmer also use for a beautiful maiden.

Special thanks to Mr. Bora Touch, Dr. Tel Thong, Mr. Kenneth So, and other scholars in the Cambodian Academic Network (**cancambodia.wordpress.com/**) for their helpful input.

"How much have you borrowed?"

"Six silver bars" replied Lim Seng.

"When you borrowed six silver bars," Dibsotachan continued, "you were living alone. Now go to ask for four more bars and I will serve as bond servant with you. We will then make the money we borrowed grow."

Lim Seng went to his creditor and got the four silver bars he had asked for. He took them to Dibsotachan.

She asked Lim Seng to buy silk with the four silver bars. He returned with twenty pounds of cocoons that Dibsotachan began spinning into thread. She then wove all types of fabulous fabrics with leaf brocades, animal shapes and various patterns. Her creations were more elegant and more beautiful than any known in the land.

When she finished Dibsotachan asked her husband to take her fabrics to his master. The merchant examined the silks, stroking them with admiration and excitement. No one had ever woven fabrics like these! The merchant paid great compliments to Lim Seng and in his excitement paid him fifty silver bars and, in addition to this gift, cancelled all his previous debts.

The merchant soon began sending students to learn the art of silk weaving from Lim's magical wife. With a number of students working with her, Dibsotachan began buying silk by the picul.[58] Lim Seng soon became a wealthy and respected businessman.

---

58 Monod's + Translator's Notes: Unit of weight widely used in Cambodia for bulky goods. One *picul* is approximately 60kg.

At the end of one year, Dibsotachan gave birth to a baby boy, who grew to become quite a boisterous child. As soon as he could crawl, he began building battlements in the ground. When he could stand, he was always drawing pictures in the dirt, constantly inscribing the images of animals and people. He was always hyperactive and never sat still. For this reason, his mother called him Popusnokar (Preah Pusnokar).[59]

When this child reached the age of five, the term of Dibsotachan's sentence reached its end; her six years' stay on earth had been completed. She walked into the garden, picked six flowers, put them on her pillow and then flew back to her celestial residence in Indra's heaven.

As mealtime came, Lim Seng wondered why his wife did not come. He went into her room and saw the six flowers. He understood the message immediately. He was in tears with desperation over Dibsotachan's departure. All the neighbors sympathized with his distress. Popusnokar ran everywhere looking for his mother, calling for her with his shrieking voice and weeping grievously with his father.

During this period in the kingdom of Cambodia, King Pudesraja died without an heir thus ending the Prah Thong dynasty. The

---

59 Monod's Note: The meaning of this word disturbs me. With great reservation, I ask myself if it could not come from *bhâta*, brilliant, and *nagara*, city. The verb *bhâ*, shine, has over time lost its aspiration: perfect *babhau*. However, this etymology is the more uncertain due to the variety of Cambodian spellings of this character's name; some spell Popusnoka, others Prah Pusnokar.

Translator's Note: In Khmer, Preah Pusnokar (from Sanskrit *Visvakarma*) = principal celestial engineer/architect. I use the name Preah Popusnokar throughout the translation, since it is better known to all Cambodians. In Khmer, *ropus* = hyperactive. This may be a pun: i.e. Popus-Ropus.

In India, the descendents of the five sons of Lord Vishwakarma form the Vishva Brahmin caste that includes priests, engineers, architects, sculptors, temple builders and artists. This group also includes five sub-castes; blacksmiths, carpenters, coppersmiths, goldsmiths and sculptors.

only people with any connection to royal blood left were Krong Huv and Kray Huv so the succession to the throne was unclear.[60]

At that time, there was a poor man who made a living by selling firewood that he collected from the forest. One day, while he was collecting his usual bundles of firewood, he was caught by a torrential rain. He went to take refuge in a shrine built for the *Neakta*.[61]

At that moment, Indra, King of the Devas, transformed himself into two roosters, one white and one black. The black rooster came to perch on the main beam of the hut, while the white rooster came to sit on the roof. After a while, the white rooster started crowing. The black rooster, which could speak the human language, said:

"Who dares to crow over my head like this? What kind of power do you have?"

"I have great power!" the white rooster answered. "If a human eats my flesh, he will be crowned as a king!"

The black rooster replied:

"If a man eats my head, he will be the supreme head of all the Buddhist monks! If a woman eats my drumstick, she will become a queen! If a man eats my breast, he will be crowned as king! So, do not treat me with disrespect!"

The white rooster then flew off while the black rooster remained on the beam. The man quietly approached the black rooster, caught it, killed it, and took it home. The man whispered the secret he

60 Monod's Note: All of these names seem to be purely legendary.

61 Translator's Note: *neakta* = spirits who guard the land in traditional Cambodian beliefs. *Neakta* shrines are normally huts built on stilts under a big tree in the village or in nearby woods. A large stone representing the spirit is placed inside the hut.

had learned to his wife who was thrilled. She happily cooked the rooster, set it on a platter and made preparations to eat it. But her husband said to her:

"Soon we will be wearing crowns! We should therefore take this platter with us to the river so we can bathe ourselves and put on fine clothes before we eat this rooster."

The husband and wife went down to the river, placing the platter of food on the bank at the water's edge while they happily went swimming. When they got out of the water they could no longer find the platter. The waves had swept the platter into the water current and it had disappeared.

That day, a *mahout*[62] named Tia brought several elephants to bathe in the river downstream. When he saw the food platter drifting towards him, he picked it up and took it to the head monk in a nearby monastery, who recognized the magical nature of the bird. He immediately took the head and consumed it. Then the monk gave the breast meat to Tia and gave the drumstick to Tia's wife, Neang Vong, but he told them nothing.

Tia and Vong returned to their home.

Meanwhile, the man and his wife who had lost the food platter searched for it in vain. Thinking that someone had stolen it when they were bathing, they cursed the alleged unknown thief.

Three days later, the council of ministers met and said:

"For some time now our country has had no king. Let us outfit the royal elephants with armor and invoke the *devas* to guide the animals in a search. When an elephant finds a man capable of

62 Translator's Note: *Mahout* is an elephant handler, derived from the Hindi words *ma-haut* and *mahavat*.

sitting on the throne it will bow down, lifts the man up upon its head and bring him here. We will then immediately prepare for his coronation."

After the meeting they decorated the elephants with rich armor and other ornaments and turned them loose to wander at will. The elephants headed straight towards the home of the mahout Tia and his wife, *Neang* Vong. The lead elephant bowed before them, lifted both onto its head and returned to the palace. The ministers immediately organized the coronation ceremonies according to tradition. Mahout Tia took the name Tevong Aschar for his reign.[63]

Prince Krung Huv and Prince Kray Huv were very disappointed by this turn of events and moved to Bakan in the province of the

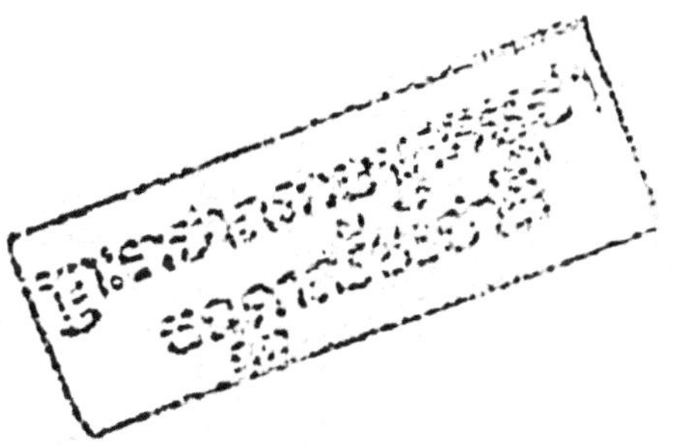

63 Monod's Note: This name seems purely legendary.

Translator's Note: A Khmer language version of this tale comments that Devong Aschar could be derived from the husband's name Tia and the wife's name Vong. *Aschar* means marvelous or wonderful and indeed they had an unusually marvelous destiny. If we consider that they became king and queen through the divine work of Indra, the appropriate name would be Deva-Vong-Aschar (*deva* = divine, *vong* = lineage, *aschar* = marvelous).

Boddisattva[64] where they built a new *prasat*[65] and refused to pledge allegiance to the new king.[66]

On seeing that the new queen was childless, Indra said:

"I will give Queen Vong a son of my own blood who will perpetuate the dynasty of the Cambodian kings forever."

One day as Queen Vong left the great palace, Indra flew overhead in the sky. Humans cannot see Indra, only a streak of bright blue light across the sky. Alarmed people began shouting:

"The light is falling! The light is falling!"

Indra showered the queen with garlands of flowers and returned to his celestial home.

Queen Vong became pregnant and later gave birth to a boy. She named him Preah Ket Mealea[67] which means 'garland of lights.'

---

64 Translator's Note: Monod made a mistake in calling Pursat (the French transliteration of Pôsat) the Bodhisattva province (as did other French scholars including Paul Pelliot and George Coedès). The name of Pôsat town and province came from the original words *Pô rosat* meaning drifted (*rosat*) Bodhi tree (*Pô*). Legend has it that one day a group of people saw a Bodhi tree (*Ficus religiosa*) strangely drifting upstream, against the river current. They picked it up and planted on the land nearby and called the place Pô rosat. As time went by, the name lost the *ro* sound and became simply Pôsat. The Cambodian spelling for *sat* is very much different from s*attva*, which relates to the Buddha. The meanings of Pôsat and Bodhisattva are very different and should not be confused with each other (*Dictionnaire Cambodgien* 1967). For people who can't read Khmer characters, the pitfall lies in the spelling. Both Pôsat and Bodhisattva involve the Bodhi tree.

65 Translator's Note: All ancient Cambodian monuments or the residence of the king with a tower, even if it only has a ground floor, are called *prasat*.

66 Translator's Note: Stone inscriptions K451 & Ka64 mention that the Malyang people (who no longer exist) in Pôsat province rebelled against King Jayavarman II.

67 Monod's Note: In Preah Ket Mealea, Mr. Aymonier sees the legendary name of Jayavarman II who reigned over Cambodia from 802-869. He informed us that, according to the Sdok Kok Thom inscriptions, this king came from Java. Therefore, he would not have been born in Cambodia as the legend says.

Meanwhile, at the home of Lim Seng, the young Popusnokar searched everywhere for his mother, but could not find where she went. A bitter sadness overwhelmed the boy's heart.

By the age of ten, he had become a diligent student. One day he asked his father:

"Who, in fact, is my mother?"

His father answered:

"Your mother was an *aspara*. She came down to live on earth for only six years before returning to her celestial world. That abode is very far away and I do not know where your mother is, my son."

The boy remained silent, but he constantly thought of his mother. He decided to go searching for his mother until he found her, though his journey would be exhausting. His father tried to persuade him not to go but nothing could deter him from his mission. The young Popusnokar travelled through many forests and plains, eating only wild fruit from the trees. His clothes were torn into rags. But his destiny was favorable. One day, the *apsaras* came down from the heavens to play on a densely wooded mountaintop. His mother Dibsotachan was in the group and, as always, she was picking flowers to make a bouquet.

When Popusnokar saw the beautiful maidens, he thought to himself:

---

For Mr. Bergaigne, Jayavarman II would be Mahapativarman, son of Indravarman I, the dates of whose reign are still unknown. We also do not know the immediate predecessors of Rajendravarman I.

Mr. Georges Maspéro thinks that the name Preah Ket Mealea reminds Cambodians of the memory of the great kings who built Angkor.

Translator's Note: Jayavarman II's actual birthplace of is still disputed among modern scholars.

"It has been many years since I have passed through regions inhabited by people. For many years, I have not seen a single human being! My clothes were torn to pieces and I had nothing to replace them with. I'm only covered by leaves taken from trees. Suddenly I see a group of exceptionally beautiful women. I wonder where they come from? Are they not, perhaps, *apsaras*?"

With this thought, Popusnokar hid himself in a bush. When the women approached, he raised his hands and prayed:

"If these women are apsaras and if my mother is not among them, may they all fly back to their celestial home. However, if my mother is among them, I pray that she cannot fly back with the others!"

After saying his prayer, Popusnokar ran out towards the clearing where the *apsaras* were frolicking. Surprised at the sight of a human boy, all the nymphs flew off in haste, but Dibsotachan was unable to fly away. Popusnokar rushed to hold her in his arms, squeezing with all his might.

"Alas!" Dibsotachan groaned in agony, "What new curse falls upon me? I have served my sentence and been freed from the human world and now I'm grabbed by a human again!"

"Mother! Mother! I am your son!" Popusnokar cried out. "When my mother vanished, I was filled with desperation and sadness. I searched for her everywhere in vain. When my father, Lim Seng, looked in her room he found only six flowers on her pillow. He immediately understood that she had returned to her celestial world. Since then, his sorrow has been so deep that it defies description. All our neighbors cried along with us. Since then, the thought of finding her again has never left my heart. When I grew up, I asked father's permission and I began my search. I thought I might die of hunger and exhaustion. Now, I have found my mother. I beg you to return with me."

Having heard the adolescent's words, Dibsotachan recognized that the boy hugging her really was her son. She cried compassionately and said:

"My child, your mother had no dislike for your father and you. She constantly thinks of you both; her memory of all the humans she lived among is still clear. But your mother is an *apsara* who cannot live a human life.

"Every day, your mother goes to fulfill her duties in the presence of the divine Indra, begging him to bless you and your father. Every day, your mother begs Indra to give his blessings of happiness to all humans. My dear son, your mother cannot return to earthly life with you. But thou hast searched for your mother and thou hast found her. Your mother will take you to bathe in the fragrant waters of Indra's garden to cleanse you of all human odor. Afterwards, I will take you to the palace to present my son to Indra."

Dibsotachan gave her scarf to Popusnokar, who put it on to rid himself of his clothes made from foliage. Then, carrying her child on her hip she flew through space. She bathed him in the fragrant waters and took him into her home where she gave him appropriate clothing. She fed him a celestial meal and took him to Indra's palace.

Popusnokar's heart overflowed with joy. But when he entered Indra's audience chamber, he was so impressed by the ineffable beauty and mystery of the place that he began shaking, his legs bent double, and he fainted! At that moment, Indra entering the hall, saw the boy and asked Dibsotachan:

"Who is this human? Why do you bring him into my palace?"

Dibsotachan replied:

"He is my son, the son who was born when I went down to earth to marry Lim Seng."

"Young man, get up!" commanded Indra.

Popusnokar came to his senses and bowed before the king of the gods. Indra led the young man into his palace, and asked him a thousand questions about the human world where he lived. Indra was greatly pleased with Popusnokar's answers.

Bowing before Indra, Dibsotachan said:

"My son is particularly skillful at drawing figures, at carving, and at building temples and fortresses that attract the admiration of humans. However, he has never had a teacher; he did all these things out of his own ideas."

"True!" replied Indra. "Whoever has knowledge without a teacher, is like a blind man. He progresses alone but has no one to guide him. Thus, you must take the young man to meet the *devaputra*[68] who are in charge of my workshops. Under their direction, he will learn a variety of crafts. Afterwards, the young man can return to his earthly world because, as a human being, he cannot stay here indefinitely."

---

68 *Deva* = celestial males similar to angels in the West; *putra* = son. *Devaputra* = male *Devata*, sons of the god *Indra*.

Popusnokar went to stay with the *devaputra* who were specialists in art and construction. He learned design, sculpture, and music under the guidance of the *devaputra*. He learned to build ships that can go on dry land. He learned to engrave gold and silver, and to forge iron. He knew how to make a solution that when poured over clay, could turn it into stone. The young man had learned and retained all the knowledge that the *devaputra* taught him. And the *devaputra* encouraged him with the following remark:

"All the works that you now know how to build will endure for thousands of years, whereas our work here lasts only for the reign of a single king. Here, if a king is crowned and charges us to construct a *prasat*, we build it for him instantly. But upon the day that this king passes away, his *prasat* will also disappear at the same time as his life. Your power is much superior to ours."

The *devaputra* reported to Indra, describing the excellent results Popusnokar achieved from their teachings. Indra was very pleased and acknowledged that Popusnokar will become the teacher of all humans who are Buddhists.[69]

Indra thereby decreed:

"All human builders must make an offering to Popusnokar before they start a building. The offering must consist of a bottle of alcohol, one silver *baht*, four sections of banana trunk decorated with betel leaves and areca nuts, five *hath*[70] of white cloth, a bowl

---

69 Translator's Note: Most of the kings who built Angkor were Hindus, and most of the temples were originally dedicated to Hindu gods. A notable exception was Jayavarman VII who, along with his queens Jayarajadevi and Indradevi, were devout Buddhists. After the decline of the Angkor period, Cambodia adopted Hinayana Buddhism as the kingdom's primary religion.

70 Translator's Note: *Hath* is a traditional unit of measure from the elbow to the tip of the middle finger, thus approximately 18 inches. It is similar to the cubit in Western cultures.

of rice and one candle. If anyone begins any building without making an offering to Popusnokar, he will not be able to see in the light of day, as if his eyes are covered by cataracts."

While Indra was talking, he suddenly remembered Preah Ket Mealea. Immediately, he flew down to Cambodia. It was nighttime on earth. Everyone was dazzled by the brilliant light and wondered what engulfed the sky. Indra landed in the royal temple and the guards ran to inform King Tevong-Aschar:

"An unknown being has descended from the heavens! It has the appearance of a man, but it is blue and shining bright as fire. It has entered the royal *prasat*".

King Tevong-Aschar hurried to the *prasat*. He recognized Indra and bowed before him.

"King Tevong-Aschar," asked Indra. "Does your majesty know my son?"

"No my Lord, I do not know him."

"What omen occurred when Preah Ket Mealea was born?" Indra asked.

"There was a blue light across the sky!" the king replied. "And then garlands of flowers fell upon the queen who later found herself to be pregnant."

"Pregnant with my son!" said Indra.

King Tevong-Aschar then called Preah Ket Mealea to the temple. Indra took the boy, sat him on his lap, and said:

"In the past my name was Makhmanubbh.[71] I built the roads, dykes, bridges and *sala*.[72] I did many charitable works making donations to the poor. With these good deeds, I was reincarnated as Indra. This is why I show my mercy to the Kingdom of Cambodia, a newly founded nation that did not yet have a powerful ruler.

"This is why I have begotten you, my son, to live a long and happy life. But in today's world, the life of humans is too short. It is rare that anyone lives to be one hundred years old. So I will bring you to my palace to bathe in a celestial pool to give you a long life."

Indra carried Preah Ket Mealea on his hip and flew back to his divine kingdom where he had a pool in his garden. Indra made Preah Ket Mealea bathe in the pool seven times a day for seven days. Afterwards, Indra brought Preah Ket Mealea into his palace. There, he invited seven Brahmans to recite incantations and sprinkle the divine water on Preah Ket Mealea to give him a lifespan of four hundred years.

When the ceremonies were complete, Indra had his coachmen harness his divine chariot to take Preah Ket Mealea throughout his palace so he could see all its wonders.

After Preah Ket Mealea saw all that he desired, the coachman took him to see Indra's celestial stables.

Upon Preah Ket Mealea's return, Indra asked:

"Are you pleased with what you have seen?"

"I am filled with wonder!" answered Preah Ket Mealea.

---

71 Monod's Note: Sanskrit: *makha* = vigorous; *manusa* = man (?).

72 Translator's Note: *sala* = open air building. In the story it may refer to the *dharmasalas*: shrines, possibly "rest houses," along main travel roads that have existed since the time of Angkor.

Indra said:

"Thus, I give you the Kingdom of Cambodia. If you have seen a *prasat* here that you want to reproduce in Cambodia, just think of it in your mind. I will send an architect who will build it in your kingdom!"

At the time, Preah Ket Mealea was only twelve years old. He was quite in awe of Indra. He thought:

"In my kingdom, I would not dare to build a *prasat* that is as beautiful as the palace of Indra. If I copy his, he might certainly be offended." With this in mind, Preah Ket Mealea said:

"I would like to have built a *prasat* that is as beautiful as your oxen stable!"

Indra laughed saying "Is that stable beautiful in your eyes?"

Indra then called Popusnokar and said "As a human you cannot stay in heaven indefinitely. I will send you to Cambodia were you will build the palace of my son, and you must make it far more beautiful than my oxen stable. When you have finished building it, I will go down to the earth to preside over my son's coronation and shower him with glory."

After Popusnokar carefully examined the stable, Indra ordered a carriage to be harnessed to take Preah Ket Mealea and Popusnokar down to earth to the Kingdom of Cambodia.

Once there, Popusnokar immediately began building the *prasat*. The year was 620 Buddhist era.[73] Popusnokar had people digging moats and piling the dugout earth as high walls. Then he took

73 Translator's Note: This is 77 AD in the Gregorian calendar. Archaeologists generally agree that Angkor Wat was built between 1115-1150 AD, during the reign of King Suryavarman II.

various carved objects and impressed them on the earth walls in all directions.

A young man named Sovan, who was a son of a village chief, came to work for Popusnokar. When Sovan had learned his trade sufficiently well to oversee the building work, Popusnokar sailed a junk towards the sea to collect shells to make lime for plastering the *prasat*. On his way back, when he reached Samrong Sèn, district of Kompong Lèng, the junk sank. Popusnokar raised the boat up again, but did not pick up the shells. This is the reason why there are piles of shells buried in Samrong Sèn village to this day. For many years, people in the village had taken these shells to make lime, but a large quantity of shells still exist to the present day.[74]

Later, Popusnokar sailed again to the sea to collect shells, but this time he took several junks with him in order to bring back considerable quantities of shells. Afterwards, he sailed out with three junks to search for sesame seeds. On his way back, a storm capsized one of the junks at Koh Kamnhan west of Daun Trie.[75]

Popusnokar emptied all the sesame seeds from the junk and made them petrified into an island. For this reason, the soil in Koh Kamnhan Island has the pure black color of the sesame seeds with no mixture of any other type of soil.

Popusnokar took the sesame seeds from the other two junks to make a formulation that he used to plaster the *prasat* he had built with mud. The mud turned immediately into stone. Popusnokar

---

74 Translator's Note: For modern archaeological verification of this legend see the work of LY Vanna: *The Archaeology of Shell Matrix Sites in the Central Floodplain of the Tonle Sap River, Central Cambodia: The Shell Settlement Site of Samrong Sen and Its Cultural Complexity*. 2002, PhD Thesis, Department of Foreign Studies, Graduate Program in Area Studies, University of Sophia, Tokyo.

75 Translator's Note: I have yet to locate these places.

did not build the *prasat* in the same way as we all do by making scaffolding and planting columns one by one. He took mud to build the five-stories of the *prasat* all at once, and then plastered it with his magical formulation. Afterwards, the whole *prasat* turned into stone. That is why the roof arches have no rafters, beams, or columns to support them.

When the building work was completed, Popusnokar painted all the sculptures with appropriate colors. He made the admirable *prasat* as beautiful as Indra's stable.

Preah Ket Mealea was very pleased with the *prasat* and he praised Popusnokar a great deal. He asked Popusnokar to build many more *prasat* decorated with marvelous sculptures.

Indra, accompanied by numerous *devata*, descended to Earth to preside over his son's coronation. He named him Arithpulpoháno Preah Ket Mealea and called the Khmer country Kampuchea (Cambodia) as it is known today.

Later on, Preah Ket Mealea noted that one of the *prasat's* towers was leaning so he asked Popusnokar to straighten it. The latter replied:

"Your Majesty has only to ask a woman to beat the tower with a gourd the tower will be straight again."

Preah Ket Mealea was very angry and shouted:

"How can you say something like that? The *prasat* towers are all in stone, and you tell a woman to hit it with a gourd to straighten it."

Popusnokar was also angry with His Majesty, but out of respect for the king, Popusnokar said nothing and sent a woman to beat the *prasat* tower with a ripe gourd, and the tower stood upright again.

Sometime later, Preah Ket Mealea gave Popusnokar three piculs[76] of iron and asked him to make a royal sword as a symbol of the king's power. Popusnokar smelted the iron down, reducing and purifying it until only the hardest and best part remained, but this was only enough to make a small sword. Its blade was as thin as a rice leaf, but it was extremely sharp.

For example, if one cut a man into two pieces with this sword, one would not see that he had been cut in two, and would think that one had missed him. The man could even talk as usual. Only when pushed would the man fall in two pieces!

If one filled a jar with water, one could cut it into two without a single drop of water leaking out. Only when one pushed the jar, would it fall apart in two pieces, spilling the water out!

Popusnokar carefully dipped the sword in water to anneal it and then presented it to Preah Ket Mealea. Seeing the size of the sword, the king was enraged and bitterly scolded Popusnokar in front of all the ministers:

"You have stolen my three piculs of iron for your personal use! That is why this sword is so small!"

Now furious as well, Popusnokar replied:

"I will not stay in Cambodia anymore. I am returning to China!"

Popusnokar got up and left while dragging the sharp edge of the sword across the floor. After he had left, everyone saw that the floorboard was cut in half where the sword was dragged. Preah ket

76 Translator's note: picul = approx. 60kg.

Mealea immediately ordered people to run after Popusnokar to ask for the sword, but Popusnokar refused and threw the sword into the Great Lake (Tonle Sap). He then boarded a junk and sailed towards China, his native country. Once there, he then taught his countrymen his craft.

That is the story of Popusnokar. Few knew it. Because of this, people wrongly believed that *Prasat* Angkor was built by the *devata*.[77]

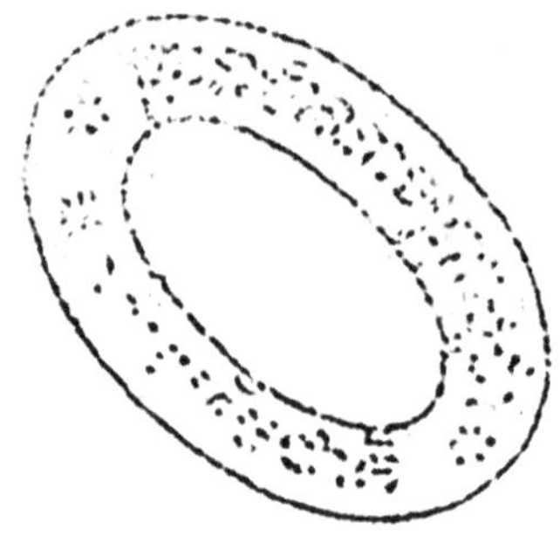

77 Translator's note: In light of this account, it is puzzling that Zhou Daguan, the Chinese diplomat who visited Angkor in AD 1296, mentioned a legend that the mythical Chinese architect, Lu Ban, built *Prasat* Phnom Bakheng in one night, and that *Prasat* Angkor Wat was Lu Ban's tomb.

Lu Ban was a Chinese carpenter, inventor, engineer and philosopher in the 5th century BC. He was responsible for some of China's most amazing architecture, particularly dragon design motifs in ancient temples. Due to his extraordinary structures, Lu Ban attained the mythical status of a god.

In Angkor, scholars agree that *Prasat* Phnom Bakheng — built in the late 9th century AD — was King Yasovarman's state temple. Angkor Wat — built in the early 12th century AD — may have been the mausoleum for King Suryavarman II. The two monuments were built more than 200 years apart.

# Appendices

## Guillaume Henri Monod

Biographical Profile

Timeline

Bibliography

## Complete Original French Text

***Légendes Cambodgiennes***

*que m'a contées le Gouverneur KHIEU*

# Guillaume Henri Monod Biographical Profile

**Kent Davis and Solang Uk**

Like other notable authors of his era in French Indochina, details about the personal life, feelings and final fate of Guillaume Henri Monod remain a mystery. We hope the information below will help other admirers learn more about this man, his descendents and his archives.

Our primary sources for factual information are the detailed annual directories of personnel published by the colonial administration (i.e. the Annuaire général de l'Indo-Chine française). In those we find our author listed with literary peers like George Groslier and Roland Meyer. That data enabled further genealogical research in Europe.

We invite researchers or relatives with questions or information to contact us through our website: www.NagaPrince.com.

Guillaume-Henri Monod was born in London on Friday, January 1, 1875. While "January 1" birthdays often appear when the actual date is unknown, his New Year's Day birth is credible, judging from the varied birthdates recorded for his siblings.

He was the third child of Albert Edouard and Laure Eugénie (née Mayor De Montricher) Monod, who married in Marseille on July 20, 1870. All their children were born in London, with the first being Madeleine Isabelle on Oct. 21, 1871. She was followed by three brothers: Raymond Emile on July 12, 1873; Guillaume-Henri on Jan. 1, 1875; and George Ambroise Walter on May 5, 1876.

Albert's father (G.H.'s paternal grandfather), Frédéric Jean Joël Gérard Monod was born May 17, 1794 in the tiny municipality of Monnaz (2009 population 396) in the western Swiss canton of Vaud. Indeed, this branch of the Monod family is rooted in Switzerland near Lake Geneva going back to at least the 16th century.

Frédéric's father, Gaspard Joël Monod, was born in Geneva on Jan. 27, 1717. Gaspard's father, David-Bernard Monod, was born in the Morges District in 1672, and his father, Abraham Christian Monod, was born in the Vevey District on May 7, 1642. Others with the Monod family name are found in France and the UK, but no direct relationships are clear at this time.

Getting back to how England became the birthplace of G.H. and his siblings, we find that his grandfather (Albert's father), Frédéric, married Marie Louise Constance de Coninck in Copenhagen on May 3, 1821. The cause for the end of that marriage is unknown, but on Sep. 10, 1839 Frédéric married Suzanne Smedley in Merseyside, Liverpool, beginning the family's U.K. association. Their son Albert was born in 1845, ostensibly in the UK, but this is not certain.

The records show that Frédéric died on Dec 30, 1863, followed by Suzanne on Nov. 21, 1867. Both, however, died in Île-de-France, as the metropolitan area of Paris was then known. Why their son Albert and his new bride from Marseille returned to London in 1870 to start their family is not known.

As for Guillaume-Henri Monod himself, we only know what can be inferred from official records and his works, as detailed in the following Timeline and Bibliography.

In 1897 he joined the Geological Society of France. For many years, he maintained his membership, and was listed as their only member in Cambodia into the 1920s. On Feb. 12, 1898, at the age of 23, he began working with the Indochina Administration. On Dec. 15, 1900 he was listed as 'administrator student' (Elève administrateur) with no mention of the school name. Following a decree on Feb. 17, 1901, he served in 1902 as Deputy Geologist in the Direction de l'Agriculture et du Commerce de l'Indochine. On Aug. 21, 1901, he was promoted to the rank of Administrator (civil servant) grade 4. On Apr. 5, 1905, he was promoted to administrative chief of Pursat Province, Cambodia.

He received a series of Civil Service promotions until an unexplained "job interruption" from May 14, 1913 to Aug. 1, 1914. As WWI only began on July 28, 1914, it is unknown if this had anything to do with the war. We do know that Monod served valiantly and received the Croix de Guerre medal (date uncertain). A later book by his friend Prince Areno Iukanthor notes that Monod was "severely wounded during the war" and served as the "former commander of the occupation troop at Saarbrücken," a German city near the French border.

It is unclear when he returned to Cambodia. On Jan. 1, 1917, he was promoted to Civil Service Administrator Grade 1. We do not know where Monod married, who he married, or if he had children. Only the charming dedication to the original 1922 edition of this book suggests that he had a wife or companion in Cambodia.

Apart from his publications there are no other records until his retirement on Oct. 10, 1925 at the age of 50. A decree dated Oct. 26, 1925 documents his award of the Grand Cross as a Knight of the Legion of Honor (Chevalier de la Légion d'honneur).

We do know he was alive in 1931 when he published Le Cambodgien – Comment ils Pensent (later translated as The Cambodian). A brief passage appeared that year in a book by Areno Iukanthor (Prince Norodom Arun Yukanthor) that at least gives us a pleasant image of his retirement saying "our dear friend Guillaume Monod currently spends his brightest days in Aix-en-Provence, reading the Khmer version of the Ramayana."

His final book in 1943, Contes Khmers (Khmer Tales), includes his dedication and devoted homage to Princess Pingpeang Yukanthor, suggesting he participated in its publication at age 68.

Despite this diverse collection of family information and facts, we find ourselves knowing very little about Monod. We could not locate a single personal document, his signature, or even his photograph. Finally, we do not know where, when or how he died, or where he rests today.

So, for the time being, much of the truth about our author largely remains among the legends that he loved so much.

# Guillaume Henri Monod Timeline

1845, May 12: Henri's father, Albert Edouard Monod is born.

1870, July 20: Albert Monod marries Laure Eugénie Mayor De Montricher in Marseille, France.

1871, Oct. 21: Birth of sister, Madeleine Isabelle Monod in London (died Oct. 28, 1966).

1873, July 12: Birth of brother, Raymond Emile Monod in London.

**1875, Jan. 1: Guillaume Henri Monod born in London, UK.**

1876, May 5: Birth of brother, George Ambroise Walter Monod in London.

1897: Joins the Société géologique de France (www. sgfr.org)

1898, Feb. 12: Entered the l'Administration de l'Indochine.

1900, Dec. 15: Administration student (élève Administrateur) – No school name is noted, but he may have been a trainee student at a school preparing administrators for colonial service.

1901, Feb. 7 (or 17): Decreed Deputy geologist, Direction de l'Agriculture et du Commerce de l'Indochine.

1901. Aug. 21 (or 28): Promoted to Administrator Grade 4.

1902: Publication of his first two geographical papers. (see Bibliography)

1905, April 5: Administrator, Grade 4. Chef of Pursat province, Cambodia.

1906: The Société géologique de France lists him as "Résident de France, Pursat (Cambodge)" as their only member in Cambodia.

1907, Jun. 15: Administrator Grade 3

1908, Aug. 1: Administrator Grade 3

1911, July 1: Administrator Grade 2

1911: Report - Pursat Province, Cambodia. (see Bibliography)

1912: The Société géologique de France lists him as "Résident de France, Kompong-Thom (Cambodge)."

1913, May 14 - 1914, Aug. 1: Job interruption ("Interruption de service du 14 mai 1913 au 1er août 1914").

1914, July 28 – Nov. 11, 1918: The dates of World War 1 (concluding with Armistice) included Monod's service for which he received the Croix de Guerre. The exact dates, rank and actions of his participation are unknown.

1917, Jan. 1: Promoted to Administrator Grade 1 of the Civil Services, transferred to the Agence économique de l'Indochine en France in Paris – Head of Press Service.

1922: Book - *Légendes cambodgiennes.* (see Bibliography)

1923: Article - *Le Sophea Lièvre.* (see Bibliography)

1923: Article - *Quelques mots sur les Cambodgiens.* (see Bibliography)

1924: Article - *Les chemins de fer en Indochine.* (see Bibliography)

1925 (circa): Introduction - *Ruines d'Angkor.* (see Bibliography)

1925, Oct. 10: Official date of retirement.

1925, Oct 26: Upon his retirement, in recognition of his long standing service to France, he was awarded the rank of Chevalier de la Légion d'honneur.

1928: Article - *La bibliothèque royale du Cambodge.* (see Bibliography)

1924: Article - *Les chemins de fer en Indochine.* (see Bibliography)

1931: Book - *Le Cambodgien.* (see Bibliography)

1931: Areno Iukanthor mentions Monod living in Aix-en-Provence.

1943. Book - *Contes Khmers.* The opening dedication of this book suggests that Monod (age 68 at the time) was alive for this publication. (see Biography and Bibliography)

**No further records of his life or date of death were found. Date discrepancies above result from differences between editions of the *Annuaire général de l'Indo-Chine française.***

# Bibliography

## The Works of

## Guillaume Henri Monod

**Descriptive notes provided as available.**

1902. *Notes sur quelques points en litige au sujet des formations de la Chine méridionale et du Tonkin*. Marseille: impr. P. Stuard. (9 p.; In-8°)

1902. *Notice sur les gisements de charbon en Indo-chine*. Publications de la Direction de l'Agriculture et du commerce de l'Indo-Chine. F. H. Schneider. (22 p.)

1911. *Notice sur la circonscription de Pursat*. Phnom Penh. (110 p.)

1922. *Légendes cambodgiennes: que m'a contées le Gouverneur Khieu*. 148 p., Paris: Bossard. (148 p. : ill. ; 17 cm.)

1923. *Le Sophea Lièvre* (*Sôphea Tonsai*) Paris: *La Revue du Pacifique*. (In-8°)

1923. *Quelques mots sur les Cambodgiens*. Paris: *La Revue du Pacifique*. (In-8° , 31 p.)

1924. *L'administration indochinoise*. Paris.*

1924. *Les chemins de fer en Indochine*. Article extr. de: *La Revue du Pacifique*. 3e annee, no. 2, Février 1924. (pp. 108-124: carte dépl. ; 24 cm.)

1925 (circa). Introduction to *Ruines d'Angkor*. Saïgon, Edition Photo Nadal. (203 p.: chiefly ill.; 18 x 24 cm.)

1926. *La petite collection orientaliste*. Paris.*

1928 *La bibliothèque royale du Cambodge*. Paris: *La revue du Pacifique*, n°1, 15 Janvier 1928. (pp. 12-14)

1930 (circa). Introduction to *Ruines d'Angkor.* Braun: Paris.

1931. *Le Cambodgien*. Paris : Larose.

1940 (circa). Introduction to *Ruines d'Angkor.* Saïgon: Edition Photo Nadal. (207 p.: chiefly ill. ; 24 x 32 cm)

1943. *Contes Khmers.* Mouans-Sartoux: Publications Chitra, C.-A. Högman. (303 p., 21 cm.)

1970. *Hors des routes fréquentées.* NOTE: From 1909 to 1927 a French language collection of legends and articles by G.H. Monod appeared in *Le Figaro* and *Le Feu* newspapers. (Book 73 p., 8vo S.l.)*

1970. *The Cambodian.* English translation of 1931 original by Keith Botsford. New Haven, Conn: Human Relations Area Files.

1975. *Les classiques de l'Orient.* Paris. Article extr. de: "La Revue du Pacifique", 4e année, no. 4, Avril 1925. (pp. 327-370 ; 24 cm.)*

1985. *Contes Khmers.* Paris: Centre de documentation et de recherche sur la civilisation khmère. (303 p. : ill. ; 20 cm.)

*** These citations are listed on Worldcat.org by BIU Langues Orientales, Paris, 75007 France**

# Original French Text:

## *Légendes Cambodgiennes:*

### *que m'a contées le Gouverneur Khieu*

**Guillaume Henri MONOD**

# Introduction

**Les peuples sont comme le rossignol de la chanson;**
**Ils chantent bien tant qu'ils ont le cœur gai.**

ANATOLE FRANCE.

LES coutumes, au Cambodge, sont immuables, parce que toutes reposent sur des légendes extrêmement anciennes qui sont devenues, dans l'esprit des Cambodgiens, l'origine presque sacrée de leurs traditions.

Le Gouverneur Khieu est un homme d'une haute intelligence; il connaît à fond la littérature cambodgienne; il en sourit parfois, mais en parle volontiers. C'est un de mes plaisirs d'avoir avec ce Khmèr de longs entretiens, au cours desquels je cherche à sonder, guidé par lui, les profondeurs, mystérieuses pour nous Occidentaux, de la très vieille âme cambodgienne.

Dans le choix des contes que j'offre aujourd'hui, j'ai cherché à varier les genres pour donner une idée générale de la littérature populaire cambodgienne.[1] Certaines de ces histoires peuvent paraître enfantines, comme « Le Beau-père qui cherche un gendre ». D'autres, comme « Kung le Courageux », montrent une réelle psychologie. Toutes sont amusantes et donnent, sur les mœurs, les coutumes, la mentalité, les idées religieuses cambodgiennes, des renseignements qui me paraissent présenter de l'intérêt. Toutes font ressortir la fertilité de l'imagination khmère, qui se plaît à accumuler les incidents, à compliquer souvent les situations, et à sortir non sans adresse d'intrigues assez difficiles à résoudre, comme dans les aventures d'Alev par exemple.

---

1 Le texte de plusieurs de ces contes a été lithographié à Saigon en 1878 (Textes Khmers, avec traduction sommaire, par Aymonier). Cet ouvrage étant introuvable aujourd'hui, je n'ai pu examiner les variantes qu'il présente avec les textes de Khieu.

Les idées cosmogoniques du Cambodge sont exploitées dans le conte des « Perdrix mâle et femelle ».

Enfin j'ai pensé que la légende décrivant la fondation d'Angkor ne manquerait pas d'intérêt. Les Khmers actuels, ne pouvant concevoir l'activité prodigieuse déployée par leurs ancêtres les grands bâtisseurs, ont expliqué par des interventions surnaturelles la construction de cet immense et admirable monument. Comme leurs autres contes, ils ont animé celui-là par des incidents amusants, et y ont donné libre cours à leur esprit poétique.

Mon intention, dans ces pages, n'est pas de me livrer à un travail savant au sujet des Satra Khmers. Je ne crois pas d'ailleurs que l'on puisse désigner un texte authentique de ces contes, qui se sont répétés de bouche en bouche, et qui ont été rédigés par divers copistes avec des variantes parfois importantes. Je me propose de les retracer tels qu'ils m'ont été racontés, m'attachant avant tout à leur conserver, dans la mesure du possible, leur charmante naïveté, la fraîcheur de la langue cambodgienne, les images, souvent infiniment délicates et gracieuses, qu'a su trouver l'esprit artiste des Khmers. Je me suis à peine cru permis d'atténuer la netteté des expressions ou la trivialité des plaisanteries qui émaillent ces contes. J'ai seulement tenu la plume pour écrire, sous la dictée du Gouverneur Khieu, la traduction des légendes qu'il me racontait. J'aime trop ces histoires pour avoir jamais osé y ajouter ou en retrancher un seul mot.

**G. H. Monod.**

# Artifices Féminins

### *Meayea Srey*

DANS les histoires de la plus haute antiquité, il est raconté qu'il y avait un mari et une femme vivant en ménage depuis longtemps. La femme avait un amant qu'elle menait sans cesse coucher dans la maison conjugale.

Un jour le mari s'était absenté pour aller déterrer des tubercules dans la forêt ; à l'heure de la forte chaleur, il entra se reposer dans une construction élevée aux *Neakta*.[2]

Il se trouva que le même jour la femme, affolée d'amour pour son amant, et prise d'un violent désir d'être débarrassée de son mari, alla porter des offrandes aux *Neakta*; le mari la voyant entrer fut fort surpris.

« Que vient-elle chercher ici? » se dit-il.

Il se cacha derrière le dos d'une statue qui représentait un *Neakta* et attendit en silence.

La femme alluma des baguettes d'encens, et fit cette invocation aux *Neakta*:

« Je ne veux plus de mon mari. J'en ai pris un autre. Je supplie les *Neakta* de faire mourir mon mari; en reconnaissance je leur offrirai un cochon. »

Le mari répondit de sa cachette, en déguisant sa voix:

« Si tu as un amant et que tu veuilles sans peine faire mourir ton mari, retourne chez toi, procure-toi une poule couveuse avec ses œufs, fais-les cuire, et donne-les à manger à ton mari: il mourra. »

La femme, convaincue que cet avis lui avait été réellement donné par le *Neakta*, s'empressa de rentrer chez elle; elle acheta une poule couveuse et ses œufs, les fit bouillir dans l'intention de se délivrer de son mari en les lui faisant manger, puis de vivre avec son amant.

Au crépuscule, le mari rentra; il demanda:

« As-tu quelque chose à me donner à manger? J'ai grand'faim. »

La femme lui apporta la poule et une marmite de riz. Le mari dévora le tout ;

---

2 Sanskrit: *Neaktamchara*, génies.

puis il fit le malade, se coucha en gémissant. Sa femme, convaincue que son mari trépassait comme l'avaient annoncé les *Neakta*, ouvrit la porte, fit entrer son amant, et alla s'étendre avec lui sur la natte.

Tandis que les amoureux se disaient des mignardises, le mari se dressa sur son séant, appela sa femme et lui dit:

« Je tremble de froid! Va puiser de l'eau; tu la mettras sur le feu pour me donner un bain. »

L'amant, effrayé en voyant le mari se relever, et n'ayant aucune possibilité de fuir, s'introduisit dans une grande jarre vide qui se trouvait auprès de la natte et s'y cacha en attendant que le mari se soit rendormi.

Le mari avait fort bien vu le manège, mais il ne souffla mot et fit semblant de rien. Il cria à sa femme:

« J'ai froid, j'ai froid! Vite fais chauffer l'eau, je me baignerai; le bain hâtera l'œuvre de la mort! »

La femme, entendant son mari appeler la mort, fut tout heureuse de voir ses prières si exactement exaucées.

Quand une grande bassine d'eau fut bouillante, le mari dit à sa femme:

« Va chercher une cruche d'eau froide pour la mélanger avec celle-ci. »

La femme sortit avec une cruche. Aussitôt qu'elle eut disparu, le mari se leva, prit le chaudron qui bouillait sur le feu, et le vida dans la jarre où était blotti l'amant, qui mourut sans un cri. Son coup fait, le mari se recoucha, jouant toujours le malade et gémissant.

La femme revenant vit la tête de son amant émerger de la jarre; ceci provenait de la crispation de ses muscles ébouillantés. La femme lui dit à voix basse: « Baisse-toi! il ne dort pas encore! »

Son amant ne bougea pas. Elle étendit la main pour le repousser dans la jarre; une oreille lui resta dans les doigts. Elle comprit que son mari avait fait mourir son amant en l'inondant d'eau bouillante; mais elle ne dit rien, elle traîna la jarre vers son mari et posa l'eau froide auprès. Le mari ne prit pas le bain; il dit:

« Je me sens mieux. Allons-nous coucher! »

ଓ ❀ ଛ

La femme ne savait comment faire disparaître le cadavre de son amant. Elle pensa:

« Dans ce village se trouvent quatre voleurs qui jour et nuit commettent des larcins dans toutes les maisons. Je vais faire emporter le cadavre par ces maraudeurs qui iront l'abandonner dans la forêt! »

Elle alla emprunter plusieurs *sampot hol*[3] et des casaques en soie, et les étendit comme pour les faire sécher autour de sa maison.

Les quatre voleurs virent cet étalage et pensèrent entre eux:

« Comment, cette femme que nous avions crue très pauvre possède de pareilles choses ? A la nuit nous viendrons sans faute la voler. »

Dans la soirée, la femme détacha les étoffes qu'elle avait mises à sécher, les replia et alla les rendre à qui les lui avait prêtées. Puis, avec une longue corde, elle attacha solidement et à tours redoublés le couvercle de la jarre dans laquelle se trouvait le cadavre. Cela fait elle sortit.

Les quatre voleurs voyant la maison vide s'y faufilèrent, fouillèrent tous les recoins, ne trouvèrent rien qui valût la peine d'être volé. Ils cherchèrent à ouvrir la jarre, mais le couvercle était bien attaché. Ils pensèrent:

« Tous les objets précieux sont certainement dans cette jarre. Ne perdons pas de temps à l'ouvrir ici. Emportons-la telle qu'elle est ! »

Ils glissèrent deux bambous sous les cordes, en placèrent les extrémités sur leurs épaules, et emportèrent leur butin dans la forêt.

Quand ils furent très loin du village, ils coupèrent les cordes et découvrirent la jarre. L'un des voleurs, tâtant avec la main, toucha les cheveux du mort. Il s'écria:

« Oh! C'est plein de soie filée! »

Le second tâta à son tour; il rencontra l'oreille arrachée, les yeux, le nez; il s'écria:

« C'est un cadavre! »

Le troisième ne voulut pas le croire. Il y mit la main à son tour, toucha la poitrine, reconnut que c'était en effet un mort; tous quatre s'enfuirent en fureur, se voyant joués par une femme qui leur avait fait emporter à grande fatigue un cadavre. Ils dirent entre eux:

---

3 Le *sampot* est une bande d'étoile que les Cambodgiens des deux sexes portent à la façon d'une culotte bouffante. Le *sampot hol* est en soie à fleurs de couleurs variées.

« Nous surveillerons cette femme; si jamais nous la rencontrons seule, nous la saisirons et nous la rosserons pour la corriger et lui enlever toute envie de nous tromper à nouveau. »

ಬ❀ಚ

Quelque temps après, la femme se rendait à la rivière pour faire des emplettes, car une jonque-bazar chinoise venait de mouiller à la berge.

Au milieu de sa route, la femme se trouva en présence des quatre voleurs ; ceux-ci, d'un commun accord, se précipitèrent vers elle, l'insulte à la bouche, pour la battre d'importance. Mais elle leur dit:

« Eh quoi, si vous me battez, quel avantage en retirerez-vous ? Accompagnez-moi plutôt : je vais recevoir de l'argent que me doit le batelier chinois. Quand je serai payée, nous partagerons mon argent. »

Les quatre voleurs se rendirent à ces raisons et se mirent en route avec la femme. Elle leur fit ces recommandations:

« Vous resterez tous quatre sur la berge pendant que je descendrai seule sur la jonque.[4] Quand vous me verrez vous faire signe de la main, venez à bord et vous aurez beaucoup d'argent. »

Elle descendit dans la jonque et dit au maître du bateau:

« Les quatre hommes que j'amène avec moi sont des esclaves qui m'appartiennent. Si vous voulez les acquérir, je suis disposée à vous les vendre.

— Je veux bien, dit le Chinois; combien en demandez-vous?

— Deux barres d'argent chacun.

— Je vous offre une barre et demie par homme.

— J'accepte, dit la femme. Je remonterai à terre pendant que vous les ferez descendre. Mais faites attention, ils voudront me suivre. Dès qu'ils seront à bord, faites-les enchaîner solidement. »

Le Chinois paya le prix convenu. La femme sortit du rouffle[5] à l'arrière de

4 Les Cambodgiens disent toujours à l'inverse de nous: descendre à bord d'un bateau, monter à terre. Ceci tient à ce que les berges des cours d'eau cambodgiens, soumis à de très grandes variations de niveau, sont toujours élevées; on les descend pour s'embarquer.

5 Un superstructure pouvant être fermée sur le pont d'un bateau.

la jonque et fit signe aux voleurs de descendre en leur montrant l'argent qu'elle venait de recevoir. Eux, convaincus qu'elle les appelait pour le partage convenu, descendirent pendant qu'elle disparaissait sous le rouffle. Mais à peine étaient-ils sur le bateau qu'ils furent saisis par les matelots et enchaînés à fond de cale.

Pendant ce temps, la femme, sortant du rouffle par la porte opposée, était remontée à terre et avait disparu.

༄❀༄

La nuit surprit la femme alors qu'elle était encore loin de son village. N'osant, par peur du tigre, poursuivre son chemin dans l'obscurité, elle grimpa sur un grand arbre qui se trouvait au bord du chemin, se pelotonna dans les hautes branches et s'endormit.

Les quatre voleurs, enchaînés au fond de la jonque, dirent entre eux:

« Cette femme a vraiment de l'intelligence! Après nous avoir fait emporter le cadavre dans la forêt, voici qu'elle nous a vendus. Aura-t-elle toujours le dernier mot avec nous? »

Ils firent des efforts avec une énergie doublée par la colère, brisèrent leurs chaînes, regagnèrent la berge et se sauvèrent dans la nuit.

Le hasard les fit passer au pied de l'arbre sur lequel avait grimpé la femme. A leur tour ils décidèrent d'y monter pour y passer la nuit. Trois d'entre eux s'installèrent sur les maîtresses branches. Le quatrième monta jusqu'au faîte de l'arbre, où il trouva la femme. Bouillant de fureur, il lui dit:

« Ah! te voilà, misérable! Cette fois ton compte est bon; tu vas mourir! Tu te fais un jeu de nous tromper. Maintenant sauve-toi si tu peux ! »

La femme fit briller son argent aux rayons de la lune et dit tout bas:

« Taisez-vous donc ! Que les trois autres ne sachent pas que je suis ici! Prenez-moi pour femme; nous avons de l'argent pour vivre; je saurai vous en procurer d'autre. Vous aurez plus de bénéfice à me garder comme compagne qu'à me faire du mal! »

Le voleur ne souffla plus mot; il se glissa auprès de la femme, l'entoura de ses bras et lui dit:

« Petite sœur, on peut dire que tu as de l'astuce!

Deux fois tu as joué tes frères aînés ! Mais notre destinée nous a marqués pour être mari et femme. A nous deux nous n'aurons pas de peine à vivre aux dépens d'autrui. »

Parlant ainsi il la couvrait de baisers. Elle se laissait faire sans protester. Puis elle lui dit d'un ton chagrin:

« J'ai peur que vous ne m'aimiez pas sincèrement. Moi je vous aime de tout cœur.

— Ton frère aîné t'aime véritablement. Tu ne connais pas le cœur de ton frère. Veux-tu que je m'engage par un serment? Que veux-tu que je fasse pour te prouver mon amour?

Si vous m'aimez au point que nous n'ayons qu'un seul cœur, nous allons nous embrasser la langue! »

Elle tira la langue la première et se pencha vers le voleur qui l'embrassa. Le voleur fit de même à son tour, mais la femme, s'approchant comme pour l'embrasser, saisit entre ses dents la langue de son amoureux, la mordit de toutes ses forces, au point de la déchirer; puis elle le poussa des deux mains; il tomba du haut de l'arbre sur le sol en poussant des cris inarticulés.

Les trois autres voleurs, entendant ce tapage, s'imaginèrent que le Chinois de la jonque s'était mis à leur poursuite avec ses gens; ils sautèrent de l'arbre, criant:

« Alerte ! Sauvons-nous ! Le Chinois nous poursuit! »

Celui qui avait la langue déchirée les appela, disant:

« La femme est sur l'arbre! Venez l'attraper! »

Mais sa langue était coupée; ses paroles étaient inintelligibles. Ses compagnons, ne comprenant pas ce qu'il disait, crurent entendre parler chinois; ils ne songèrent qu'à sauver leur vie et s'enfuirent dans la forêt.

La femme descendit alors de l'arbre, serrant son argent dans son écharpe; elle l'apporta à son mari et vécut paisiblement avec lui par la suite.

# Le Beau-Père Qui Choisit un Gendre

## *Apuk Khmek Rus Kon Prasa*

ON dit qu'autrefois il était un vieux et une vieille qui avaient une fille remarquablement belle. Dans quel pays vivaient-ils? Je ne sais. C'est une histoire qui s'est transmise de bouche en bouche jusqu'à moi.

Ces deux vieux avaient fait serment qu'ils ne donneraient leur fille qu'à un prétendant qui pourrait s'abstenir absolument de jurer.

Un jeune homme de belle apparence s'en vint un jour demander la main de la jeune fille. Les parents répondirent:

« Oui, nous te la donnerons, ne te mets pas en peine. Tu entreras à notre service et tu nous obéiras.[6] Si tu es capable de ne jamais jurer, nous te la donnerons. Nous te posons d'avance nos conditions: ne nous reproche pas ensuite d'être fourbes! »

Le jeune homme répartit:

« Je puis très bien m'abstenir de jurer. Je suis disposé à faire tout ce que vous voudrez et vous obéirai en tout.

— C'est bien, dit le père, si tu peux éviter de jurer, va en paix. Demain matin, tu entreras au service de ton beau-père. »

Le lendemain, le vieux fit préparer par sa fille le déjeuner du galant. Lorsque celui-ci se fut restauré, il lui dit:

« Mon gendre, va prendre les buffles et tu iras labourer la rizière. Tu laboureras jusqu'à ce que ces pierres que tu vois en bordure du chemin gémissent. Alors tu dételleras les buffles. »

Le jeune homme alla chercher les buffles, les attela à la charrue et se mit à labourer. Il travailla du lever du jour à midi, mais les pierres ne gémirent point.

---

6 C'est une coutume dans le peuple cambodgien que le prétendant, lorsqu'il est agréé par les parents de la jeune fille, entre à leur service pour quelques mois.

Les buffles ne voulaient plus marcher, mais les pierres restaient silencieuses. Le garçon avait chaud, avait faim; il ne put résister, il s'écria:

« Satanées pierres, quand donc gémirez-vous? »

Il ne prononça que ce seul juron, mais le vieillard, qui était caché derrière les pierres, apparut et dit:

« C'est bon, dételle les buffles et va-t'en chez toi; je te refuse ma fille; tu ne peux te retenir de jurer. »

Le jeune homme délia les animaux et se retira fort penaud.

Bientôt après un autre garçon se présenta; le vieux lui tint le même discours qu'à son prédécesseur. Mais cette fois le jeune homme eut plus de malice; il alla labourer la rizière, emportant avec lui un paquet de riz. Lorsqu'il eut labouré jusqu'à ce que le soleil fut haut dans sa course, il arrêta les buffles, mangea, et se remit à l'ouvrage.

A midi passé, les pierres n'avaient pas encore gémi.

Les buffles étaient exténués et ne pouvaient plus marcher. Arrivé près des pierres, il dit:

« Chères pierres, gémissez. Les buffles n'en peuvent plus, ayez pitié d'eux. Il ne s'agit pas de moi, j'ai de quoi manger; je puis sans peine labourer jusqu'à la nuit. Mais ces buffles, ayez-en compassion; ce sont des animaux, et ils appartiennent à mon beau-père! »

Toutes ses supplications ne firent pas gémir les pierres. Mais il se garda de jurer, car il se doutait que le vieillard l'écoutait en cachette. Longtemps, il implora les pierres. Enfin, le père vit ses buffles à bout de force; il en eut pitié parce qu'ils lui appartenaient : il se mit à gémir derrière les rochers. Aussitôt, le jeune homme détela les bêtes et vint à la maison de son beau-père, qui lui fit préparer à dîner par sa fille. A la tombée du jour, le beau-père le congédia:

« Mon cher enfant, rentre chez toi. Demain matin tu reviendras. »

Le jeune homme prit congé et retourna chez lui.

Mais lorsque la nuit fut tout à fait tombée, il revint à pas de loup se poster sous la maison[7] du vieux pour écouter ce qu'il dirait à sa femme.

---

7 Les maisons au Cambodge sont construites sur pilotis.

Or, voici ce qu'il entendit:

« Celui-là sait s'abstenir de jurer; mais il a un mauvais physique. Il ne convient pas pour notre fille. Faisons donc en sorte de le mettre en colère et de l'amener à jurer pour pouvoir la lui refuser. »

La femme répondit:

« C'est facile. Tu te mettras dans un sac; dans un autre nous mettrons du riz. Demain matin, je lui dirai que tu es allé couper du bois dans la montagne, et je lui commanderai de porter les deux sacs jusqu'au sommet. La charge sera fort lourde; il se mettra en colère et jurera. Toi, dans le sac, tu l'entendras: tu pourras alors le congédier. »

Ayant ainsi conversé, les parents de la jeune fille s'endormirent. Le jeune homme avait tout entendu.

Au lever du jour il alla reprendre son service chez ses beaux-parents. La femme lui montra deux sacs liés aux deux bouts d'un fléau et lui dit:

« Mon cher enfant, ton père est allé couper du bois sur la montagne ; il te fait dire de prendre cette charge de riz et de le suivre au plus vite. Il est parti à jeun avant le jour. Emporte ces deux sacs, dépêche toi de monter au sommet de la montagne, et là tu prépareras le déjeuner de ton père. »

Le jeune homme prit la charge et sortit.

Arrivé au pied de la montagne, il commença de monter. Mais la charge était pesante; il redescendit.

« O mon cher beau-père, il aura bien faim! disait-il tout haut en marchant, mais je ne puis monter rapidement, c'est tellement lourd. Qui donc pourrait porter une pareille charge jusqu'en haut? Si cependant mon beau-père n'a pas pitié de moi et qu'il m'injurie, j'accepterai ses reproches sans murmurer! »

Ce disant il était revenu dans la plaine. Il avisa des herbes très sèches, y déposa son fardeau et s'éloigna. Mais aussitôt il revint sans bruit et mit le feu tout autour de la charge. Le vieux, enfermé dans son sac, était entouré de flammes; la chaleur arrivait jusqu'à lui; il tremblait de tous ses membres, épouvanté à la pensée de mourir consumé. Mais il ne pouvait pas sortir.

Le garçon fit semblant de revenir de loin tout courant et s'écria:

« Eh, qui a allumé ce feu qui va brûler mon fardeau? Comment aller le prendre? Il est au milieu du brasier! je ne peux en approcher! »

Criant ainsi, il se tenait en dehors des flammes.

Lorsque le feu atteignit presque les sacs, il se précipita et traîna sa charge hors de l'incendie. Le vieux était couvert de brûlures; le garçon délia les sacs, il vit son beau-père en piteux état; il joua la surprise et s'écria:

« Eh, cher père, pourquoi ne m'avoir pas averti? Il s'en est fallu de peu que vous perdiez la vie dans les flammes, que vous laissiez veuve ma chère belle-mère! »

Le beau-père se vit joué et fut fort en colère; mais il ne savait que faire. Il se leva et rentra chez lui clopin-clopant. Pendant tout le jour il resta couché, soignant ses brûlures et les contusions qu'il avait reçues lorsqu'il avait été traîné loin du feu.

Le soir venu, il renvoya le garçon jusqu'au matin. Comme la nuit précédente, le jeune homme vint écouter causer les deux vieux.

« Comment faire, dit le mari, pour congédier ce garnement? Il est plein de finesse; mais je ne veux pas lui donner ma fille! »

Il raconta son aventure;

« Trouve un moyen de le congédier! »

La femme répondit :

« Voici: tu feras le maître et lui ordonneras de faire le chien; tu l'emmèneras chercher des tortues. S'il n'en rapporte pas, ou si, courant à quatre pattes, il ne peut pas te suivre, nous le mettrons à la porte!

— C'est bien pensé, femme! dit le mari. Dès demain je suivrai ton conseil. »

Le garçon, renseigné, rentra se coucher.

Avant le chant du coq, il prit des tortues et alla les attacher par-ci, par-là, dans les herbes de la plaine où le beau-père avait décidé d'aller chasser.

A l'aurore, il se rendit chez le vieux qui lui dit:

« Mon fils, nous allons chercher des tortues. Seulement nous n'aurons pas de chien. Tu vas le remplacer: tu seras le chien, je serai ton maître. Nous tâcherons de trouver une ou deux tortues et nous reviendrons les manger ici.

— A vos ordres », dit le garçon.

Le père prit une musette de riz, un bambou plein d'eau et sortit; le jeune homme, à quatre pattes, le suivait en courant. Arrivé à la plaine où il avait attaché les tortues, il galopa en avant, entra dans les herbes, détacha sans être vu une tortue et se mit à aboyer. Le vieux se hâta d'approcher; il vit son gendre qui tenait une tortue entre ses dents. Le chien quêta de droite et de gauche, et rapporta sept ou huit tortues.

A midi, le vieux eut faim; il ouvrit sa musette et se mit à manger. Le gendre, faisant toujours le chien, aperçut un troupeau de buffles ; il se précipita, mordit les bestiaux aux jambes ; les buffles s'enfuirent dans les champs de riz mûr. Le vieux courut faire sortir chien et buffles des récoltes. Lestement, le garçon vint manger toutes les provisions de son beau-père. Celui-ci, à son retour, ne trouva plus rien; furieux, il voulut frapper le chien, mais il était trop fatigué pour l'atteindre. Il avait faim, la route était longue. Il s'efforçait de marcher l'estomac creux. Il ne pouvait s'en prendre à son gendre, puisqu'il était chien. Arrivé chez lui, il mangea et renvoya le jeune homme.

Cette nuit-là, de sa cachette habituelle, le gars entendit le vieux raconter tout ce qui s'était passé à sa femme, qui lui dit:

« Il t'a joué étant le chien. Demain fais le contraire: c'est toi qui seras le chien et lui le maître. Tu lui rendras la pareille. »

Le matin, le garçon, instruit de ce qu'il devait faire, prit l'eau et le riz et partit suivi du vieux qui trottait à quatre pattes. Le jeune homme marchait vite pour que son beau-père ne puisse le suivre. Bientôt il s'écria:

« Qu'est-ce donc que ce chien? Il est toujours derrière. Comment trouvera-t-il ainsi des tortues? »

Il frappa le chien pour le faire marcher en avant.

Mais le vieux ne pouvait courir dans les herbes. Il se traînait toujours suivant le sentier derrière son gendre ; il ne trouvait point de tortues. Le garçon le rossa à lui faire perdre la respiration. Mais le vieux, tout honteux, n'osait rien dire.

A midi, le garçon s'arrêta pour manger. Il s'écria:

« Qu'est-ce que c'est que ce chien qui ne sait pas trouver de tortues? qui marche toujours derrière son maître? Il ne sait que manger et dormir! »

Le garçon avala le riz et la viande, ne jetant au vieux que les os qu'il ne pouvait pas même ronger, car il n'avait plus de dents. Le beau-père, assis, affamé, regardait manger son gendre. Quand le repas fut fini, le garçon donna au vieux un coup de rotin et dit:

« Allons! rentrons à la maison. Il n'y a rien à faire avec un chien pareil! » Et il se mit en route.

Le vieux, exténué, ne pouvait plus suivre à quatre pattes. Il se remit debout et marcha tout honteux derrière.

En arrivant le garçon dit:

« Mère, nous n'avons point de tortues. Le chien ne vaut rien ! »

Il prit congé et s'en retourna chez lui.

Lorsqu'ils furent rentrés dans leur chambre, le vieux et la vieille s'entretinrent des événements de la journée. Le vieux raconta comment il avait été maltraité et privé de nourriture. La vieille dit:

« Nous ne pouvons lui donner notre fille. Et nous ne réussissons pas à le congédier!

— Il est laid, dit le vieux ; il ne peut convenir à notre jolie fille! Mais tous mes efforts pour le mettre en colère et le forcer à jurer sont stériles ! Imagine quelque chose qu'il ne puisse accomplir, qui lui fasse perdre patience et nous donne un prétexte pour le renvoyer!

Voici, dit la femme. Avant le jour, tu mangeras, tu chiqueras ton bétel, et tu te cacheras dans ce panier. Dans un autre nous mettrons du sel. Quand ce mauvais sujet viendra, je lui dirai que tu es allé faire des achats au marché et qu'il doit te rejoindre avant midi. Le marché est trop loin pour qu'il puisse arriver à temps. En chemin, fatigué de sa charge et se croyant seul, il jurera sûrement. »

— Tu as raison, » dit le vieux, et ils s'endormirent. Le garçon, comme de coutume, avait surpris leurs projets.

Quand il se présenta le matin chez ses beaux-parents, la vieille lui donna la lourde charge à porter et lui fit les recommandations convenues.

Le jeune homme se mit en route, pensant:

« Cette fois, il faut que je fasse en sorte qu'on me donne la fille. J'en ai assez de ces épreuves! »

Arrivé à moitié route, il posa sa charge et dit.

« Le couvercle de ce panier est bien mal attaché! »

Il prit une corde, enferma solidement son beau-père; puis il se remit à marcher.

Il atteignit une rivière que franchissait un pont de bois. Il posa ses deux paniers tout au bord du pont; un rien suffisait à les faire tomber.

« Malheureux que je suis ! s'écria-t-il, l'heure avance ! Mon cher beau-père va être en colère! Mais ma charge est si lourde! Comment pourrai-je arriver à temps? Il faut que je me repose un instant sous ces arbres là-bas, puis je me remettrai en route! »

Il dit et s'éloigna. Il choisit une grosse bûche et revint vers le pont, imitant avec le morceau de bois la démarche pesante d'un éléphant; déguisant sa voix, il se mit à crier :

« Qui a posé cette charge au milieu du pont? Mon éléphant va l'écraser! Vite qu'on l'enlève. »

Tout en parlant il frappait lourdement en cadence le tablier du pont.

Le vieux, enfermé dans son panier, crut que c'était vraiment un éléphant qui venait et qui allait l'écraser. Tout à coup, il sentit un choc. Les deux paniers, comme poussés par le pied de l'éléphant, tombèrent dans l'eau. Le malheureux était suffoqué, tremblait, secouant sa prison, pensant qu'il allait mourir.

Le jeune homme le laissa boire un moment, ayant d'avance attaché les paniers avec un rotin qui les empêchait de s'enfoncer. Puis il fit semblant de venir de loin, criant:

« Eh ! Qui a osé faire passer un éléphant et jeter ma charge dans l'eau? Misère de moi! que va dire mon beau-père? Je suis déjà en retard et voici que tout le sel est mouillé! »

Comme il retirait la charge de l'eau, il vit l'un des paniers secoué par les tremblements de son beau-père; il dit :

« Oh ! Les poissons sont déjà entrés! Hélas! tout est trempé! Je vais ouvrir les paniers et les mettre à sécher. Mais le sel sera fondu! Bien vite je vais le rapporter à ma belle-mère qui en fera de la saumure pour mon cher beau-père! »

Ce disant, il ouvrit un des paniers et y trouva son beau-père.

« Oh! cher père, dit-il, pourquoi n'avez-vous pas crié? Pourquoi ne m'avez-vous pas fait savoir que vous étiez là dedans? Voyez comme vous avez risqué d'être noyé. Quelqu'un a conduit ici un éléphant, je ne sais d'où, et la bête vous a poussé dans l'eau avec le pied ! »

Le vieux l'écouta sans mot dire et regagna sa maison dans un silence rageur. Il se sentait berné et à bout d'invention; il n'osa plus tendre de nouveaux pièges. Il accorda sa fille en mariage au garçon.

Nous avons raconté cette histoire pour qu'elle serve de leçon à ceux qui ont des filles à marier. S'ils veulent leur donner un mari, qu'ils célèbrent le mariage. S'ils ne le veulent pas, qu'ils le disent franchement. Mais qu'ils n'imitent pas les duperies de ce vieux qui voulait choisir un gendre. D'abord, ce n'est pas honnête, et puis ils n'auront jamais le dernier mot avec les amoureux.

# Histoire d'Alev

### *Ruong Alev*

IL y avait autrefois un homme appelé Ngeh; sa femme s'appelait Ngoh; ils avaient un fils qui s'appelait Alev.

A l'âge de sept ans, cet enfant, qui était plein d'intelligence, se rendit compte de la simplicité de ses parents qui n'avaient aucune idée pour améliorer leur sort et vivaient dans une grande misère. Il leur dit:

« Si nous sommes si pauvres, c'est parce que nous n'exerçons aucun métier, nous ne travaillons pas comme les autres. A la saison des pluies, faisons des rizières; en saison sèche, cultivons un jardin. Moi j'irai travailler aux champs avec mon père. S'il a besoin de nourriture, d'arec, de bétel, ou de quoi que ce soit, je viendrai à la maison chercher ce qu'il faudra et le rapporterai. »

Les parents approuvèrent cette proposition. Au jour Ngeh se rendit aux rizières avec l'enfant.

Quand il fut resté un certain temps aux champs, Alev fut pris du désir de manger des gâteaux.

« Pour cela, se dit-il, il faut que je trompe mes parents! »

Il dit à Ngeh :

« Père, je vais à la maison chercher de l'arec et du bétel.

— Vas-y, » répondit Ngeh.

Alev s'en fut. A moitié route, il entra dans une pagode, se prosterna devant les bonzes et les pria de lui raser la tête. Puis il prit congé et se dirigea vers la case de ses parents. Il couvrit sa tête de son écharpe, et entra en faisant semblant de pleurer. Sa mère, le voyant sangloter, lui demanda:

« Mon petit, pourquoi pleures-tu ainsi? »

Alev redoubla ses sanglots. Sa mère se jeta sur lui, le prit dans ses bras, enleva l'écharpe qui lui couvrait le visage, et vit sa tête rasée. Elle fut saisie d'inquiétude. « Pourquoi, mon enfant, ta tête est-elle rasée ainsi? Quelle est la cause de tes larmes?

— O ma mère, mon père est mort! »

*Neang*[8] Ngoh éclata en pleurs et en gémissements, se rappelant avec désespoir combien douce avait été sa vie depuis qu'elle s'était unie à son mari.

« Mère, dit Alev, ne vous désespérez pas ainsi! Si vous ne faites que pleurer, comment préparerez-vous la cérémonie de mon père?

— Ton père a-t-il déjà été enterré ? demanda-t-elle.

— J'ai chargé les gens du voisinage de préparer l'inhumation avec pompe. »

*Neang* Ngoh se mit en toute hâte à préparer des gâteaux, des pâtisseries, et dit à son fils:

« O mon petit, prends toutes ces sucreries et va faire les offrandes sur la tombe de ton père. Je n'ai pas la force d'y aller moi-même! Si j'allais avec toi, si je voyais la rizière que ton père a mise en culture, l'endroit où on l'a mis, la tombe qu'on lui a faite, ma douleur serait trop amère! Va, mon enfant, va sans moi! »

Alev se réjouit parce que sa ruse avait si bien réussi. Il se hâta de préparer sa charge dans deux paniers attachés aux deux extrémités d'un bambou qu'il plaça sur son épaule et s'éloigna.

Arrivé à moitié chemin, il déposa sa charge, s'assit à l'ombre d'un manguier, et se mit à dévorer les gâteaux. Lorsqu'il en fut rassasié, il en restait encore. Il remit ce reste dans les paniers pour l'apporter à son père.

En approchant de la cabane de Ngeh, il fit de nouveau semblant de pleurer. Son père le voyant dans les larmes, voyant sa tête fraichement rasée, l'interrogea:

« Qu'y a-t-il, mon petit? Pourquoi pleurer ainsi? Pourquoi tes cheveux sont-ils rasés?

— Oh! Mon père, ma mère est morte! C'est pour son deuil que ma tête est rasée. Nos parents, nos voisins, ont fait les cérémonies de l'ensevelissement, ont fait les offrandes de gâteaux. J'en ai apporté pour que mon père ait sa part. »

Ngoh, qui était un homme simple et facile à tromper, crut son fils et pleura de compassion sur sa femme.

---

8 *Neang* - Appellatif des femmes. En cambodgien, on ne dit pas le nom d'une personne sans le faire précéder d'un appellatif : A pour les petits garçons, Me pour les petites filles, Chau pour les hommes, *Neang* pour les femmes, *Neak* pour les personnes de qualité, etc....

« Oh! Mon fils, désormais ton père ne retournera jamais dans son village bâti au bord du fleuve! Ton père ne quittera plus ces rizières ! Il ne veut plus revoir les lieux où il vécut heureux avec ta mère. »

Alev, enchanté d'avoir si bien fait tomber ses parents dans le piège, se réjouit dans son cœur.

Au bout de quelques jours, Alev dit à Ngeh:

« Cher père, nous voici tous deux seuls; notre existence est pénible. Personne ne s'occupe de préparer notre nourriture; personne ne nous tisse des vêtements. Vous devriez prendre femme, dans le seul but d'avoir quelqu'un qui fasse nos aliments, qui puise l'eau, qui décortique le riz. Nous ne serions plus aussi misérables! »

Ngoh répondit:

« Hélas! Mon petit, il n'y a pas un mois que ta mère est morte, et tu m'engages déjà à me remarier! Tu n'as pas de regrets de ta mère? Ne me mépriserait-on pas ? On dirait: sa femme est morte depuis quelques jours à peine, et déjà il veut se remarier ! J'aurais honte! Je ne veux pas prendre une autre femme. »

Mais Alev ne faisait que supplier son père sans cesse.

Un jour Ngeh revenait exténué de la rizière. Alev lui dit:

« Mon père, vous êtes à bout de forces, parce que vous n'avez pas de femme pour vous seconder et soutenir vos efforts. Souvenez-vous des préceptes; nos ancêtres nous ont enseigné: si un homme n'a pas de femme, quand il va à la forêt, il néglige la maison; s'il s'occupe à la maison, il néglige les travaux extérieurs. Comment aurez-vous de quoi nous nourrir? Vos seules forces n'y suffisent pas.

— Et qui donc, répond Ngeh, irait demander pour ton père la main d'une femme?

— Ne vous mettez pas en peine, mon père. Je me charge d'aller chercher une femme pour vous. Occupez-vous seulement de notre maison.

— Fais comme tu l'entendras », répondit Ngeh.

Alev fit aussitôt ses préparatifs, et se rendit auprès de *Neang* Ngoh sa mère. Il demeura auprès d'elle deux ou trois jours, puis il lui dit:

« Ma chère mère, nous voici seuls tous deux. Moi je ne suis qu'un enfant, je ne suis pas capable de pourvoir à nos besoins. Vous, vous êtes une femme, une veuve. Je connais un homme qui voudrait vous épouser. Prenez-le pour mari, à seule fin qu'il prenne soin de nous, qu'il allège notre misère. »

*Neang* Ngoh répondit:

« Mon enfant, il n'y a que quelques jours que ton père est mort, et tu oses me dire de prendre un autre mari? Ce n'est pas bien! De plus tout le monde me tournerait en dérision; on dirait: qu'est-ce donc que cette femme qui, à peine veuve, songe déjà à se remarier?

— Ma mère, vous vous préoccupez de ce que diront de vous nos voisins. Est-ce qu'ils se préoccupent de nous venir en aide? Ils ont de l'argent; subviennent-ils à nos besoins?

« Lorsque j'étais aux rizières, j'y ai rencontré un homme qui ressemblait exactement à mon père. Il m'aimait comme son propre fils. Il m'a demandé: As-tu tes parents? Je lui ai répondu: J'ai perdu mon père; je n'ai plus que ma mère. Il m'a dit: Je voudrais épouser ta mère. Mais y consentirait-elle? Si elle m'accepte, notre mariage sera célébré selon les règles qui nous ont été enseignées par nos ancêtres. Si elle me repousse, je ne sais comment elle pourra subvenir à vos besoins à tous deux. »

Alev insista, supplia tant et si bien que *Neang* Ngoh finit par lui dire:

« Fais comme tu l'entendras! »

Alev se réjouit dans son cœur et se dit : « Je vais à nouveau manger des gâteaux! » Il fit diligence pour orner la maison, et dit à sa mère:

« L'homme dont je vous parle veut faire ce mariage sans retard. Je vais par la campagne chercher des poules, des canards, des fruits, des légumes; puis j'irai avertir celui qui veut vous épouser de faire tous les apprêts du mariage. »

Alev s'en alla aux rizières, et dit à Ngeh:

« Mon père, j'ai demandé pour vous la main d'une femme. Elle a le visage, les yeux, la taille, la voix, le teint qu'avait ma mère. Je l'ai déjà installée dans notre maison. Préparez donc sans retard tout ce qu'il faut pour le mariage. »

Ngeh courut chez ses voisins, les pria de l'aider à préparer des mets, des gâteaux, des sucreries; il acheta des viandes, des poules, des canards, des légumes de toutes sortes, des fruits. Alev ne faisait que manger des friandises tout le jour. Il dit à Ngeh:

« La femme que j'ai demandée pour vous ne consent à célébrer le mariage que de nuit. De jour, elle ne veut pas vous épouser. »

Ngeh, dans sa sottise, acceptait tout ce que proposait Alev. Il prit ses dispositions pour célébrer le mariage la nuit.

Le soir venu, il pria ses voisins de l'aider à transporter ce qui avait été préparé pour la cérémonie.

On fit cuire le riz, des mets variés; les uns apportèrent des fruits, d'autres des friandises de toutes sortes, et allèrent les présenter à l'épousée selon la coutume.

*Neang* Ngoh de son côté s'était fait aider par ses voisines pour faire les préparatifs d'usage.

Alev ne songeait qu'à manger à satiété des gâteaux. *Neang* Ngoh, entendant la voix de celui qui approchait, mais ne voyant pas dans la nuit son visage, était remplie d'étonnement.

« C'est exactement la voix de mon Ngeh aimé! » pensait-elle.

L'étonnement de Ngoh n'était pas moindre. Il pensait:

« La voix de ma fiancée est semblable à celle de ma douce *Neang* Ngoh! »

Il pénétra dans la maison, vit la femme qui l'attendait.

« Mais elle est toute pareille à *Neang* Ngoh, ma femme! » s'écria-t-il.

— Mais il est tout pareil à Ngeh, mon mari! » dit-elle.

— C'est Ngeh!

— Ce n'est pas Ngeh!

— C'est Ngoh!

— Ce n'est pas Ngoh! » criaient les parents, les voisins.

Cependant Ngeh et Ngoh s'examinaient mutuellement; ils se rendirent compte qu'Alev les avait joués et se sauvèrent tout honteux. Alev se voyant découvert alla se cacher. Dès le lever du jour il se rendit dans une pagode où il implora l'hospitalité.

Ngeh et Ngoh reprirent leur vie commune.

⁂

Alev étudiait avec zèle à la pagode. Un beau jour, il se dit:

« Je vais tromper quelque bonze qui ait beaucoup d'argent, lui en soutirer, et l'apporter à mes parents. » Il s'en vint auprès d'un jeune bonze qui était fort beau et lui dit en secret:

« Seigneur bonze, une femme vous aime; c'est une jeune fille d'une extrême beauté. »

Le jeune bonze, entendant ces paroles, eut le cœur heureux et fut saisi de désir. Il répondit:

« S'il est certain que tu me dises la vérité, je te donnerai un bat d'argent.

— Seigneur, attendez jusqu'à ce soir. Quand la nuit sera noire, je vous conduirai dans un lieu que je vous montrerai; puis j'y amènerai la jeune fille. »

Alev quitta la cellule du bonze et se rendit au village voisin. Il va trouver un jeune marchand chinois et lui dit:

« Chinois, aimerais-tu que je te procure une jeune fille charmante ?

Certes oui!

Si tu la désires, combien m'offres-tu d'argent pour te la faire avoir?

— Je te donnerai un bat d'argent.

— C'est bien peu! Si tu me donnes deux bat, je te ferai avoir une jeune fille de la plus grande beauté et d'une extrême blancheur.

— C'est convenu.

— Eh bien, attends qu'il fasse nuit ; je te conduirai auprès d'elle. »

Alev retourna à la pagode. Lorsque le jour eut baissé au point que deux personnes se regardant ne puissent se reconnaître, Alev mena le bonze dans une cabane isolée et lui recommanda:

« Quand j'amènerai la jeune fille, couvrez avec le plus grand soin votre tête avec votre robe, pour qu'elle ne reconnaisse pas à votre crâne rasé que vous êtes bonze, car alors elle n'oserait vous approcher. »

Ayant dit, Alev vint à la maison du Chinois et appela celui-ci pour lui parler secrètement:

« J'ai amené près d'ici la jeune fille dont je t'ai parlé; je vais te conduire auprès d'elle. Mais aies bien soin, avant d'entrer, de couvrir complètement ta tête avec une écharpe, car si elle voyait la façon dont tes cheveux sont rasés, ta tresse, tes pommettes saillantes, elle reconnaîtrait que tu es un Chinois et te repousserait. »

Il accompagna le Chinois jusqu'auprès de la cabane dans laquelle attendait le bonze.

« La jeune fille est là, murmura-t-il. Paye-moi la somme convenue! »

Le Chinois se pencha à l'entrée de la cabane; il vit le bonze assis, la tête drapée dans sa robe; il n'eut pas de doute que ce ne fût une jeune fille ; il remit deux bat à Alev, qui les serra dans sa ceinture, s'esquiva au plus vite et rentra à la pagode.

Le bonze et le Chinois, restés ensemble dans la cabane, croyaient chacun se trouver avec une femme; mais ils ne tardèrent pas à s'apercevoir qu'Alev les avait joués; tout honteux ils se séparèrent.

Alev attendait le bonze dans sa cellule; quand il le vit entrer, il lui réclama la somme promise.

« Tu m'a trompé et tu oses me réclamer de l'argent!

Certes tu ne recevras rien de moi!

— Si vous ne me donnez pas mon argent, Seigneur bonze, je dévoilerai au Seigneur guru votre tentative incontinente; je vous dénoncerai à tous les habitants du village et des environs ; vous serez couvert de honte et méprisé de tous. De plus le tribunal ecclésiastique vous fera passer en jugement. Il sera publiquement exposé que vous m'avez loué pour vous procurer une femme, que mon salaire a été fixé à un bat d'argent, et que vous m'avez refusé ce que vous me deviez alors que j'avais pour ma part rempli mes engagements. Je ne vous laisserai pas de repos. Je vais de ce pas porter plainte auprès du Seigneur guru. »

Le bonze, effrayé des menaces d'Alev, lui donna immédiatement un bat d'argent. Mais Alev ne l'accepta pas. Il dit:

« Quand nous sommes convenus de mon salaire, vous m'avez promis un bat d'argent - de l'argent plein le bat dans lequel vous prenez chaque jour votre nourriture.[9] Mesurez-moi un plein bat d'argent; je l'accepterai en paiement. Si vous ne me remettez cette quantité d'argent, je vais rendre compte au Seigneur guru de notre différend. Il vous chassera ignominieusement de la pagode. Et je porterai plainte devant le tribunal ecclésiastique, vous serez jugé; vous recevrez la bastonnade sur la tête, puis vous serez réduit à l'état d'esclave de la couronne, vous serez employé à recueillir de vos mains le fourrage des éléphants. »

---

9 Il y a ici un jeu de mots : un bat d'argent est le nom d'une ancienne monnaie cambodgienne. Ce mot est encore usité au Siam pour désigner le tical, Bat est aussi le nom de la marmite dans laquelle les bonzes reçoivent les aliments qui leur sont donnés par les fidèles. Le bonze avait promis à Alev une pièce d'un bat. Alev lui réclame une pleine marmite d'argent: un bat plein d'argent.

Le bonze, épouvanté, supplia Alev:

« Laissez-moi aller chercher de l'argent ; ne dites rien au Seigneur guru; ne portez pas plainte devant le tribunal ecclésiastique; je vais m'efforcer de réunir de l'argent, je vendrai jusqu'à mes vêtements de bonze pour parfaire la somme!

— Allons, dit Alev, donnez-moi seulement autant d'argent que je pourrai en porter pour aller chez mes parents, et je vous tiens quitte! »

Le bonze, tout heureux, remplit d'argent une musette, et le supplia de ne pas le dénoncer.

« Aie pitié de moi, ne ternis pas ma réputation!

— Chassez la crainte de votre cœur, Seigneur bonze, je ne dirai rien à personne. »

Emportant l'argent, il prit congé du bonze.

৩ ❀ ৫

Alev retourna auprès de ses parents. Près de la maison il rencontra sa mère et lui cria:

« Ma mère, couds une grande bourse!

— Et pourquoi faire coudre une grande bourse? » demanda *neang* Ngoh.

Alev lui montra ce qu'il apportait.

*Neang* Ngoh courut dire à Ngeh qu'Alev apportait une pleine musette d'argent. Ngeh vint aussitôt et, voyant la somme importante que lui donnait son fils, il perdit la rancune qu'il avait conçue contre lui pour l'avoir trompé. Le père et la mère embrassèrent Alev.

« D'où as-tu tant d'argent? demanda Ngeh. Comment l'as-tu acquis?

— Quelle difficulté y a-t-il à l'acquérir? Il suffit d'aller par les villages montrer aux habitants certaine partie de son corps ; tous donnent de l'argent: les uns donnent un bat ; d'autres deux, ou trois, ou davantage. Ainsi il est facile de recueillir beaucoup d'argent. Si vous voulez en faire l'essai, allez au marché. Montrez cette partie de vous-même une fois à chaque passant, et vous obtiendrez plus d'argent que vous ne pourrez en rapporter. »

Ngeh, dans sa sottise, suivit le conseil de son fils.

Il se planta devant une maison et fit voir ce qu'Alev lui avait dit de montrer. Les habitants de la maison, indignés, le rouèrent de coups et le chassèrent. Il s'enfuit et recommença son exhibition devant une autre maison où il fut battu comme la première fois. Il prit sa course pour rentrer chez lui.

Alev l'attendait à moitié route. Il vit son père revenir en courant du village. Il se trouva qu'au même moment un Cham venait loin derrière Ngoh par le même chemin, portant une charge de soie à fleurs et de boîtes en argent. Alev cria à Ngeh:

« Attention, père! Les gens du village vous courent après pour vous battre! Coupez à travers champs et vous leur échapperez! »

Ngeh, se retournant, vit un homme le suivant de loin avec un bambou sur l'épaule. Il crut que c'était en effet un homme du village qui le poursuivait; pris de peur, il se jeta à travers champs comme le lui conseillait Alev.

Celui-ci attendit le Cham avec l'intention de le tromper à son tour. Il lui dit:

« Grand frère, courez aider à l'attraper! Si vous y arrivez, nous chiquerons ensemble le bétel! »

Le Cham regarda dans la direction que lui indiquait Alev. Il aperçut un homme qui courait, et supposa qu'il poursuivait quelque daim. Il confia sa charge à Alev et se précipita à la suite de Ngoh. Celui-ci, voyant le Malais qui courait derrière lui, se crut poursuivi et força sa course.

Alev, cependant, porta vivement la charge à sa mère, la lui fit cacher, et se sauva.

Le Cham finit par rejoindre Ngoh; il comprit qu'il avait été trompé, revint sur ses pas et chercha son bien. Mais Alev avait disparu. Désolé d'avoir perdu sa charge, et ne pouvant s'en prendre à personne, il se mit à la recherche d'Alev.

Alev s'était enfui. Il arriva dans un village extrêmement éloigné, où il rencontra une vieille femme qui, aidée de sa petite fille, chargeait son petit bien sur un sampan pour aller se fixer dans une autre région où habitait sa famille, car la jeune fille était nubile et d'âge à être mariée.

Alev, dont le cœur fut attiré vers la jeune fille, se mit en devoir de les aider à transporter sur la jonque leurs objets. Voyant le bon cœur d'Alev, la vieille lui demanda:

« Jeune homme, où vas-tu?

— Je demande la permission de vous accompagner, répondit Alev.

— Comment t'appelles-tu?

— Mon nom est: Mongendre[10] dit Alev. Où que vous vous rendiez, permettez-moi de vous suivre. »

La vieille se réjouit dans son cœur, pensant qu'Alev aiderait à ramer le sampan.

Tout étant disposé à bord du bateau, Alev se mit à l'aviron. La vieille s'assit, pagayant à l'avant. La jeune fille s'installa au milieu; elle souriait, les yeux fixés tantôt sur sa grand'mère, tantôt sur Alev.

Après avoir ramé un moment, Alev fit semblant d'avoir oublié son coupe-coupe.

« Oh, vieille, dit-il, j'ai laissé mon coupe-coupe sur la berge derrière nous, car toute mon attention était portée sur vos affaires. J'ai oublié ce coupe-coupe qui est un souvenir précieux de mes parents. Permettez-moi de tourner le bateau et d'aller le chercher. »

Il vira de bord et rama vers, le point de départ.

Quand il l'eut atteint, il dit à la grand'mère:

« Vieille, voulez-vous avoir la bonté de monter sur la berge et de prendre mon couteau. Je l'ai laissé auprès de la souche où nous avions réuni vos paquets. »

Dès qu'elle eut disparu sur la berge, Alev remit le bateau dans le courant avec la plus grande célérité, abandonnant la vieille. Il ramait de toutes ses forces, aidé par le courant.

Quand la grand' mère eut vainement cherché le coupe-coupe, elle revint à la rivière, mais n'y trouva plus le sampan. Explorant du regard le cours d'eau, elle aperçut Alev emmenant le bateau qui déjà avait gagné de la distance. Désespérée,

---

10 Ici encore il y a un jeu de mots. Alev répond: Je me nomme *chau* Prâsa: Prâsa veut dire gendre, *chau* est l'appellatif des hommes - mais désigne aussi les enfants au deuxième degré, *chau* Prâsa veut donc dire à la fois: le garçon nommé Gendre et: petit gendre, comme nous disons: petit-fils, petit-neveu par rapport aux grands-parents ou grands-oncles et grand'tantes. Le jeu de mots étant intraduisible nous avons traduit *chau* Prâsa par Mongendre et nous ferons dans la suite dire à la vieille: ma fille pour: ma petite-fille, l'expression petit-gendre étant inusitée en français.

se frappant du poing la poitrine, elle poussait des cris, pleurait, se lamentait. Elle se mit à courir le long de la berge, implorant l'aide des gens qu'elle rencontrait.

« A mon secours! Voyez là-bas, c'est Mongendre qui enlève ma fille! A l'aide! Mongendre a volé ma fille! Il l'emmène, voyez, secourez-moi! »

Les riverains entendaient ces plaintes; ils disaient entre eux:

« Le gendre emmène la fille, nous n'avons pas à nous en mêler! Le mari peut emmener sa femme si ça lui plaît ! »

Personne ne vint en aide à la vieille. Le sampan avait déjà disparu; la vieille à bout de souffle s'arrêta. Alors seulement elle expliqua aux riverains:

« Le misérable qui a enlevé ma fille s'appelle Mongendre. Mais il n'est pas le mari de ma fille. Il a volé ma fille, il a volé mes biens! »

Les riverains comprirent trop tard de quoi il s'agissait. Alev avait déjà gagné une telle avance qu'ils ne pouvaient plus songer à le poursuivre.

Pendant ce temps, Alev ramait toujours. La nuit venue, il cajola de douces paroles la jeune fille.

« Ton frère aîné t'a enlevée parce qu'il a le cœur plein d'amour pour sa petite sœur. Ton frère aîné a le désir de t'épouser. »

Mais elle ne faisait que sangloter et pleurer sa grand'mère avec laquelle elle avait toujours vécu.

« Ma grand'mère me cherche, dit-elle. Elle ne me trouve pas. Ne s'est-elle pas déjà jetée à l'eau et noyée de désespoir? Que sais-je? Ou bien dans sa nostalgie de sa petite-fille, elle ne prendra aucune nourriture et mourra. Ramenez-moi vers elle. Si vous ne me ramenez pas vers ma grand'mère, je vais me noyer sous vos yeux. »

Alev aborda dans une forêt solitaire, et dit tendrement:

« Si je vous ai enlevée, c'est par amour, c'est pour que vous soyez ma femme. Si vous vous jetez à l'eau, que me restera-t-il à aimer?

— Si vous m'aimez, pourquoi n'avez-vous pas demandé ma main selon la coutume?

— Mon cœur est impatient, ô mon aimée. Comment aurais-je pu faire ma demande selon la coutume et supporter tous les délais qu'elle comporte? Si encore j'avais été certain que vous me seriez accordée. Mais si j'étais repoussé, qu'aurais-je pu faire? C'est pour cela que je vous ai enlevée, pour vous conduire au pays de mes parents, de mes ancêtres, et célébrer notre mariage selon la coutume. Mais ne vous affligez pas, mon aimée. Votre frère aîné vous ramènera auprès de votre grand'mère. Cessez d'être attristée! »

A force de douces paroles, Alev calma le cœur de la jeune fille qui finit par s'endormir à son côté.

❧ ✿ ☙

Au jour, Alev reprit l'aviron et poursuivit sa route.

Il tomba au milieu de cinq cents brigands qui attendaient en embuscade les voyageurs naviguant sur la rivière pour les dévaliser. Ne pouvant les éviter, Alev dirigea son bateau au milieu de leur troupe, et dit au chef des brigands:

« Vous tous, malgré votre grand nombre, vous n'osez piller que les voyageurs isolés qui vont modestement gagner leur vie. Moi, je ne m'attaque pas à si petite proie. Je pille des villes, des royaumes, j'attaque des groupes importants; à moi seul, je me rends maître de leurs capitales, de leurs provinces. Car je sais des incantations grâce auxquelles les sabres ne me blessent pas, le feu ne me brûle pas, des incantations qui me rendent invulnérable, invincible. Je m'en viens maintenant de piller une ville d'où j'ai enlevé cette jeune fille après avoir mis à sac la cité entière. Si vous ne me croyez pas, demandez à cette femme! »

Les brigands, entendant Alev se vanter de la puissance que lui donnaient les formules magiques qu'il possédait, furent pris du désir de s'instruire auprès de lui.

« Puisqu'il en est ainsi, enseignez-nous à tous les incantations. Consentez à être notre maître en formules magiques. Aidez-nous de vos conseils et opérons de concert.

— Si vous êtes disposés à apprendre, je puis vous enseigner mon art, répond Alev. La seule difficulté est de trouver un lieu convenable et à l'abri de toute surprise. Cherchons donc une île, éloignée de toute côte; nous y établirons sans risques un lieu de réunion. »

Alev et les brigands se mirent à la recherche d'un îlot isolé dans la mer. Ils en trouvèrent un qui était bordé d'une belle plage de sable. Alev aborda et chercha un endroit approprié, caché aux vues du point où était amarré leur bateau. Il réunit les brigands et leur dit:

«Maintenant, si vous voulez que je vous enseigne des formules qui vous donneront une puissance illimitée, il est indispensable que, quand je vous commanderai de faire une chose, vous la fassiez aussitôt avec un parfait ensemble. C'est à cette seule condition que mes incantations auront leur vertu. »

Tous les brigands s'engagèrent à obéir exactement.

Alev leur commanda de construire un terre-plein, portant un autel orné de lianes, de fleurs, de baguettes d'encens, de parasols rituels à sept étages. Puis il fit creuser dans le sable un grand bassin, assez profond pour qu'un homme y perde pied.

Ces préparatifs terminés, Alev commanda aux cinq cents brigands de se raser la tête. Puis il leur dit:

« Pour donner son pouvoir à l'incantation que je vous enseignerai, il faut que vous alliez déposer dans la jonque tous vos vêtements; ensuite vous plongerez tous ensemble complètement sous l'eau, et sans revenir à la surface, sans reprendre votre respiration, vous réciterez la formule chacun sept fois de suite. Vous devrez la retenir très exactement et la réciter sans y rien changer, faute de quoi elle perdra sa vertu pour chacun de vous. Tenez-vous prêts, pendant que je vais me recueillir dans la forêt. »

Alev attendit que les brigands soient revenus sans vêtements de la jonque, puis il descendit au mouillage, et dit à voix basse à sa femme:

« Écoute bien ce que je vais te dire et sois attentive: tire autant que tu pourras le câble de l'ancre. Quand tu me verras venir en courant au rivage, lève immédiatement l'ancre et laisse-moi faire pour le reste. »

Puis il fit un détour par la forêt et rejoignit les brigands. Il leur enseigna une longue formule dépourvue de sens, qu'il leur fit répéter plusieurs fois jusqu'à ce qu'ils la disent sans erreur.

La nuit venue, il leur dit:

« Il faut que vous plongiez bien exactement tous ensemble et que tous ensemble vous reveniez à la surface. Ainsi vous acquerrez tous les bienfaits de la formule. Êtes-vous prêts... Plongez!... »

Au même instant Alev courut au rivage, leva l'ancre, ouvrit la voile, prit le vent, et cingla vers le large.

Quand les cinq cents brigands revinrent à la surface, ils cherchèrent des yeux

Alev et ne le virent pas. Ils se demandaient: Où donc est le Seigneur notre maître?

Ils sortirent du bassin et se rendirent au terre-plein, mais ne le trouvèrent pas; ils l'appelèrent; il ne répondit pas. Enfin ils allèrent au rivage; ils ne trouvèrent pas Alev, mais s'aperçurent que leur jonque avait disparu. Ils se rendirent compte qu'ils avaient été trompés. Aucune embarcation n'existait dans l'île pour poursuivre Alev.

Les cinq cents brigands allèrent couper des bambous dans la forêt et construisirent des radeaux pour regagner la terre ferme.

Alev et sa femme filaient bonne allure, naviguant à l'aise dans la jonque des brigands et emportant tous les biens des cinq cents voleurs. Ils allèrent à pleine voile toute la nuit, tout le jour, et abordèrent le soir dans un village. Mais Alev remarqua que dans ce village il n'y avait pas un homme; il n'y avait que des femmes et des enfants. Il se douta aussitôt que c'était le village des brigands qu'il avait abusés. Il mouilla son ancre.

Les femmes des brigands ne reconnurent pas que c'était la jonque de leurs maris, car ceux-ci avaient quitté isolément et à pied le village, et n'avaient que plus tard rencontré cette jonque qu'ils avaient pillée et capturée.

Alev, après avoir jeté l'ancre, prit une planche noircie et de la craie, descendit à terre, et se mit à tracer des signes cabalistiques, faisant semblant de consulter le sort.

Les femmes et les enfants des brigands s'approchèrent, virent les signes qu'il traçait et crurent que vraiment il savait la cabale. Ils demandèrent:

« Sauriez-vous, par votre art, nous dire où sont nos maris, où sont nos pères? Voici longtemps qu'ils nous ont quittés et nous sommes sans nouvelles d'eux.

— Et quelle difficulté y a-t-il à vous satisfaire? Ne me dites rien; il me suffit de faire des calculs, d'aligner des signes, et je puis tout savoir. Quoi que vous vouliez apprendre, vous n'avez qu'à apporter des baguettes d'encens, du bétel, de l'arec, et à garder un complet silence pour me laisser interroger le sort. »

Les femmes des brigands coururent dans toutes les maisons avertir leurs compagnes. Toutes apportèrent des baguettes d'encens, des branches fleuries, de l'arec, du bétel, des bananes, de la canne à sucre, qu'elles vinrent offrir à Alev.

Celui-ci prit son tableau noir; il fit semblant d'interroger les esprits. En réalité, il calculait le temps qu'il faudrait aux brigands pour avoir construit des radeaux et revenir à leur village. Il dit aux femmes:

« Vos maris reviendront tous ensemble après-demain. Mais auparavant un danger vous menace: la nuit prochaine, des fantômes nus et la tête rasée viendront dans votre village, chercheront à entrer dans vos maisons, pour y répandre une terrible épidémie de petite vérole. Il faut donc que vous preniez vos mesures pour éteindre ce fléau. »

Les femmes des brigands, effrayées, demandèrent à Alev comment il leur serait possible d'éviter la maladie.

« C'est très facile, répondit Alev. Au crépuscule, réunissez-vous, femmes et enfants, à la porte de chaque maison, tous armés de solides bâtons. Quand vous verrez accourir les fantômes nus et la tête rasée, frappez jusqu'à ce qu'ils s'enfuient. N'en laissez pas entrer un seul dans vos cases. »

Les brigands accostèrent le lendemain près de leur village. Mais, n'ayant point de vêtements, ils restèrent cachés dans la forêt tant qu'il fit jour; à la nuit tombante, ils s'approchèrent du village, et coururent chacun vers sa case. Mais les femmes et les enfants, les prenant pour les fantômes annoncés, les reçurent à grands coups de bâton, frappant de toutes leurs forces jusqu'à ce qu'ils tombent à terre blessés, meurtris ; certains s'évanouirent, d'autres eurent des membres cassés.

Enfin les femmes reconnurent leurs maris, les enfants reconnurent leurs pères; tous, en larmes, racontèrent aux brigands ce qui s'était passé; à leur description, les brigands n'eurent pas de peine à reconnaitre Alev. Mais que pouvaient-ils faire, roués de coups, blessés, et ne sachant pas dans quelle direction poursuivre leur ennemi.

Alev cependant était resté caché auprès du village; il avait entendu le retour des brigands, les vociférations des femmes, la bastonnade, les cris des maris. Alors il s'était hâté vers la jonque, avait mis à la voile, et se dirigeait vers le village de sa femme.

❧ ❀ ❧

Lorsqu'ils eurent atteint le hameau, Alev et sa femme se mirent à la recherche de leur grand'mère ; l'ayant trouvée, Alev se prosterna devant elle, implora son pardon et lui offrit tout ce qu'il avait dans sa jonque. La vieille grand'mère, voyant ces richesses, pardonna, se prit d'affection pour Alev, et l'accepta pour devenir véritablement son gendre. Il fit construire une maison et engagea de nombreux domestiques pour servir sa femme et sa grand'mère.

Au bout de quelque temps, il prit congé des deux femmes, disant qu'il voulait aller voir ses propres parents. La grand'mère aimait de tout cœur son petit-fils par alliance; mais elle n'osa pas le détourner d'aller rendre visite à son père et à sa mère.

« Ne reste pas trop longtemps absent! lui recommanda-t-elle. Reviens vite, car tu nous laisses isolées sans personne sur qui nous puissions compter. »

Sa femme voulut aller avec lui:

« Je veux aller faire la connaissance de ta mère, de ton père, de tes parents. Et puis, je ne veux pas être séparée de toi. C'est une triste situation pour une femme d'être loin de son mari. Elle n'a personne pour la défendre, pour la garder. On la traite de veuve, on la tourne en ridicule. Je veux aller avec toi.

— Ma chérie, ton frère aîné voudrait aussi t'emmener avec lui. Mais songe à ta grand'mère, qui est vieille, qui peut tomber malade. Jour et nuit elle serait seule, sans personne pour la soigner, pour s'occuper d'elle, personne à qui nous puissions nous fier. Elle a tant souffert quand nous l'avons abandonnée; maintenant elle est heureuse. Mais si tous deux nous la quittons de nouveau, elle en mourra sûrement. Nous avons une fois commis une lourde faute; ne la commettons pas à nouveau. »

Sa femme, émue de compassion pour sa grand'mère, consentit à le laisser partir seul. Elle prépara son bagage et des provisions de route, et lui demanda combien il emmènerait de serviteurs et de voitures.

« Je n'en prendrai point, dit-il. Ton frère aîné partira seul. »

Il ne voulait pas emmener de domestiques, parce qu'il songeait à prendre femme en chemin et aurait craint que ses gens ne disent qu'il était déjà marié.

« J'ai l'habitude de voyager seul, ajouta-t-il. Si j'emmenais des hommes, des charrettes, des bœufs, des buffles, mon voyage serait lent; il ne s'accomplirait pas aussi rapidement que le désire mon cœur. »

Il mit seulement de l'argent dans une écharpe, emporta des vivres pour la route, et prit congé de sa grand'mère et de sa femme.

« Si tu trouves tes parents en bonne santé, lui dit sa grand'mère, hâte-toi de revenir! »

ꕥ

Alev arriva auprès de Ngeh et de *neang* Ngoh qui étaient son père et sa mère, et leur donna l'argent qu'il avait apporté. Ses parents eurent le cœur réjoui. Ils demandèrent:

« Où donc étais-tu, toi qui as si longtemps disparu?

Ta mère ne faisait que regarder le chemin par lequel elle espérait voir venir son fils!

— Je travaillais pour gagner ma vie, reprit Alev.

Car vous, mes parents, vous ne songez pas à trouver une profession comme tout le monde.

— Agis selon ton cœur, mon enfant. Tes parents gagnent assez pour leur subsistance. Ils prennent soin de leurs biens pour te les laisser. Mais si tu veux travailler de ton côté, à ton aise! »

Alev resta quelques jours auprès des siens, puis il se remit en route.

Il arriva dans une ville royale, grande et très peuplée. Il alla visiter le palais royal; puis il examina les habitations des dignitaires et des riches particuliers. Il remarqua une maison de grande dimension, au toit élevé, dans laquelle étaient accumulées de splendides richesses ; elle possédait des hangars pour les voitures, des étables remplies de bœufs, de buffles, d'éléphants, de chevaux; des serviteurs nombreux allaient et venaient. De magnifiques jardins étaient ornés de fleurs de toutes sortes: des bassins, où jouaient des poissons d'argent et d'or, étaient couverts de lotus blancs, de lotus roses, de nénuphars, de fleurs aquatiques variées; enfin il y vit une jeune fille de grande beauté. Alev eut l'amour dans le cœur et désira obtenir cette jeune fille. Il alla se présenter au maître de la maison, qui était un riche négociant, et lui demanda de le prendre comme client,[11] s'engageant à remplir toute fonction qui lui serait confiée.

Cet homme puissant éprouva de la sympathie pour Alev. Il l'interrogea:

« D'où es-tu? Où demeurent tes parents?

— Je suis d'un pays fort lointain; mon père et ma mère avaient de grandes richesses, de nombreux serviteurs, des bœufs, des buffles, des éléphants, des chevaux, une belle maison comme la vôtre, Seigneur. Mais tous deux sont tombés

---

11 Littéralement: neveu. Ce terme, dans l'ancienne civilisation cambodgienne, correspond à peu près à ce que représentait celui de client dans l'ancienne Rome.

malades et sont morts. Mon cœur s'est resserré; je n'ai pas voulu rester là où j'avais coutume de vivre avec ma mère, avec mon père. J'ai quitté ma maison, mes biens; j'ai fait un long voyage; permettez-moi de demeurer avec vous, Seigneur; tout ce que vous me donnerez à faire, je le ferai de mon mieux. »

Le négociant accepta de garder le jeune homme auprès de lui.

Alev se levait au jour, balayait la maison, prenait soin de tous les objets de valeur, mettait chaque chose à la place la plus appropriée ; il s'efforçait à s'occuper de tout comme s'il se fût agi de ses biens propres.

Son maître, voyant son activité, son dévouement constant, se prenait de plus en plus d'amitié pour lui; il lui donna autorité sur toute la domesticité. Quand il se rendait à l'audience du roi, il se faisait accompagner par Alev.

Au bout d'un certain temps, Alev connut tous les dignitaires, tous leurs clients, jusqu'aux ministres.

En public, il affectait la niaiserie; si quelqu'un le tournait en dérision, grand ou petit, jamais il ne se fâchait; il ne discutait jamais avec personne.

Plus tard, il fréquenta assidûment le tribunal, suivant les débats, écoutant les sentences prononcées par les juges. Il apprit ainsi à connaître les lois, les coutumes.

Alev ramassait avec soin tous les papiers que l'on jetait, s'ils portaient des cachets. Il se procura ainsi l'empreinte des cachets de chacun des ministres, de tous les grands dignitaires, des fonctionnaires de tout ordre, qui avaient des richesses. Il reproduisit avec de la cire l'empreinte de tous ces sceaux, puis sculpta des cachets semblables à ces empreintes; ensuite il écrivit des reconnaissances de dettes, d'après lesquelles tous les hauts fonctionnaires lui auraient emprunté les uns cent barres d'argent, d'autres deux cents barres, d'autres cinquante, et revêtit ces reconnaissances des cachets qu'il avait sculptés.[12] Il plia ces lettres, en remplit une boîte.

Lorsqu'il sortait de la maison, il apportait cette boîte à la femme de son maître, la priait de la lui garder, et lui recommandait de ne permettre à personne de l'ouvrir. A son retour, son premier soin était d'aller redemander sa cassette.

Au bout de quelque temps, la femme du négociant, piquée de curiosité, se

---

12 Autrefois au Cambodge les fonctionnaires ayant des cachets distinctifs de leur fonction ne signaient aucune pièce; ils se contentaient d'y apposer leur cachet.

demanda ce que pouvait contenir ce coffret. Elle l'ouvrit, le trouva plein de papiers soigneusement pliés; ces papiers étaient des reconnaissances de dettes, montrant que tous les dignitaires, tous les fonctionnaires avaient emprunté de l'argent à Alev. Le total de ces billets représentait une somme extrêmement élevée. Elle fut très surprise, et s'en vint montrer le contenu du coffret à son mari; celui-ci, après l'avoir examiné, lui dit:

« Quand Alev est venu ici, je l'ai interrogé sur ses parents. Il m'a répondu qu'ils étaient morts, mais que de leur vivant ils avaient de grands biens, autant que nous-mêmes. Voyant qu'il a prêté tellement d'argent aux personnages de la Cour, je reconnais qu'il m'avait certainement dit la vérité quand il m'avait parlé de sa fortune. Son intelligence, son caractère, dénotent qu'il a de la naissance. Il prend soin de tout ce qui nous appartient; il sait tout ce que nous avons dans la maison; il est comme notre fils.

« Voici notre fille en âge d'être mariée. Elle nous a déjà été demandée par les fils des principaux personnages de la Cour. Mais ils n'étaient pas selon notre cœur et nous ne l'avons pas donnée. Je la donnerais volontiers à Alev. Mais nous serions tournés en dérision, car Alev est venu seul et orphelin, sans que personne connaisse son origine. D'autre part j'aimerais l'avoir pour gendre, car sa conduite, son caractère sont parfaits, parce qu'il a montré le plus grand dévouement en s'occupant de nos intérêts comme s'ils avaient été les siens propres.

« J'ai beau examiner la question, elle est bien difficile à résoudre!

— Quant à éviter qu'on nous tourne en dérision, c'est facile, répondit la femme. Nous n'avons qu'à faire le mariage la nuit, avec très peu de cérémonie, — juste assez pour que les génies ne se mettent pas en colère. Ces jeunes gens seront ainsi mariés secrètement. Si on vient plus tard à l'apprendre, qui pourra nous critiquer? Tout le monde doit de l'argent à Alev ! »

Le riche négociant approuva les paroles de sa femme, et consentit au mariage dans les conditions qu'elle avait proposées. Il appela le jeune homme et lui dit:

« Depuis que tu es entré dans ma maison, j'ai vu que ta pensée, ton cœur, tes soins, se sont portés sur mes affaires comme si tu avais été mon propre fils. En récompense je te donne en mariage ma fille chérie. »

Alev eut le cœur rempli de bonheur.

Son maître appela la jeune fille, lui prescrivit de faire les salutations aux ancêtres, de faire les offrandes aux génies suivant la coutume qui nous vient de l'antiquité, et la donna pour épouse à Alev.

Deux ou trois jours après le mariage, la femme d'Alev lui dit qu'elle allait se rendre à l'audience royale. Alev lui répondit:

« Je serai au tribunal.[13] Quand tu passeras devant, si tu me vois t'appeler de la main, tu mettras du bétel sur une coupe et viendras déposer cette coupe devant moi. Puis tu me salueras et nous nous retirerons ensemble. »

Ayant fait ces recommandations à sa femme, Alev s'habilla d'un vieux sampot et d'une vieille veste, et alla s'asseoir au tribunal. Tous les hauts dignitaires, tous les fonctionnaires, les pages, les juges s'y trouvaient réunis. Ils étaient venus à dos d'éléphant, à cheval, avec de nombreuses suites.

Voyant Alev assis dans ses misérables vêtements, les dignitaires, par dérision, lui frappaient la tête. lui donnaient des coups dans le dos, lui tiraient les bras, pour lui faire faire des bouffonneries comme il avait l'habitude de le faire sans jamais se fâcher contre personne. Mais ils ne savaient pas combien Alev avait d'intelligence. Ils le prenaient pour un malheureux vivant d'aumônes. C'est pourquoi ils se moquaient de lui.

La fille du riche négociant vint à passer dans son palanquin, suivie de serviteurs portant des boîtes à bétel en or, des plateaux en argent; elle regarda Alev qui ne fit aucun signe; elle poursuivit sa route vers le palais. Les dignitaires, la voyant passer, disaient:

« Elle est la plus belle de toutes!

— Les fils des princes eux-mêmes n'ont pu obtenir sa main!

— Heureux qui l'aura pour femme! »

Chacun renchérissait sur ce qui était dit par les autres.

Alev prit à son tour la parole et dit:

« Vous dites, Seigneurs, que tous les plus hauts personnages ont demandé cette jeune fille sans pouvoir l'obtenir. Attendez, Seigneurs, qu'elle ressorte du palais. Je l'appellerai et elle viendra m'offrir du bétel à chiquer! »

---

13 Les tribunaux cambodgiens, ou *Sala chumnum*, sont des constructions sur pilotis, mais sans cloisons. De simples colonnes supportent le toit au-dessus du plancher. On peut donc voir de l'extérieur ce qui s'y passe et inversement.

Les dignitaires prirent ces fanfaronnades pour une nouvelle bouffonnerie, car ils voyaient toujours Alev faire le fou en leur présence, et ils ignoraient que rentré chez lui il était loin d'être fou. Ils se moquaient de lui; ils ignoraient combien Alev était fin. Ils dirent;

« Nous ferions bien le pari que cette jeune fille ne répondra pas à ton appel. Mais comment parier avec toi? Tu n'as rien à mettre comme enjeu!

— Ne vous mettez pas en peine de cela. Si je perds le pari, je m'engage par écrit à être votre esclave ma vie durant. Vous m'emploierez à ce que bon vous semblera, je vous obéirai en tout. »

Les dignitaires et fonctionnaires se réjouirent, désirant avoir Alev pour esclave, comptant qu'il les amuserait de ses saillies.

« Il a perdu la raison, disaient-ils, s'il croit que cette belle jeune fille répondra à son appel! Tenons le pari avec lui. Il sera notre esclave à tous; chacun le prendra à son tour; nous nous amuserons de lui. Qu'il écrive dans des billets tout ce qu'il a la prétention de gagner de nous! Que nous importe: il est sûr de perdre. Nous pouvons mettre l'enjeu qui lui passera par la tête! »

Ils lui donnèrent tous des billets lui disant:

« Inscris autant d'or ou d'argent qu'il te plaira; inscris des éléphants, des chevaux, leurs harnachements, tout ce que tu voudras. »

Alev remplit soigneusement les billets, portant, suivant ce que possédaient ses antagonistes, des chevaux, des éléphants ou de grandes sommes d'argent. Tous apposèrent leur cachet en riant et se moquant de lui. Il enveloppa les billets dans une écharpe; il écrivit à son tour l'engagement, s'il perdait le pari, de se mettre en servitude à vie chez les gagnants et remit son billet au ministre du Palais; puis il s'assit à l'entrée du tribunal.

Au bout d'un moment, on vit la jeune fille revenir du palais. Alev lui fit signe de la main et lui cria de lui apporter du bétel. Elle descendit en toute hâte de sa litière, plaça du bétel sur une coupe d'or et vint le présenter à Alev. Celui-ci prit le bétel, puis il se leva, fit placer sa femme sur le plus beau des éléphants qu'il avait gagnés, installa ses serviteurs sur les autres, sur les chevaux, monta sur un éléphant à grandes défenses, et se mit en route avec sa suite.

Les dignitaires, les fonctionnaires qui avaient perdu le pari étaient muets de stupeur. Ils avaient les yeux blancs d'émotion, et pleuraient leurs montures favorites, harnachées d'or et d'argent, et tous les biens qu'ils avaient perdus.

La surprise du beau-père fut aussi grande en voyant arriver son gendre et sa fille en un si pompeux convoi. Tous les serviteurs de la maison se pressaient aux fenêtres pour voir leurs jeunes maîtres.

Le négociant interrogea Alev.

« J'ai commencé à me faire payer les dettes contractées envers moi », répondit le jeune homme.

Le beau-père, le cœur plein de joie, pensa: « Vraiment personne ne nous tournera en dérision! »

Le négociant et sa femme chérirent Alev plus encore que par le passé.

Chaque jour, Alev allait recevoir des parieurs les sommes qu'ils mirent longtemps à lui payer complètement. Peu à peu il prit sur lui le soin de régler toutes les affaires de ses beaux-parents et leur évita toute peine et tout souci.

Lorsque son beau-père, chargé d'années, atteignit le terme de son âge, Alev se trouva être le principal négociant de la capitale.

༄ ❀ ༄

Nous avons dit l'histoire d'Alev telle qu'elle a été répétée de génération en génération. Si quelqu'un vient à la lire, qu'il ne se moque point de nous.

# Kung le Courageux

## *Kung Hean*

AUTREFOIS vivait un homme qui avait deux femmes. Il s'appelait Kung, et ses deux femmes s'appelaient Am et Kom.

Un jour, Kung emmena Am et Kom en voyage: ils allaient faire une visite à des parents dans une province éloignée. Il se trouva que la région était désolée par un tigre féroce qui pourchassait sans cesse hommes et bestiaux. Kung atteignit une grande forêt voisine du village où il se rendait; le tigre s'y trouvait; du plus loin qu'il aperçut le voyageur, l'animal bondit en poussant des rugissements épouvantables. Kung, tremblant de tous ses membres, s'alla cacher dans un arbre creux, à moitié évanoui de peur. Am et Kom unirent leurs efforts et, à coups de gourdin, tuèrent le fauve. Kung, voyant la bête morte, sortit de sa cachette, prit un bâton et frappa à tour de bras le cadavre du tigre. Ses femmes s'indignèrent:

« Tu n'es pas un homme, tu es une femmelette! et tu es un lâche de frapper ce tigre qui est déjà mort. »

Kung se tourna furieux, insulta ses femmes et leur dit:

« Jamais personne n'a vu des femmes tuer un tigre. Seuls les hommes ont un tel courage! »

Kung coupa une liane, attacha la bête, puis, aidé de ses deux femmes, l'emporta dans le village. Tous les gens du pays, à ce spectacle, se réunirent en masse, fort joyeux. Ils demandèrent:

« Comment avez-vous fait pour tuer cette bête?

Elle était terrible! Combien n'a-t-elle pas dévoré d'hommes, de buffles et de bœufs! C'est nous rendre un service immense que de nous en délivrer!

- Kung, dirent les deux femmes, aperçut le tigre et courut se cacher dans un arbre creux. Nous deux, femmes, nous avons réussi à tuer la bête féroce! » Kung, entendant ces paroles, proféra contre ses femmes de violentes injures.

« Jamais, s'écria-t-il, aucune femme n'a eu ni l'audace, ni la force de tuer un tigre. Vous le savez bien, vous tous, gens de ce village! »

Et, plein d'orgueil, il raconta comment il s'y était pris:

« Le tigre était là, moi, je me trouvais ici. J'ai saisi une matraque de cette façon, j'ai frappé ainsi, le tigre est tombé là. »

En parlant, Kung mimait toutes ses passes d'armes, sautant de droite et de gauche, brandissant son bâton, s'époumonant pour faire admirer ses prouesses aux villageois.

Tous les assistants étaient remplis de respect pour Kung et décidèrent d'un commun accord de l'appeler Kung le Courageux.

La renommée de cet homme valeureux parvint jusqu'aux oreilles du roi, qui l'éleva à de hautes dignités.

Or, il advint qu'un crocodile redoutable s'établit dans la rivière qui baignait la capitale. Chaque jour, il happait quelque sujet de Sa Majesté; personne n'osait plus s'approcher de la rivière; le commerce fut arrêté; les bateaux se balancèrent à vide sur leurs amarres; tout le pays était dans la désolation.

Le roi, mis au courant de la situation, donna l'ordre à Kung le Courageux d'aller capturer le crocodile. Kung fut bouleversé d'épouvante. Mais comment eût-il pu discuter les commandements du monarque? Il répondit:

« Que Votre Majesté ne s'inquiète pas. Je suis à ses ordres ! »

Il s'en retourna chez lui et dit en pleurant à ses femmes:

« O vous qui m'êtes chères, je vous fais mes adieux!

« Le roi m'a commandé d'aller me saisir d'un crocodile effroyablement méchant qui hante le fleuve! Cette fois, il est certain que je suis perdu. Cette maudite bête va me dévorer. Lorsque j'ai combattu le tigre, c'était sur la terre ferme, j'avais tous mes moyens. Mais aujourd'hui, quelle force aurai-je sous l'eau? Je ne verrai même pas. Et c'est le roi qui commande: je ne puis qu'obéir. Je n'ai plus qu'à me jeter à la rivière et à me laisser manger. »

Kung réunit ses enfants, ses clients, tous ses parents et leur fit ses adieux. Il était blême de peur, ses dents claquaient. Puis il se mit en route; il avait de la peine à marcher car ses jambes flageolaient. Une sueur froide ruisselait entre ses épaules. Il titubait d'épouvante.

Arrivé sur la berge, il aperçut le crocodile qui flottait endormi, tout près du rivage.

Les gens du pays, ayant appris que Kung le Courageux allait détruire le monstre, s'étaient réunis en foule sur la berge.

Kung avisa au bord de l'eau deux arbres qui avaient poussé d'une même souche, et formaient entre eux une fourche. Il s'y assit un instant, cherchant à rassembler ses esprits. Le crocodile endormi flottait à la surface à deux mètres de lui. A sa vue, la gorge de Kung se serra, il perdit la respiration, ses cheveux se dressaient sur sa tête. Brusquement il se leva, il était à bout, il voulait à tout prix en finir. Fermant les yeux, il se précipita dans les flots.

Le crocodile, réveillé en sursaut, fit un effort prodigieux pour sauter sur la berge. Le hasard voulut qu'il retombât dans la fourche que formaient les deux arbres. Il était pris comme dans un étau, et ne pouvait ni avancer, ni reculer.

Kung le Courageux revenant à la surface, ouvrit les yeux, supputant le nombre de secondes qui lui restaient à vivre, et vit le crocodile ainsi pris au piège. Il cria à ses enfants de saisir une lance et de le transpercer. Lorsque l'animal fut bien mort, Kung osa l'approcher.

« Voyez, dit-il, quelle est ma force et quel est mon courage. J'ai nagé sous l'eau jusqu'à ce terrible animal, et je l'ai jeté sur la berge avec assez d'adresse pour qu'il soit emprisonné. »

Tous les assistants furent convaincus qu'il disait vrai et le couvrirent d'éloges. Il rentra dans la ville, porté en triomphe, et vint faire au roi le récit de son haut fait. Le roi lui accorda de nouvelles dignités en récompense de ses éminents services.

La réputation de Kung le Courageux fut dès lors établie sans conteste.

A quelque temps de là une guerre éclata; un voisin ambitieux envahit les terres du roi, qui aussitôt confia à Kung le commandement de toutes ses armées.

Kung le Courageux était pour le coup anéanti. Il rentra chez lui et se traîna jusque sur sa natte; il ne prit aucune nourriture; il était incapable d'articuler une parole; ses yeux étaient révulsés de terreur.

Ses deux femmes s'approchèrent de lui.

« Ami, dirent-elles, pourquoi vous couchez-vous ainsi sans manger? Que vous arrive-t-il pour vous mettre dans cet état lamentable? »

Kung rassembla toute son énergie pour répondre:

Le roi a chargé votre frère aîné de mener ses armées à la guerre. Votre frère tremble de mâle peur. Il ne sait comment éviter d'obéir aux ordres qu'il a reçus, et pourtant il ne veut pas aller au combat.

— Ne vous épouvantez donc pas ainsi, dirent les femmes; nous vous accompagnerons. nous vous viendrons en aide, nous vous le promettons; levez-vous, venez vous restaurer; prenez votre bain comme à l'ordinaire et calmez votre cœur. »

Kung le Courageux, remonté par ses femmes, se leva, prit un bain et mangea. Puis il fit ses préparatifs pour aller combattre les armées ennemies.

Lorsque le moment fut venu, il prit congé du roi et partit en guerre, accompagné de ses deux femmes. Kung était à califourchon sur la tête d'un éléphant, Am et Kom assises derrière lui. Son armée l'entourait de toutes parts; les corps de troupe marchant en bon ordre, musique en tête et oriflammes au vent.

Lorsque les ennemis furent en vue, qu'il n'y eut plus de doute sur la rencontre, Kung fut aveuglé par la peur. Dans son affolement il enfonça son harpon dans la tête de son éléphant, qui partit en trombe, se précipita à travers les divisions, dépassa toute l'armée sans que les soldats puissent le suivre, et fonça dans les rangs ennemis.

Les assaillants voyant Kung le Courageux s'élancer ainsi au milieu d'eux, furent convaincus que, pour oser s'exposer ainsi, il devait être doué d'une puissance surnaturelle: ils s'enfuirent, se disloquèrent en une déroute folle, jetant bas leurs armes, abandonnant les animaux, les bagages, ne songeant qu'à sauver leur vie.

Kung le Courageux, devant cette stupéfiante victoire, reprit tout son aplomb. Il réunit les grands officiers et leur vanta son audace. Certains d'entre eux se montrèrent sceptiques, car ils remarquèrent, sur la tête de l'éléphant qui portait Kung, des traces manifestes de sa peur.

« Eh, dit Kung, qu'est-ce que cela prouve? Est-ce au milieu de la mêlée qu'on va s'arrêter pour une colique? Le vrai courage consiste à ne songer à rien qu'à la victoire quand on est en présence de l'ennemi. »

Toute l'armée entendit ce discours. Quelques-uns - ceux qui avaient de l'intelligence - comprirent ce qu'il fallait penser de la bravoure de Kung. Mais le plus grand nombre manquait de perspicacité; on fit à Kung une longue ovation.

Kung le Courageux rentra en triomphateur dans la capitale. Il alla se prosterner devant le roi, et lui conta comment les ennemis s'étaient dispersés à son approche.

Le roi se réjouit de tout cœur. Il combla Kung d'honneurs, en fit le premier dignitaire du royaume, lui décerna ses plus hautes récompenses, et lui offrit des présents magnifiques.

Kung se montra plus que jamais orgueilleux de sa force et de sa valeur.

Cette histoire nous a été contée par des vieillards qui la tenaient de leurs aïeux. Si quelque curieux vient à la lire, qu'il ne se moque pas de nous qui l'avons redite selon nos anciens.

# Histoire de la Perdrix Femelle et de la Perdrix Mâle

*Ruong Totea Gni Chhmol*

ON raconte qu'il y avait un jour deux perdrix, une femelle et un mâle, qui étaient mari et femme. Ils habitaient une forêt. La femelle devint enceinte. Quand le temps fut révolu, les deux oiseaux construisirent un nid de feuilles et d'herbes, bien caché dans une touffe épaisse pour le dérober à la vue des ennemis, et la femelle pondit deux œufs. Elle les couva avec le soin le plus vigilant; il en sortit deux petits, une femelle et un mâle. La mère les soignait et les réchauffait sous elle; si elle venait à s'éloigner, le mâle prenait sa place ; ils se relayaient ainsi sans cesse, sans jamais abandonner un instant tous deux à la fois les petits.

Quand les oiselets commencèrent à pousser quelques plumes, l'affection de leur mère fut plus grande encore. Rien ne saurait lui être comparé.

Il se trouva que la saison sèche dura plus que de coutume. Toutes les herbes furent brûlées; les feuilles des arbres jonchaient la terre.

Un chasseur prit son arbalète et alla chasser dans la plaine. Voyant les herbes sèches, il y mit le feu pour obliger les animaux qui s'y trouvaient à se sauver et pouvoir tirer sur eux. Le feu s'étendit avec violence jusqu'à la forêt ; tout le ciel était obscurci par la fumée. Arbres et bouquets de bambous devenaient la proie des flammes; des langues de feu s'élevaient au haut des airs. L'incendie faisait un bruit semblable à celui d'un violent ouragan.

La perdrix mâle prit son vol et s'éleva au-dessus des hautes futaies pour se rendre compte de ce qui arrivait. Elle vit la forêt qui brûlait et l'incendie qui s'approchait, poussé par un vent violent. Elle cria de toutes ses forces:

« Perdrix chérie de ton frère aîné, laisse tes petits et viens immédiatement me rejoindre! Vois comme la forêt brûle! Vois les flammes s'élever jusqu'au ciel! » La femelle vola regarder; le feu s'approchait rapidement; elle ne pensa qu'à ses petits:

« O chéris de votre mère, dit-elle, à peine êtes-vous venus au monde, vous ne savez pas encore voler; vous allez être dévorés par le feu sans qu'il soit possible de vous secourir. Votre mère est au désespoir. Elle n'a pas de mains pour vous emporter. Elle ne vous quittera pas; elle sera consumée avec ses deux petits. »

Elle dit à son mari:

« Le feu va atteindre incessamment notre nid; mes petits vont succomber. Je ne veux pas les abandonner dans leurs souffrances ; je mourrai avec eux. Quant à toi, que veux-tu faire?

— Je veux aussi rester auprès de nos petits et mourir avec eux. »

Tous deux descendirent sur leur nid. Le feu approchait avec une rapidité extrême. La mère couvrait les petits; le père couvrait la mère. Ils étaient épouvantés et tremblaient de tous leurs membres. La chaleur devint intolérable; la perdrix mâle ne put pas la supporter; elle s'élança dans les airs. La femelle, levant la tête, vit son mari qui l'abandonnait avec ses petits; elle pensa:

« La parole des mâles n'est pas ferme. Quand je viendrai à renaître,[14] sous quelque forme que ce soit, je demande à ne jamais avoir affaire à un mâle. Que je ne devienne pas dans une autre vie la femme d'un mari qui ne tient pas sa parole. »

Aussitôt qu'elle eut prononcé ce vœu, le feu l'atteignit et la fit mourir avec ses petits.

Le mâle, qui se tenait en l'air au-dessus du nid, vit succomber sa femme et ses petits. Son cœur fut plein de pitié. Il pensa:

« O combien ma femme a été fidèle à sa parole! Elle a dit qu'elle préférait périr avec ses petits; la voici morte en effet. Il ne convient pas que je survive seul, violant ma parole. Il convient que je fasse le sacrifice de ma vie auprès des miens.

« Quand ma femme reprendra vie pour commencer une autre existence, quelle que soit sa nouvelle condition, je demande à renaître dans la même et à redevenir son mari à travers toutes mes existences successives. »

---

14 La cosmogonie cambodgienne admet la migration des âmes. Tout être vivant a une âme qui après la mort monte au *Sthan Suor* [du sanscrit *Sthana Svur* ou *Svarga*] (paradis) ou descend au *Sthan Norok* [*Sthana Naraka*] (enfer], d'où elle vient reprendre naissance dans un nouveau corps pour un autre *cheat* (*jata*), existence. Les âmes peuvent animer tour à tour des êtres vivants quelconques, animaux ou hommes.

Ayant fait ce souhait, il se laissa tomber du haut des airs sur le cadavre de sa femme et fut brûlé à son tour.

❀

Le mâle, qui n'avait pas été dès le début fidèle à sa parole, revint au monde sous la forme d'un enfant, fils d'un homme misérable, qui habitait le royaume de Peareanosey[15] situé aux confins du monde.

Il était devenu un petit garçon; mais il avait une apparence affreuse; son corps était couvert d'excroissances, de loupes grosses comme le pouce; il était tout à fait privé d'intelligence. Pour cette raison, son père le nomma Turpolpheap.[16]

La femelle, qui avait tenu sa parole, reprit naissance dans le sein de *neang* Nanteartevi, première femme du roi Promteat, qui régnait sur le royaume de Peareanosey. Elle vint au monde sous la forme d'une fille admirablement belle. On n'aurait pu trouver de par le monde aucune femme plus belle qu'elle. C'est pourquoi ses parents lui donnèrent le nom de Chonbatkalyani.[17]

Quand elle fut d'âge à savoir parler, elle n'adressait la parole qu'aux femmes, mais jamais à un homme; même au roi son père elle ne disait jamais un seul mot.

A mesure qu'elle grandissait, elle devenait de plus en plus belle. Si un homme la voyait, il ne songeait plus qu'à rester en admiration devant elle, sans vouloir s'éloigner.

Son esprit égalait sa beauté. Elle connaissait les caractères d'écriture, les préceptes religieux, les préceptes coutumiers. Elle savait résoudre toutes les énigmes. Peu de personnes l'égalaient en intelligence.

Le roi son père, voyant qu'elle ne parlait jamais à aucun homme, ne savait comment il pourrait la marier.

Après avoir longuement réfléchi, il fit construire devant son palais une tour environnée de jardins agréables; il assigna cette tour comme résidence à sa fille. Puis il fit publier par tout le royaume, par tous les pays étrangers, grands et petits, que sa fille habitait cette tour. Il invitait tous les hommes, rois, dignitaires,

---

15 En sanskrit: *Banarasi* = Bénarès.

16 Pheap, sanskrit: *Bhava* = être, personne; Turpol, sanskrit: *durbala* = faible, frêle, laid.

17 Transcrit en sanskrit ce nom devient Janapadakalyani ; *Jana*: être humain; *Pada* : signe, marque ; *Kalyani*: belle, ravissante, aimable.

simples particuliers, à venir se promener dans les jardins attenants, déclarant que si un homme quel qu'il soit était capable de faire prononcer seulement trois paroles par Chonbatkalyani, il lui donnerait la princesse en mariage et l'élèverait à la dignité d'Obbarach.[18] Si la princesse prononçait les trois paroles, les tam-tam et les gongs l'annonceraient aussitôt à grand bruit, et celui qui aurait remporté la victoire serait amené au palais pour être présenté à Sa Majesté, qui le recevrait pour gendre.

Chacun était libre de venir tenter l'épreuve. Il était seulement défendu, pour arriver à faire parler la princesse, de l'effrayer, d'user de violence, ou d'entrer dans la tour.

Cette proclamation fut répandue dans toutes les régions. Des hommes innombrables vinrent dans les jardins. Pour attirer l'attention de la princesse, les uns avaient revêtu des vêtements magnifiques; d'autres faisaient des armes, d'autres luttaient, faisaient des assauts de boxe, conduisaient des chevaux ou disputaient des courses en chars; chacun cherchait à se mettre en valeur à sa façon.

La princesse se tenait sans cesse en haut de sa tour, regardant tous ces jeux, — mais elle n'avait pas un sourire, elle ne prononçait pas un mot.

∞ ❀ ∞

La proclamation du roi parvint aux oreilles de Turpolpheap. Il dit à sa mère:

« O mère, on dit que la fille du roi ne parle jamais à un homme et que Sa Majesté a fait venir tous les hommes pour se livrer à des jeux ; si l'un d'eux obtient que la princesse lui parle, il sera son époux. Je voudrais aller voir ces jeux, et apprendre qui aura obtenu la main de cette jeune fille. Veuillez me donner deux bols de riz et une marmite; je vais à la tour.

— O chéri de ta mère, ton corps est laid; tu es très pauvre; tu n'as que le seul sampot que tu portes; tous ceux qui sont là-bas sont de beaux jeunes hommes splendidement habillés. N'y va pas, tu serais tout honteux de toi-même. Ce n'est pas à toi que viendrait à échoir la princesse!

—Je ne désire pas obtenir Chonbatkalyani! Je veux seulement aller voir les

---

18 Le titre d'Obbarach, que l'on a le tort de traduire habituellement en français par: second roi, ce qui ne correspond à aucune réalité, est le titre conféré au premier prince de la cour cambodgienne.

divertissements. Depuis ma naissance, je n'ai jamais vu de joyeuse réunion. Ayez la compassion de me laisser y aller! »

La mère, prise de pitié, donna une musette de riz, trois poissons secs, du sel, du *prahok* ,[19] deux assiettes et une petite marmite à son fils, et lui fit ces recommandations:

« Vas-y, mon garçon, et reviens vite. Ne reste pas longtemps, toi qui n'es jamais entré dans une grande ville! »

Turpolpheap prit ses provisions et se mit en route avec la foule.

Soudain une pluie violente se mit à tomber. Il fut trempé; tremblant de froid, il chercha un abri. Mais les gens qui étaient dans les divers hangars le repoussèrent et ne le laissèrent pas entrer, lui montrant du doigt un kiosque situé au pied de la tour. Tout transi, Turpolpheap courut se réfugier dans le kiosque.

Quand la pluie cessa, il demanda du feu pour se réchauffer. Mais il n'alluma qu'une seule bûche, il ne souffla pas le feu, qui brûla un instant et s'éteignit. Turpolpheap se dit à lui-même:

« Je ne comprends pas quel est ce feu qui a peur du bois! »

La princesse Chonbatkalyani, qui était sur la tour, dit:

« Ce garçon est-il fou de vouloir allumer une bûche seule? Comment brûlerait-elle? Il n'a qu'à mettre plusieurs bûches, alors son feu brûlera! »

Turpolpheap leva les yeux et vit la princesse; il alla chercher une brassée de bois sec, souffla sur le brasier, qui fit une belle flamme. Il resta assis auprès et se réchauffa; pour sécher ses vêtements mouillés, il s'approchait si près du feu qu'il se sentit brûler. Il sauta en arrière, puis revint contre le foyer, se brûla encore.

Chonbatkalyani dit:

« Il est vraiment fou! Pourquoi ne change-t-il pas de sampot pour sécher celui qui est mouillé? »

Turpolpheap mit son écharpe en guise de sampot, sécha le sampot ; puis il le remit et fit sécher l'écharpe.

Une fois habillé de sec, Turpolpheap voulut manger. Il coupa dans une branche deux piquets qu'il enfonça dans le sol et fit un joli brasier entre ces piquets. Puis

---

19 Le *prahok* est une pâte faite de poisson pilé avec de la saumure.

il prit sa marmite pour aller puiser de l'eau dans un bassin. Mais ce bassin était couvert de lentilles d'eau. Turpolpheap posa la marmite sur la rive; des deux mains il écarta les plantes aquatiques sur un espace suffisant pour atteindre l'eau, puis il alla prendre sa marmite. Pendant ce temps les lentilles s'étaient étendues de nouveau et couvraient l'eau. Turpolpheap remonta poser sa marmite sur la berge, descendit écarter les plantes d'eau, qui se refermèrent comme la première fois avant qu'il n'ait repris la marmite. Il recommença le manège plusieurs fois sans pouvoir puiser d'eau.

La jeune fille vint au bord de la terrasse et dit agacée:

« Il est incontestablement fou! Comment puisera-t-il jamais de l'eau en s'y prenant ainsi! Il n'a qu'à tenir sa marmite d'une main; de l'autre il écartera les plantes flottantes, et ainsi il atteindra facilement la surface de l'eau! »

Turpolpheap fit ce que disait la princesse; il remplit sa marmite, y versa du riz, la posa sur les deux piquets qu'il avait plantés. Aussitôt qu'il la lâcha des mains, elle se renversa, se vida, éteignit le feu. Turpolpheap s'efforça de ranimer la flamme, retourna remplir d'eau la marmite, y remit du riz, la reposa sur les piquets, — elle se renversa de nouveau. Il recommença plusieurs fois avec le même résultat.

La princesse, qui s'impatientait à suivre des yeux son manège, dit:

« Vraiment ce garçon est complètement fou! Qui n'a jamais songé à poser une marmite sur deux piquets! Il n'a qu'à planter trois piquets comme tout le monde et sa marmite ne se renversera pas! »

Turpolpheap se conforma aux paroles de la jeune fille et put cuire son riz; il remua avec sa cuiller, qu'il glissa ensuite dans sa ceinture. Quand l'eau eut bouilli le temps nécessaire, il chercha sa cuiller pour égoutter le riz, mais il ne savait plus où il l'avait mise. Il courait de tous côtés pour la chercher, mais sans la trouver. Se parlant à lui-même il s'écria:

« Où donc ai-je-mis ma cuiller que je ne puis trouver ? Mon riz va se perdre! »

La princesse dit:

« Il a mis sa cuiller dans sa ceinture et la cherche partout! »

Turpolpheap entendant ces mots retrouva sa cuiller, égoutta le riz, le mangea, puis remit sa marmite dans sa musette.

A ce moment un gouverneur de province qui avait un attelage de bœufs trotteurs avec lequel il prenait tous les jours part à des courses dans le parc, appela Turpolpheap et lui demanda:

« As-tu des chevaux ou des bœufs? »

— Je n'en ai point, Seigneur!

— Alors attelle mes bœufs à mon char et fais-leur faire un tour.

— Je n'ai jamais conduit d'attelage!

— Fais toujours! Si tu casses le char, peu importe, je ne te réclamerai rien! »

Turpolpheap emmena les bœufs, sortit la voiture, et attela les bêtes. Il en mit une la tête tournée vers la voiture, l'autre tournée en sens inverse, monta sur le char et voulut faire partir les animaux, mais ceux-ci ne pouvaient pas marcher. Turpolpheap s'arma de l'aiguillon, piqua la tête d'un des bœufs, la croupe de l'autre. Les deux bêtes firent des bonds désordonnés. Tous les hommes qui étaient à l'entour furent pris d'une gaieté bruyante, Chonbatkalyani se mit à rire et s'écria:

« Il est plus fou qu'on ne saurait croire! Tout le monde attelle les deux bœufs la tête tournée vers le timon, ainsi seulement il leur est possible de traîner le char! »

Elle avait à peine prononcé ces paroles que les tam-tam et les gongs se mirent à résonner à grand fracas.

Turpolpheap n'avait certes pas agi par ruse réfléchie, mais véritablement par sottise.

La princesse entendant le bruit des tam-tam et des gongs fut soudain comme réveillée en sursaut: elle n'avait nullement pensé adresser la parole à Turpolpheap; elle était convaincue qu'elle s'était parlé à elle-même. Elle pensa:

« Pour quelle raison frappe-t-on ainsi les instruments ? Je n'ai parlé à personne! »

Cependant les femmes qui étaient placées auprès de la princesse, les secrétaires placés dans l'enceinte extérieure, chargés les uns et les autres de noter les paroles de la princesse, allèrent se prosterner aux pieds du roi Promteat et lui dirent:

« Depuis le commencement de ces fêtes, l'auguste fille de Votre Majesté n'a pas dit un seul mot à aucun homme. Or voici que soudain elle a parlé à plusieurs reprises à un individu affreux, tout couvert d'excroissances. Notre cœur s'est serré: nous ne voulions pas noter ses paroles, nous ne voulions pas frapper tam-tam et gongs; mais à six reprises elle s'est adressée à cet homme, et les ordres de Votre Majesté étaient formels! »

Le roi répondit:

« S'il en est ainsi, allez chercher cet homme. Si laid qu'il soit, la princesse lui a parlé, il sera son époux; le roi n'a qu'une parole! »

Les officiers du palais coururent appeler Turpolpheap et lui dirent;

« Sa Majesté ordonne que tu viennes te présenter à elle! »

Turpolpheap, effrayé, se mit à trembler de tous ses membres; il se prosterna et demanda aux officiers:

« Seigneurs, pourquoi le roi me fait-il appeler? Ai-je fait quelque chose de répréhensible?

— Nous n'en savons rien. Viens vite! »

Turpolpheap fut amené devant le roi; Sa Majesté fut remplie de tristesse en le voyant; mais le roi ne pouvait se dédire. Il ordonna à ses officiers de mener Turpolpheap au bain, de l'habiller de somptueux vêtements prélevés sur les magasins royaux et de le ramener devant le trône.

Le plus grand des *tevoda*[20] préposés par Indra à la garde du palais royal, réfléchit et se dit:

« Cet homme a été affligé d'un aspect repoussant parce qu'il n'a pas eu le cœur immédiatement droit à la fin de sa précédente existence. Sa laideur a été une punition infligée jusqu'à ce qu'il ait acquis la fermeté, alors son apparence extérieure doit redevenir belle. L'épreuve a suffisamment duré. Je vais aller au paradis chercher de l'eau de grâce et je la répandrai sur lui. »

Le *tevoda* s'en alla chercher de l'eau de grâce dans une burette d'or. Au moment où les officiers du palais amenèrent Turpolpheap au bain, le *tevoda* répandit l'eau sur son corps; toutes ses tares disparurent aussitôt; sa couleur devint semblable à l'or; il fut soudain plus beau que tous les hommes, aussi beau qu'un *tevoda*.

Les officiers furent stupéfaits; ils disaient entre eux:

« L'homme que nous avons amené était affreux; il a suffi de le plonger dans

---

20 En sanskrit *deva*. Les êtres du Paradis. C'est à tort que l'on traduit habituellement *tevoda* par dieux, le bouddhisme étant monothéiste.

l'eau pour qu'il devienne d'une beauté exceptionnelle. Toutes ses excroissances ont disparu. Cela est invraisemblable. Cet homme s'appelle-t-il vraiment Turpolpheap, ou bien comment s'est-il substitué à l'autre?

— Je suis bien réellement Turpolpheap. »

Les officiers ne pouvaient le croire. Ils s'interrogeaient avec anxiété les uns les autres.

Ils revêtirent le jeune homme de riches vêtements; sa beauté en fut accentuée. Toutes les femmes qui le virent eurent le cœur ému; les hommes eux-mêmes reconnaissaient combien il leur était supérieur en beauté.

Les officiers firent leur rapport au roi:

« Voici l'homme si laid que nous avons mené au bain; en sortant de l'eau il est devenu tel que Votre Majesté le voit. Nous ne saurions expliquer ce prodige. »

Le roi considéra Turpolpheap et se réjouit dans son cœur. Mais son étonnement fut extrême et il craignit que ses officiers se soient entendus pour faire disparaître Turpolpheap et lui substituer un autre homme. En conséquence, il pensa que le jeune homme devait être conduit de nouveau à la tour où il tenterait une seconde fois l'épreuve. Si la princesse lui adressait les trois paroles prescrites, le mariage serait aussitôt célébré.

Tandis que le roi songeait ainsi, les *tevoda* qui étaient les gardiens de l'épée sacrée, ceux qui gardaient le diadème royal, la personne du roi, les diverses parties du palais, s'entretenaient entre eux; ils disaient:

« Turpolpheap est devenu beau physiquement; mais il est resté inintelligent. Donnons-lui de l'esprit qui lui permette de se faire adresser la parole par Chonbatkalyani.

— Je veux, dit un des *tevoda*, pénétrer dans son cœur et être son intelligence.

— Je veux, dit un autre *tevoda*, m'introduire dans l'escalier de la tour.

— Et moi, je vais entrer dans la natte sur laquelle la princesse est assise.

— Et moi, j'entrerai dans son coussin.

— Et moi dans son bol d'or.

— Et moi dans sa coupe ciselée.

— Et moi dans l'épingle d'or de sa coiffure.

— Et nous emploierons la finesse de notre esprit à faire que Chonbatkalyani parle à Turpolpheap. »

Les *tevoda* allèrent se placer chacun où il l'avait dit. Mais ils étaient invisibles à nos yeux humains.

Le roi, ayant résolu dans son cœur ce qu'il convenait de faire pendant que les *tevoda* se concertaient entre eux, s'adressa au jeune homme:

« Turpolpheap, dit-il, je désire que tu ailles encore une fois éprouver ma fille. J'irai moi-même écouter. Si la princesse répond à tes discours, si elle prononce seulement trois phrases, je te la donnerai pour épouse. »

Le *tevoda* qui avait pénétré dans le cœur de Turpolpheap et lui donnait de l'esprit lui fit répondre:

« Je demande pardon à Votre Majesté; son humble esclave a entendu votre ordre. Mais il est peu convenable que moi qui ne suis qu'un homme du peuple je me permette d'aller éprouver la princesse, de lui adresser la parole. Ce serait manquer de respect envers le sang royal!

— Je te donne l'autorisation de lui parler selon ton cœur, répondit le roi. Garde-toi seulement d'employer la violence! »

Turpolpheap prit congé du roi, et se rendit à la tour environné d'une foule de dignitaires qui voulaient assister à l'épreuve.

II s'arrêta devant le perron, se disant tout haut à lui-même:

« Je connais les convenances; il n'est pas permis d'entrer dans une maison si le maître de cette maison ne vous y a pas invité. Je ne puis pas pénétrer dans la tour! Si l'on m'appelle, j'entrerai. »

Le *tevoda* qui s'était caché dans l'escalier répondit:

« Je vous invite, Seigneur, à monter; car moi, l'escalier, je vous prie de me fouler sans hésitation. » Turpolpheap monta; une fois dans la tour, il s'arrêta, disant:

« Je ne saurais m'asseoir sans en être prié! »

Le *tevoda* qui était dans la natte de la princesse répondit:

« Je vous invite, Seigneur, à venir ici vous asseoir sur moi qui suis une belle natte. »

Turpolpheap s'assit auprès de la princesse, mais celle-ci se détourna de lui.

Au bout d'un moment, Turpolpheap dit:

« J'ai grande envie de fumer une cigarette. Mais personne ne m'en offre! »

Le *tevoda* qui était dans la coupe ciselée glissa légèrement sur la natte jusqu'auprès du jeune homme, en disant:

« Je vous prie, Seigneur, de vouloir bien fumer une des cigarettes que je contiens. »

Turpolpheap ayant allumé une cigarette dit:

« Je sais raconter beaucoup d'histoires. Mais personne ne paraît vouloir les écouter!

— J'ai grande envie de les entendre, dit le *tevoda* qui était dans le coussin. Je vous prie de raconter, Seigneur! »

Turpolpheap dit:

« Il y a bien longtemps, quatre hommes habitant le pays khmer se mirent en route ensemble pour aller apprendre des formules magiques et des incantations auprès d'un *achar*[21] qui vivait dans le royaume de Savothi, aujourd'hui appelé Birmanie.

L'un apprit les formules qui dirigent les flèches; le second apprit l'art de *hora*, qui savent prophétiser l'avenir; le troisième à pouvoir vivre sous l'eau; le quatrième à ressusciter les morts.

Celui qui avait appris à diriger les traits tirait sans jamais manquer son but, même quand celui-ci était hors de portée de sa vue. Celui qui avait appris l'art des *hora* voyait comme avec ses yeux le futur et le passé, et non seulement ce qui était à la surface de la terre, mais ce qui avait été enfoui depuis la plus haute antiquité; par ses calculs il pouvait tout découvrir; rien ne lui restait caché. Celui qui avait appris à vivre sous l'eau pouvait rester immergé un jour entier sans être gêné. Celui qui avait appris à ressusciter pouvait rappeler à la vie tout homme, tout animal, fût-il mort depuis trois jours entiers.

Quand ils furent complètement instruits, ils prirent congé de *l'achar* et revinrent dans leur pays.

Un jour ils arrivèrent au bord d'un océan et s'arrêtèrent pour manger. L'un d'eux demanda au *hora*:

« Ferons-nous aujourd'hui quelque rencontre? »

Le *hora* fit ses calculs et prédit:

---

21 En sanskrit: *Acharya*, maître, celui qui enseigne.

« Au milieu du jour, nous verrons un *intri*[22] tenant dans son bec la fille d'un roi et volant en haut des airs. La jeune princesse est morte.

— Si ta prédiction se réalise, dit celui qui dirigeait les traits, je tuerai *l'intri*.

— S'il tombe dans la mer, dit celui qui pouvait plonger, j'irai le chercher sous les eaux.

— Si la princesse est morte, dit le quatrième, je la ressusciterai. »

Quand le soleil fut au milieu de sa course, ils aperçurent *l'intri* à une très grande hauteur; il paraissait grand comme la paume de la main.

Celui qui dirigeait les traits banda son arc, lança une flèche qui traversa *l'intri* de part en part. L'oiseau tomba dans la mer. Le plongeur alla chercher la jeune fille et la rapporta sur le rivage; elle était morte en effet. Celui qui en avait le pouvoir la rappela à la vie.

Les quatre compères se disputèrent la princesse; chacun prétendait qu'il avait à sa main plus de titre que ses compétiteurs.

Coussin, toi qui m'as demandé l'histoire, décide lequel des quatre avait raison? »

Le *tevoda* qui était dans le coussin répondit volontairement d'une façon erronée; il dit:

« A mon avis, la jeune fille doit être à celui qui l'a ressuscitée! »

Chonbatkalyani, entendant le coussin prononcer cette sentence injuste, le frappa de la main et dit:

« C'est faux! La jeune fille doit être accordée au plongeur, car celui-là le premier l'a prise dans ses bras et a vu son corps découvert. Celui qui a tiré de l'arc doit être considéré comme le père de la princesse, car il l'a sauvée de l'anéantissement; celui qui l'a ressuscitée sera sa mère, car c'est la mère qui donne la vie à l'enfant. Quant au *hora*, il sera le frère de la jeune fille, car il a seulement eu connaissance de sa venue, mais n'a pris aucune peine pour elle. »

Chonbatkalyani avait rendu une sentence certainement conforme à l'équité. Pendant qu'elle répondait à la question posée par Turpolpheap, les secrétaires notaient une parole.

༄ ✿ ༄

22 Aigle fabuleux.

Turpolpheap reprit la parole et dit:

« Je voudrais raconter une autre histoire; mais je ne sais si quelqu'un désire l'entendre.

— J'ai grande envie de l'écouter! dit la coupe ciselée. Parlez, Seigneur, je vous en prie.

— Il y a bien longtemps, dit Turpolpheap, il y avait un mari très jaloux. Il emmena sa femme sur une montagne couverte de forêts, débroussailla un espace qu'il mit en culture et vécut complètement isolé des autres hommes.

Au bout d'un certain temps sa femme mit au monde une fille. Quand l'enfant fut devenue une jeune fille, elle fut un jour aperçue par un homme qui passait par la forêt et qui s'éprit d'amour pour elle. Il la courtisa en secret tant et si bien qu'il finit par en faire sa maîtresse. Non content de cela, il devint aussi l'amant de la mère.

La mère et sa fille savaient l'une et l'autre qu'elles étaient toutes deux maîtresses de cet homme; mais elles avaient toutes deux trop de torts pour oser se les reprocher mutuellement. Le mari jaloux ne savait rien. Il fut cependant pris de soupçon lorsqu'un jour il s'aperçut que sa fille était enceinte. Mais il ne savait que penser; le cœur agité, il ne pouvait plus tenir en place; tout le jour il allait chasser à l'aventure dans la forêt.

A la même époque, il y avait dans la même région un autre mari extrêmement jaloux. Celui-là était allé apprendre d'un *achar* des incantations qui lui donnaient le pouvoir d'avaler un être humain. Ce mari, où qu'il allât, avalait sa femme pour l'empêcher de se laisser séduire.

Un jour sa femme lui demanda comment il pouvait l'avaler ainsi:

« Je sais, répondit-il, une formule magique d'une grande puissance.

— Je voudrais l'apprendre aussi, dit la femme.

— Tu n'as que faire de l'apprendre!

— Si tu ne me l'enseignes pas, je vais me pendre! »

Le mari aimait sa femme. Il lui enseigna la formule. Dès qu'elle l'eut exactement retenue, elle prit un amant, qu'elle avalait à l'approche de son mari; celui-ci ne se doutait de rien.

Un jour, le mari dit à sa femme:

« Demain, au lever du jour, fais cuire du riz et fais-en avec soin un paquet, car je te mènerai rendre visite à ma mère qui ne te connaît pas encore. »

Ayant dit, il s'endormit profondément. Le lendemain matin, il prit en bandoulière les provisions préparées, avala sa femme et se mit en toute hâte en chemin.

Au milieu du jour, il atteignit un étang situé au milieu d'une forêt inhabitée; il s'arrêta à l'ombre d'un arbre, fit sortir sa femme de son estomac et se disposa à faire avec elle son repas. Toutefois avant de manger il alla se baigner dans l'étang. L'eau était très basse; il s'éloigna du rivage cherchant la profondeur au milieu de l'étang.

Pendant ce temps sa femme fit remonter de son estomac son amant, se donna à lui, puis le fit rapidement manger et l'avala de nouveau lorsqu'elle entendit revenir son mari. Celui-ci mangea en compagnie de sa femme ; puis il l'avala et se mit en route.

La chasse avait amené en cet endroit l'autre jaloux qui soupçonnait sa fille; il s'était caché dans un fourré et avait vu le mari cracher sa femme et aller se baigner; puis la femme cracher son amant, se livrer à lui et l'avaler de nouveau; il se dit:

« Voici un mari qui sait avaler sa femme, et malgré cela elle a un amant. Moi qui abandonne tout le jour ma femme et ma fille, comment puis-je penser qu'elles sont chastes? »

Il resta dans sa cachette; il vit le mari revenir du bain, manger avec sa femme, puis avaler celle-ci et s'éloigner. Il fit un détour et vint à la rencontre du mari, à qui il demanda:

« Où allez-vous?

- Je vais rendre visite à ma mère.

— Que cette rencontre en forêt soit le début d'une amitié durable. Camarade, venez vous reposer un moment chez moi! »

Ils arrivèrent tous deux à la maison du chasseur, qui dit à sa fille:

« Mets vite du riz sur le feu, car voici un ami que j'amène. Dès que le riz sera cuit, apporte-le; nous mangerons tous ensemble. »

La femme et la fille du chasseur préparèrent le repas et mirent quatre couverts, pour l'ami, pour le chasseur et pour elles-mêmes.

Le chasseur dit:

« Le couvert n'est pas complet, il faut le compléter pour qui est dans l'estomac de mon ami! Crachez, mon ami; que nous mangions tous ensemble. »

Le mari fut fort étonné. Comment cet homme savait-il qu'il avalait sa femme? Il la fit sortir de son estomac; la fille du chasseur apporta un bol de plus. Mais le chasseur de dire:

« Il manque encore un couvert, car la femme de mon ami a encore un homme dans l'estomac! Crachez-le, je vous prie, qu'il déjeune avec nous ! »

La femme fut couverte de confusion. Mais elle ne pouvait nier; elle cracha son amant sous les yeux de son mari. Celui-ci se voyant ainsi trompé ne voulut plus vivre; il se priva de respirer et mourut. Sa femme fut prise de pitié pour son mari et de remords; elle ne voulut plus vivre, se priva de respirer et mourut. L'amant, se reprochant d'être cause de ces deux morts, ne voulut plus vivre, se priva de respirer et mourut. Le chasseur, sa femme et sa fille, l'amant de ces deux femmes, survenu au même moment, se privèrent de respirer et moururent les uns après les autres, car chacun s'accusait des malheurs qui étaient arrivés: le chasseur se reprochait d'avoir dévoilé le secret qu'il venait de découvrir; la femme et la fille se désolaient d'avoir préparé le repas qui avait retenu l'étranger; l'amant de la jeune fille et de sa mère pensait qu'en faisant de ces deux femmes ses maîtresses il avait aigri le cœur du chasseur.

Je demande qui de tous les personnages de l'histoire est responsable. Coupe ciselée, prononcez le jugement. »

La coupe ciselée eut soin de donner une mauvaise réponse. Elle dit:

« Dans cette affaire la responsabilité incombe au chasseur, car ayant surpris un secret, il n'a pas gardé le silence; il a mis au grand jour ce qui était ignoré; il a provoqué des colères et des confusions; toutes les morts qui s'en sont suivies sont imputables au chasseur. »

Chonbatkalyani, entendant sa coupe ciselée émettre un avis contraire à la jurisprudence, lui donna une tape et dit:

« Nullement! La responsabilité incombe aux femmes qui, ayant des amants, trompaient leur mari. Elles ont causé leur mort et doivent être considérées comme ayant tué leur mari. »

Le jugement de la princesse était parfaitement équitable les secrétaires notaient une deuxième parole.

༄ ❀ ༄

Turpolpheap demanda encore si personne ne désirait entendre une autre histoire. Le bol d'or le pria de la raconter. Il le fit en ces termes:

« Il y avait autrefois quatre femmes qui habitaient au Siam. Elles se réunirent pour se mettre à la recherche d'hommes intelligents dont elles feraient leurs maris. Elles firent la rencontre d'un homme assez bien de sa personne qui leur demanda:

« Où allez-vous toutes quatre?

— Nous cherchons des hommes intelligents pour les épouser, répondirent-elles.

— Moi, je suis à la recherche d'une femme intelligente pour en faire mon épouse. Nous venons à nous rencontrer ainsi peut-être est-ce notre destin de nous marier ensemble.

— Je vous accepte pour mari! dirent ensemble les quatre femmes. Mais il faut que vous veniez me chercher chez moi.

— Où est votre demeure? » Demanda l'homme. L'une des femmes montra ses cheveux; la seconde montra ses sourcils; la troisième montra ses seins; la quatrième montra son sampot, puis elles s'en allèrent toutes quatre.

L'homme s'assit, s'efforçant de comprendre les énigmes posées par ces femmes, mais il ne put rien y comprendre. Il se mit à chercher leurs maisons, mais ne les trouva pas. Il vint à passer devant un condamné qui avait été mis en croix; il poussait des cris lamentables et souffrait atrocement. Le supplicié lui dit:

« O Seigneur, j'ai soif. Faites-moi la charité de me donner un peu d'eau à boire. »

L'homme répondit:

« J'ai beaucoup de préoccupations; je ne puis aller vous chercher de l'eau. Je cherche des énigmes que je ne puis résoudre.

— N'ayez pas d'inquiétude quant à vos énigmes; je me fais fort de les résoudre. Donnez-moi seulement à boire. »

L'homme alla chercher de l'eau; le crucifié but, puis demanda quelles étaient les énigmes. L'homme lui dit le geste qu'avait fait chacune des quatre femmes quand il leur avait demandé où elles habitaient. Le supplicié répondit:

« La femme qui vous a montré ses cheveux vous indiquait par là qu'elle demeurait dans la maison où l'on file la soie. Il y a une seule maison ici où ce travail soit fait; il vous est aisé de la trouver. Celle qui vous a montré ses sourcils vous a indiqué que devant sa maison il y a une haie touffue; celle qui vous a montré ses seins a planté auprès de sa demeure un pied de citrouille qui porte deux fruits. Enfin celle qui vous a montré son sampot habite dans la maison du tisserand. »

L'homme se mit à la recherche des femmes et les trouva toutes quatre sans aucune peine. Elles lui demandèrent:

« Avez-vous deviné nos énigmes tout seul, ou quelqu'un vous a-t-il aidé?

— Le prisonnier mis en croix les a résolues, répondit-il. »

Les quatre femmes dirent:

« S'il en est ainsi, c'est le supplicié qui est intelligent! Allons demander qu'on nous le laisse enlever et soigner. Quant à celui-ci, il n'est qu'un sot et nous ne le prendrons pas pour mari. »

Elles obtinrent la permission de détacher le prisonnier de la croix et le rapportèrent pour le soigner. L'une des femmes allait dans la forêt chercher des simples; la deuxième allait chez les voisins demander du riz et du poisson pour nourrir le malheureux; la troisième faisait la cuisine; la quatrième pansait les plaies et veillait le blessé. Et il en fut ainsi jusqu'à ce que le prisonnier fût complètement guéri. Alors les quatre femmes se disputèrent l'homme qu'elles avaient soigné, chacune voulant le prendre pour mari à elle seule. La première disait:

« Si je n'étais pas allée cueillir des simples, comment aurait-on pu le soigner?

— Et si je n'avais procuré le riz et les vivres, à quoi auraient servi tes drogues? disait la seconde.

— Belle affaire d'avoir des vivres, repartit la troisième, si je ne les avais fait cuire!

— Si je n'avais pas lavé ses plaies à l'eau chaude, si je n'avais oint son corps de médicaments, si je ne l'avais soigné jour et nuit, dit la quatrième, tout le reste aurait été sans effet! »

Les quatre femmes se disputèrent tant et si bien qu'elles finirent par porter la question devant le tribunal. Mais je ne sais comment les magistrats la tranchèrent.

Je te demande, bol d'or, de nous dire laquelle des quatre femmes devait avoir l'homme pour mari? »

Le bol d'or répondit:

« Il doit être à celle qui a fait la cuisine; car sans elle il n'aurait pu se nourrir et n'aurait pas vécu!

— Bol d'or, dit Chonbatkalyani, ton jugement est injuste! Cet homme doit être donné pour mari à la femme qui lui a donné les soins, qui a lavé et pansé ses plaies, car cette femme a vu, a touché le corps de cet homme. Celle qui a fait la cuisine sera considérée comme la mère de l'homme, car c'est par ce genre de soins qu'une mère entretient la vie de son enfant. Celle qui allait cueillir les plantes médicinales tiendra lieu de père, car quand un enfant est malade, c'est au père à aller chercher les médicaments et appeler le médecin. Enfin celle qui allait demander des vivres sera la sœur ainée, car c'est à elle qu'il appartient, quand les parents sont en souci de leur enfant, d'assurer les approvisionnements nécessaires au jeune frère.[23] »

Chonbatkalyani ayant prononcé cette sentence parfaitement conforme à la justice; les secrétaires notèrent une troisième parole.

*

Turpolpheap dit encore:

« Il y a une question que je voudrais résoudre; si quelqu'un a assez d'intelligence pour le faire, je lui demande de m'éclairer, car cette énigme me préoccupe fort.

— Posez-la sans crainte, dit l'épingle d'or qui retenait la chevelure de la princesse. Je résous sans jamais me tromper toutes les énigmes.

— Celle-ci est une grave question; elle a trait à la mort:

Lorsqu'un être humain vient à mourir, que devient son âme? Est-il vrai qu'elle vienne se réincarner et vivre une nouvelle existence? »

L'épingle d'or répondit:

23 L'histoire des quatre femmes se disputant un homme a été donnée séparée à trois reprises par A. Leclère: deux fois dans ses contes Laotiens (1 vol. chez E. Leroux, 1901) sous les titres: «Le voleur et les quatre femmes » p. 90, et: « Le supplicié et les quatre prostituées » (p. 164) et dans « Cambodge, contes et légendes », (libr. Bouillon, 1885) (p. 189) Les variantes ne touchent pas le fond de l'histoire.

« Quand un être humain meurt, il est complètement mort; il ne reprend vie nulle part. Et mon affirmation est facile à contrôler: qui a jamais vu un mort renaître? On peut interroger tous les hommes de la terre, jamais aucun d'eux ne pourra répondre: « Autrefois, dans une existence antérieure, j'ai vécu sous telle forme, dans tel pays; lorsque j'ai quitté le corps que j'avais alors, je suis venu me réincarner ici. » Certes nul être humain ne peut prétendre avoir de tels souvenirs. J'en conclus que la mort nous détruit entièrement! »

Chonbatkalyani fut indignée d'entendre cette réponse ; elle enleva avec colère son épingle d'or et la jeta sur la natte, l'apostrophant ainsi:

« Épingle d'or, tu es d'une stupidité extrême. Tenir un pareil discours est un très grand péché. Buddha, notre Maître, nous le répète dans son enseignement: nous venons sur la terre dans une existence charnelle ; la série de nos incarnations successives est infinie; nos naissances et nos morts se succèdent continuellement. Mais dès l'instant où nous avons pris vie dans le sein de notre mère, nous oublions tout notre passé, nous ne savons plus d'où nous venons, notre mémoire est absolument vide. Au moment où la mort de notre corps terrestre remet notre âme en liberté, celle-ci perd de nouveau la mémoire de toute existence antérieure. Aussi longtemps que nous nous réincarnons, que nous menons des existences successives, il ne nous est pas permis de conserver le souvenir d'un état dans un autre. Si un jour nous parvenons à la connaissance suprême de Buddha, alors seulement nous retrouverons la mémoire de toutes nos vies successives.

Le Seigneur a prescrit que dans nos vies humaines nous nous efforcions de faire des œuvres pies et d'être charitables. Par faire des œuvres pies, on entend construire des pagodes, sculpter des Buddha, faire des offrandes, ou toutes choses qui sont de la religion; faire œuvre pie est encore : soulager ceux qui souffrent, aider à mettre fin aux misères, soigner les malades, venir en aide aux prisonniers.

Être charitable consiste à donner aux pauvres.

Celui qui a vécu charitable et a donné aux œuvres, se réincarne dans un beau corps, appartient à une famille respectée, est doué d'intelligence, et reçoit autorité sur les hommes, car il est digne de les commander; il jouit de grands biens.

Autour de nous, nous voyons des êtres qui sont des hommes au même titre que nous-mêmes. Comment expliquer que les uns soient puissants, d'autres comblés de richesses, d'autres doués de qualités physiques, tandis que d'autres sont misérables ou laids à voir? C'est le résultat des existences antérieures, punies ou récompensées dans l'existence actuelle. »

Chonbatkalyani fut interrompue dans son discours par les tam-tam et les gongs frappés de toutes parts, car pendant qu'elle parlait les secrétaires avaient noté quatre paroles. La princesse se tut aussitôt.

Turpolpheap lui dit alors:

« Chonbalkalyani, ô la plus belle des princesses, je suis venu vous rendre visite dans votre demeure; mais vous ne m'avez pas adressé une parole courtoise. Votre escalier, votre natte, votre coupe ciselée, votre bol d'or, votre coussin, votre épingle à cheveux, qui sont des objets inanimés, m'ont tous accueilli de façon gracieuse. Vous, princesse, vous n'avez aucun égard pour moi. Je suis cependant de tous les hommes celui que la destinée a le plus heureusement marqué; mais puisque vous vous détournez de moi, je vous demande la permission de me retirer. »

En parlant ainsi, il se levait de la natte et faisait un pas vers la porte ; mais Chonbatkalyani l'arrêta par ces mots:

« Ne vous hâtez pas de partir ! Attendez, je vais vous parler.[24] »

Les tam-tam et les gongs se firent entendre à nouveau, car les secrétaires venaient de noter cinq paroles.

Le roi Promteat fut dans une grande joie. Il célébra par des fêtes magnifiques le mariage de Chonbatkalyani avec Turpolpheap, dont il avait changé le nom, lui donnant celui de Sovanbotum;[25] il lui conféra la dignité d'Obbarach.

Après de longues années, Sovanbotum succéda à son beau-père sur le trône de Peareanosey.

---

24 L'incident de la princesse silencieuse est reproduit par A. Leclère dans la courte histoire do *neang* Panhcha Kalyaney (contes Laotiens, p.160 et 167, avec d'assez profondes variantes. Dans ce conte Laotien, le prétendant est un prince; il reproche à la jeune fille de ne pas lui avoir répondu: « Je suis le fils d'un roi régnant; elle n'a pas plus répondu à ce que je lui ai dit que sa boîte à bétel! - La princesse s'élance vers le prince, le prend entre ses bras et lui dit des choses très agréables et très sages ». Combien est mieux traitée dans le conte cambodgien l'attitude de la princesse.

25 Lotus d'or.

On demandera sans doute: est-il possible que Turpolpheap, pour avoir une seule fois tenu sa parole, ait acquis un tel mérite qu'il ait été élevé au trône?

Nous répondrons: certes non. Mais Sovanbotum et Chonbatkalyani, qui étaient mari et femme, accomplirent beaucoup de bonnes œuvres et furent très charitables pendant un grand nombre d'incarnations successives. Lorsque prendra fin la série de leurs existences encore à venir, il est certain qu'ils deviendront Buddha à leur tour.

Mais, demandera-t-on encore, comment se fait-il que ces deux êtres se soient incarnés sous forme de perdrix?

Voici la raison:

Dans une existence antérieure ils étaient hommes, mari et femme, habitant le pays de Langka.[26] Il se produisit une famine; les deux époux allèrent chercher des tubercules. Mais la forêt était très épaisse et presque impénétrable. Ils y mirent le feu; un couple de tourterelles avec deux petits furent brûlés; Sovanbotum et Chonbatkalyani se réincarnèrent dans des perdrix. Les tourterelles devenues chasseurs mirent le feu à la forêt et firent mourir dans les flammes les perdrix. La peine de nos mauvaises actions n'est pas punie dans une réincarnation, mais au cours de centaines et de centaines de vies successives.

26 Ceylan.

# La Fondation d'Angkor

EN l'an 600 de l'ère de Buddha, un Chinois nommé Lim Seng vivait dans la province de Changai.

Lim Seng avait cinquante ans; il se trouvait dans une grande misère. Ayant emprunté six barres d'argent à un négociant, il s'était mis en servitude pour dette chez son créancier; celui-ci lui avait assigné comme tâche de défricher et de mettre en culture un terrain situé sur le bord du fleuve. Lim Seng, à la saison où toutes sortes de fleurs étaient écloses, en faisait chaque jour une ample moisson qu'il apportait à son maître.

Un jour, cinq *devi* habitant le palais d'Indra prirent leur vol et vinrent s'ébattre sur la terre. Elles aperçurent le jardin tout fleuri de Lim Seng et y entrèrent. L'une d'elles, nommée Dibsodacan, cueillit six fleurs dont le parfum la charmait. Ses sœurs errèrent dans le jardin sans couper de fleurs. Au retour dans leur divin séjour, elles dévoilèrent à Indra le larcin de Dibsodacan. Indra interrogea la coupable et la condamna à redescendre sur terre où, pendant six ans, elle vivrait de la vie humaine et serait la femme de Lim Seng.

Dibsodacan, honteuse et désespérée, prit son vol, se rendit auprès de Lim Seng, lui avoua qu'elle lui avait dérobé six fleurs.

« En punition, dit-elle, Indra m'ordonne d'être six ans votre femme.

— Je suis dans la misère, répondit Lim Seng; je ne puis vous prendre pour femme. Mon maître est dur; à peine me donne-t-il ma propre nourriture, et quelle nourriture!

— N'importe! Je vous aiderai; je vous apprendrai des arts inconnus. Si vous ne me preniez pas pour femme, comment serait exécutée la sentence d'Indra? Ayez pitié de moi! »

Lim Seng accueillit Dibsodacan à son foyer. Il était fier de cette *devi* plus belle que toute femme. Bientôt un grand amour l'enflamma pour elle.

Dibsodacan, ayant vécu avec lui pendant quelques mois, constatant les difficultés de sa vie et l'honnêteté de son cœur, le prit en pitié.

« Combien avez-vous emprunté? demanda-t-elle.

— Six barres d'argent.

— Lorsque vous avez emprunté six barres, vous viviez seul. Maintenant, allez demander quatre barres de plus et je serai en servitude avec vous. Nous ferons fructifier l'argent que vous allez obtenir. »

Lim Seng se rendit auprès du négociant, son créancier, et obtint les quatre barres qu'il demandait. Il les apporta à Dibsodacan.

Elle pria Lim Seng de lui acheter de la soie pour quatre barres d'argent. Il lui apporta vingt livres de cocons; Dibsodacan les fila, puis se mit à tisser toutes sortes d'étoffes: des soies brochées de feuillages, des soies brodées d'animaux, des dessins innombrables; elle fit des tissus admirables, dépassant en beauté tout ce qui était alors connu des hommes. Puis elle chargea son mari d'apporter toutes ces soies à leur maître. Le négociant tâta les étoffes ; il fut plongé dans l'admiration. Jamais personne n'avait su tisser ainsi. Il fit à Lim Seng de grands compliments et dans sa joie lui donna cinquante barres d'argent, lui remettant de plus sa dette antérieure. Il envoya de nombreux élèves apprendre de Dibsodacan l'art de tisser la soie. Dibsodacan se mit à acheter des cocons par *piculs*[27], enseignant tout le jour à ses élèves. Lim Seng s'enrichit rapidement et devint puissant et considéré.

Au bout d'un an, Dibsodacan mit au monde un garçon. Cet enfant était très remuant. Dès qu'il put ramper, il creusait dans la terre des remparts; lorsqu'il put se tenir debout, il dessina sur le sol des animaux et des hommes. Toujours il traçait des images sur la terre. Jamais il n'était inactif mais sans cesse en mouvement. Pour cette raison, sa mère l'appela Popusnokar.[28]

Quand cet enfant atteignit l'âge de cinq ans, la peine de Dibsodacan arriva à son terme, les six années de son séjour terrestre étant révolues. Elle cueillit six fleurs qu'elle déposa sur son oreiller et s'envola vers son divin séjour.

Lorsque vint l'heure du repas, Lim Seng, étonné de ne pas voir venir sa femme, entra dans sa chambre. Il aperçut les six fleurs et comprit leur symbole. Il fondit

---

27 *Picul* - mesure commerciale valant environ 60 kilogrammes.

28 Le sens de ce mot m'embarrasse. Sous les plus grandes réserves, je me demande s'il ne pourrait venir de *Bhâta*, brillant, étincelant, et *Nagara*, ville. Le verbe *Bhâ*, briller, étinceler, perd à certains temps son aspiration: parfait *Babhau*. Mais cette étymologie est d'autant plus incertaine que l'orthographe donnée par les scribes cambodgiens au nom de ce personnage est variable ; les uns écrivent Popusnokar, d'autres Prah Pus nokar.

en larmes, désespéré du départ de Dibsodacan ; tous les voisins s'unirent à sa détresse. Popusnokar, courant partout à la recherche de sa mère, l'appelait d'une voix déchirante et sanglotait avec son père.

❦

Dans le royaume du Cambodge, le roi Pudesraja mourut sans enfants. La descendance du roi Khma Prah Thong s'éteignait. Il ne restait que Krong Huv et Kray Huv qui fussent de sang royal; la succession au trône se trouva vacante.[29]

Un jour, un malheureux qui ne gagnait sa vie qu'à ramasser dans la forêt des fagots de bois à brûler fut surpris par une pluie torrentielle. Il se réfugia dans une cabane élevée aux génies.

Indra, le roi des *deva*, prit la forme de deux coqs, l'un blanc, l'autre noir. Le coq noir se posa sur la maîtresse poutre de la cabane; le coq blanc se posa sur le toit. Au bout d'un moment le coq blanc chanta. Le coq noir, parlant le langage des hommes, dit:

« Qui donc se permet de chanter ainsi au-dessus de ma tête? Eh, quelle est ta puissance?

— Je suis très puissant, répondit le coq blanc. Si un homme mange ma chair, il montera sur le trône. » Le coq noir repartit:

« Si un homme mange ma tête, il sera roi des bonzes. Si une femme mange ma cuisse, elle sera reine. Si un homme mange ma poitrine, il règnera. Ne me traite donc pas avec mépris ! »

Le coq blanc s'envola; le coq noir resta sur la poutre. L'homme s'approcha sans bruit, saisit le coq noir, le tua et l'emporta dans sa hutte. A voix basse, il rapporta à sa femme le secret qu'il avait surpris. Elle, au comble du bonheur, fit cuire le coq, le disposa sur un plateau et se mit en devoir de le manger. Mais son mari lui dit:

« Nous voici sur le point de porter la couronne.

Emportons cette chair au bord de la rivière, délassons-nous en prenant un bain; puis nous revêtirons des vêtements propres et nous mangerons ce coq. »

L'homme et la femme descendirent à la berge, posèrent le plateau au bord de l'eau et s'ébattirent joyeusement dans la rivière. Lorsqu'ils revinrent sur la rive,

29 Ces quatre noms paraissent être purement légendaires.

ils ne retrouvèrent pas le plateau; les remous l'avaient entraîné dans le courant; il avait disparu.

Un cornac nommé Tar avait ce jour - là mené ses éléphants se baigner dans la rivière. Il vit ce plateau flotter vers lui. Très surpris, il prit le plateau et l'alla montrer au chef de la bonzerie. Le bonze reconnut la nature du coq. Il prit la tête et la mangea; il offrit à Tar la poitrine et donna la cuisse à Vong, femme de Tar, mais il ne leur dit rien.

Tar et Vong rentrèrent chez eux.

L'homme et la femme qui avaient perdu le plateau le cherchèrent en vain; pensant qu'il leur avait été dérobé, ils s'accablèrent mutuellement d'injures.

Trois jours après, les ministres se réunirent en conseil.

« Voici longtemps, dirent-ils, que notre royaume est privé de roi. Caparaçonnons des éléphants et invoquons les *deva*. Que les éléphants aillent d'eux-mêmes se prosterner devant celui qui est digne du trône, le mettent sur leur tête et l'amènent ici. Nous préparerons aussitôt le couronnement. »

Les éléphants, richement ornés, furent lâchés en liberté. Ils se dirigèrent vers Tar et Vong, se prosternèrent devant eux, les mirent sur leur tête et les ramenèrent au palais. Les ministres préparèrent les fêtes du couronnement selon la coutume. Tar prit le nom de règne de Devunagschar.[30]

Krong Huv et Kray Huv furent irrités. Ils se transportèrent à Bakan, dans la province de Bodhisattva[31], y construisirent un palais et refusèrent de se soumettre au nouveau roi.

Indra, voyant la reine sans enfants, dit;

« Je vais donner à Vong un fils de ma propre race qui perpétuera la dynastie des rois cambodgiens. »

Un jour, la reine étant sortie du palais, Indra s'envola dans les airs. Les hommes ne distinguèrent aucune forme mais virent une immense lumière bleue descendant à travers l'espace. Ils se mirent à crier;

« La lumière qui tombe! »

30 Ce nom parait être purement légendaire.

31 Pursat.

Indra fit descendre sur le corps de la reine une pluie de fleurs tressées en guirlandes et disparut.

Vong devint enceinte et mit au monde un fils qu'elle nomma Prah Kèt Mealea[32], ce qui signifie: Lumière fleurie.

❀

Popusnokar avait cherché sa mère de tous côtés et ne savait où elle s'en était allée. Une amère tristesse envahit son cœur.

Jusqu'à dix ans, il s'était appliqué à l'étude. Un jour, il demanda à son père:

« Qui donc était ma mère?

— Ta mère était une *devi*. Elle n'était venue vivre sur terre que pendant six années, puis elle est retournée à sa divine demeure. Cette demeure est fort éloignée, je ne sais où elle se trouve ! »

L'enfant garda le silence; mais sa pensée n'était occupée que de sa mère. Il décida de se mettre à sa recherche, dût-il succomber aux fatigues du chemin. Son père eut beau faire, il ne put le détourner de ce projet; Popusnokar se mit en route, traversant plaines et forêts, se nourrissant de fruits sauvages; ses vêtements s'en allèrent par lambeaux. Mais le destin lui était favorable. Un jour, des *devi* étaient venues se récréer sur une montagne boisée; parmi elles était Dibsodacan qui faisait un bouquet de fleurs forestières.

Popusnokar aperçut ces femmes si belles ; il pensa:

« Voici bien des années que j'ai dépassé les régions habitées par les hommes; voici bien des années que je n'ai rencontré aucun être humain. Mes vêtements sont tombés en pièces sans qu'il soit possible de les remplacer. Je ne suis vêtu que de feuilles cueillies aux arbres. Soudain j'aperçois des femmes en groupe nombreux;

---

32 M. Aymonier voit dans Prah Ket Mealea le nom légendaire de Jayavarman II qui régna sur le Cambodge de 802 à 869 de notre ère. Il nous apprend que, selon l'inscription de Sdok Kok Thom, ce roi vint de Java. Il ne serait donc pas né au Cambodge comme le dit la légende.

Pour M. Bergaigne, Jayavarman II serait Mahapativarman, fils de Rajendravarman Ier dont les dates de règne nous sont encore inconnues; nous ignorons également les prédécesseurs immédiats de Rajendravaman I.

M. Georges Maspero pense qu'en Prah Ket Melea les Cambodgiens résument le souvenir des grands rois bâtisseurs du Cambodge.

toutes sont d'une beauté surnaturelle. D'où pourraient-elles être venues jusqu'ici? Ne sont-elles pas des *devi* ? »

Popusnokar se cacha; lorsque les femmes furent proches, il fit cette incantation:

« Si toutes ces femmes sont des *devi* et que ma mère ne se trouve pas parmi elles, qu'elles prennent leur vol et retournent dans leur demeure. Mais si l'une d'elles est ma mère, je demande qu'elle soit empêchée de s'envoler avec ses compagnes! »

Popusnokar s'élança dans la clairière où s'ébattaient les *devi*. Surprises par l'apparition de cet enfant des hommes, elles s'envolèrent en hâte; mais Dibsodacan ne put s'enfuir. Popusnokar se précipita vers elle et la prit dans ses bras, la serrant de toutes ses forces. Dibsodacan fut saisie d'angoisse.

« Hélas! gémit-elle, quelle malédiction s'appesantit à nouveau sur moi? A peine suis-je délivrée de ma condition humaine, voici qu'un homme me saisit à nouveau!

- Ma mère, ma mère, je suis ton fils! Lorsque ma mère eut disparu, le désespoir s'est emparé de moi, je n'ai fait que pleurer, je te cherchais partout, nulle part je ne t'ai retrouvée. Mon père Lim Seng est entré dans ta chambre; il a trouvé six fleurs sur l'oreiller et a compris que tu étais retournée à ton existence divine. Son chagrin a été profond au delà de toute expression. Tous nos voisins pleuraient avec nous. La pensée de te retrouver n'est jamais un instante sortie de mon cœur. Dès que mes forces ont été suffisantes, j'ai pris congé de mon père et me suis mis à ta recherche. Je pensais mourir d'épuisement. Maintenant j'ai retrouvé ma mère! Je te supplie de revenir avec nous! »

Dibsodacan reconnut que l'adolescent qui la tenait embrassée était bien vraiment son fils, car ses paroles étaient convaincantes. Elle se mit à pleurer de compassion et lui dit:

« Mon enfant, ta mère n'a point d'aversion pour ton père. Constamment elle a pensé à toi-même et à lui; son souvenir est resté fidèle à tous les hommes au milieu de qui elle a vécu. Mais elle est une *devi* et ne peut vivre d'une vie humaine. Chaque jour elle doit aller remplir ses fonctions auprès du divin Indra dont elle implore pour toi et ton père les bénédictions. Chaque jour, elle lui demande de répandre le bonheur sur toute la région. Mon enfant, ta mère ne peut pas retourner vivre avec vous. Mais voici que tu m'as cherchée et que tu m'as retrouvée. Ta mère va prendre son enfant et le mener une fois dans sa demeure divine. Tu vas te baigner dans les eaux parfumées du bassin qui se trouve dans le jardin d'Indra et qui te laveront de ton odeur humaine, puis je te conduirai au palais et présenterai mon fils à Indra. »

Dibsodacan donna son écharpe à Popusnokar qui s'en revêtit, rejetant son vêtement de feuillage. Puis, prenant son enfant sur sa hanche, elle l'emporta à travers les airs. Elle le baigna dans l'onde parfumée, le conduisit dans sa demeure où elle lui fit revêtir des vêtements convenables, le rassasia de célestes aliments et se dirigea avec lui vers le palais d'Indra. Le cœur de Popusnokar débordait de joie. Mais lors qu'il pénétra dans la salle d'audience, il fut tellement impressionné par la beauté ineffable du lieu et par son mystère qu'il ne put se soutenir; ses jambes fléchirent, il tomba évanoui sur le sol. A ce moment, Indra sortant de son palais vint à passer.

« Quel est cet homme que tu amènes dans mon palais? demanda-t-il à Dibsodacan.

— C'est mon fils, le fils qui m'est né lorsque j'ai vécu sur la terre, mariée à Lim Seng.

— Adolescent, lève-toi! Commanda Indra.

Popusnokar reprit ses sens, se prosterna devant le roi des *deva*. Indra le fit entrer dans son palais et lui posa mille questions sur la région qu'il habitait sur terre. Les réponses de Popusnokar le satisfirent grandement.

« Mon fils, dit en se prosternant Dibsodacan, est particulièrement ingénieux à tracer des figures, à sculpter, à construire des temples ou des forteresses qui font l'admiration des hommes. Toutefois, il n'a jamais eu de maître et ne fait ces choses que selon sa propre inspiration.

— Un homme qui sait sans maître est comparable à un aveugle! Repartit Indra. Il progresse tout seul et ne peut prendre conseil. S'il en est ainsi, ton fils devra se joindre aux *devaputra* de mes ateliers. Sous leur direction, il apprendra à exécuter les travaux les plus divers et retournera ensuite dans le monde des hommes, car il ne peut, dans sa condition humaine, rester ici à demeure. »

Popusnokar se rendit auprès des *devaputra* spécialisés dans les arts et les constructions. Il apprit à dessiner, à sculpter, à faire de la musique; il sut construire des navires qui naviguent en terre ferme; il cisela l'or et l'argent, forgea le fer; il connut des solutions qui, répandues sur la glaise, la transforment en pierre. Il retenait tous les enseignements des *devaputra*. Ceux-ci l'encourageaient d'élogieuses paroles.

« Les travaux que tu sais faire maintenant pourront durer des milliers d'années, alors que les nôtres ne durent qu'un règne; si un roi monte sur le trône et nous confie la construction d'un temple, nous le construisons en un instant; mais le jour où ce roi vient à mourir, le temple disparaît au même moment. Ta puissance est donc supérieure à la nôtre. »

Les *devaputra* rendirent compte à Indra des résultats remarquables de l'éducation de Popusnokar. Indra s'en réjouit et décida que Popusnokar serait désormais l'éducateur de tous les hommes appartenant à la religion bouddhique.

« Tout constructeur humain sera tenu de faire une offrande à Popusnokar, consistant en un plateau sur lequel il placera une bouteille d'alcool, un bat d'argent, quatre morceaux de bananier portant des feuilles de bétel et des noix d'arec, cinq coudées de toile blanche, un bol de riz et une bougie. Si un homme entreprend un travail de quelque importance et ne fait pas cette offrande à Popusnokar, que ses yeux se ferment à la lumière du jour, qu'une taie les couvre. »

Tandis qu'il parlait ainsi, Indra vint à penser à Prah Kèt Mealea. Il se transporta à travers les airs au pays du Cambodge. Il faisait nuit sur la terre. Les hommes, éblouis par une lueur éclatante, se demandaient ce qui pouvait ainsi embraser le ciel. Indra descendit dans le temple royal; les gardiens coururent prévenir le roi Devungaschar.

« Un être inconnu est descendu des cieux. Il a l'apparence d'un homme, sa couleur est bleue, il brille comme du feu, il est entré dans le temple royal. »

Devungaschar se dirigea au plus vite vers le temple et reconnut Indra. Il se prosterna devant lui. « Roi Devungaschar, demanda Indra, connais-tu mon fils?

— Je ne le connais pas!

— Comment est né Prah Kèt Mealea?

— Une lueur bleue a envahi le ciel, puis des guirlandes de fleurs sont tombées sur la reine, qui par la suite se trouva enceinte.

— Enceinte de mon fils, dit Indra.

Devungaschar appela Prah Kèt Mealea. Indra le prit et le fit asseoir sur sa cuisse. Il lui dit:

« Autrefois, je m'appelais Makhmanubbh[33]; j'ai construit des routes et des digues, des sala et des ponts; j'ai distribué mes richesses aux pauvres; en récompense, je suis devenu Indra. J'ai pris en pitié le royaume cambodgien; parce qu'il est de fondation récente, aucun homme puissant n'y est né jusqu'ici. C'est pourquoi je t'ai engendré, pour te donner longue et heureuse vie. Mais les hommes, en ce temps, vivent peu d'années; rares sont ceux qui atteignent l'âge de cent ans. Je vais t'emporter dans mon palais et te baigner dans un bassin qui te fera vivre une longue existence. »

Indra prit sur sa hanche Prah Kèt Mealea, l'emporta dans son royaume divin. Dans les jardins, il y avait un bassin. Pendant sept jours, Indra y plongea Prah Kèt Meala sept fois par jour; ensuite, il le fit entrer dans son palais. Il invita sept Brahma à venir réciter des incantations et à faire des aspersions sur Prah Kèt Mealea pour lui donner une vie de quatre cents ans.

Ces cérémonies accomplies, Indra fit atteler son char divin; il confia Prah Kèt Mealea à ses cochers qui le conduisirent en volant autour du palais pour lui en montrer les beautés.

Lorsqu'il eut tout contemplé autant qu'il le désirait, Prah Kèt Mealea se fit ramener aux célestes écuries. Indra lui demanda:

« Es-tu content de ce que tu as vu ?

— Je suis émerveillé!

— Je te donne le royaume du Cambodge. Si tu as vu ici un monument que tu désires reproduire, dis-le selon ton cœur. Je t'enverrai un architecte qui le construira dans ton royaume. »

Prah Kèt Mealea n'avait que douze ans; il était très intimidé devant Indra. Il réfléchit:

« Dans mon royaume, je ne puis rien faire qui soit aussi beau que le palais d'Indra; si je voulais m'égaler à lui, il serait mécontent. »

Il dit alors:

« Je voudrais faire construire un édifice aussi beau que votre étable à bœufs ! » Indra se mit à rire.

« Cette étable est belle à tes yeux? » Il appela Popusnokar et lui dit:

---

33 Sanskrit: *Makha*, vigoureux; *Manusa*, homme (?).

« Tu es de race humaine, tu ne peux rester dans ces lieux. Je vais t'envoyer dans le Cambodge, où tu construiras le palais de mon fils; tu le feras aussi beau que mon étable à bœufs. Lorsque tu l'auras construit, je descendrai sur la terre pour présider au couronnement de mon fils et le comblerai de gloire. »

Lorsque Popusnokar eut bien examiné l'étable, Indra fit atteler un de ses chars sur lequel il fit monter Prah Kèt Mealea et Popusnokar, et les fit conduire sur la terre cambodgienne.

Popusnokar se mit aussitôt en devoir de commencer la construction de l'édifice royal; c'était en l'an 620 de l'ère bouddhique. Il fit creuser des fossés, accumuler la terre qui en provenait et mouler sur toute la surface des sculptures de toutes sortes.

Le fils d'un chef de village, appelé Sovan, travaillait sous les ordres de Popusnokar. Lorsque Sovan fut en état de diriger les travaux, Popusnokar s'embarqua sur une jonque pour aller à la mer chercher des coquillages dont il ferait la chaux pour enduire le monument. Lorsqu'au retour il atteignit Somronsèn, dans la province de Kompong Leng, la jonque coula. Popusnokar fit renflouer le bateau mais abandonna les coquillages dont il était chargé. C'est pour cela que maintenant encore on trouve une si grande accumulation de coquilles enterrées dans le sol à Somronsèn; depuis d'innombrables années les habitants de cette région emploient ces coquilles pour faire de la chaux et n'ont pas épuisé la quantité qui est encore considérable de nos jours.

Popusnokar repartit pour la mer avec de nombreuses jonques, rapporta un grand chargement de coquilles et en fit une quantité considérable de chaux. Puis il arma trois jonques pour aller chercher des graines de sésame. Une tempête fit chavirer une des jonques à Komnhanthom, à l'est de Dontri. Popusnokar fit jeter la cargaison du bateau et pétrifia les graines de sésame abandonnées dont le tas forma une île. C'est pour cela que, de nos jours encore, la terre de l'île Komnhan est noire comme la graine de sésame sans qu'aucune autre terre s'y soit mélangée.

Des graines qui chargeaient les deux jonques restantes, Popusnokar fit une préparation dont il enduisit le monument de terre qu'il avait fait construire. La terre se transforma aussitôt en pierre.

Popusnokar ne construisait pas, comme nous le faisons, en établissant des échafaudages et en dressant les colonnes une à une. Il construisit tout ensemble un monument à cinq tours entièrement en terre et l'enduisit en entier de la solution qui le transforma en pierre. C'est pourquoi dans les voûtes mêmes des toitures on ne voit ni poutres ni chevrons.

Lorsque la construction fut achevée. il peignit les sculptures de couleurs appropriées; le monument était admirable et en tout semblable aux étables d'Indra.

Prah Kèt Mealea, dans l'admiration, félicita Popusnokar et l'employa à construire un grand nombre de monuments tous ornés de sculptures merveilleuses.

Indra, escorté de *deva* innombrables, vint sur la terre, versa sur son fils l'eau du couronnement. Il lui donna le nom de Arothpulpearso Prah Kèt Mealea, et il appela le Cambodge de son nom actuel.

Les fêtes du couronnement terminées, Indra retourna dans son divin séjour avec les *deva* qui l'accompagnaient.

Par la suite Prah Kèt Mealea remarqua qu'une des tours d'Angkor n'était pas d'aplomb. Il enjoignit à Popusnokar de la redresser. Celui-ci répondit:

« Que Votre Majesté envoie une femme frapper la tour avec une citrouille mûre et elle se redressera ! » Prah Kèt Mealea, fort en colère, s'écria:

« Comment peux-tu parler de redresser avec une citrouille cette tour qui est en pierre? »

Popusnokar se fâcha à son tour et répondit:

« Si Votre Majesté ne me croit pas, que la tour reste inclinée! Et à l'avenir, que toutes les tours du genre de celle d'Angkor soient inclinées comme celle-ci. »

A quelque temps de là, Prah Kèt Mealea livra à Popusnokar trois *piculs* de fer et lui ordonna de lui forger une épée, insigne de sa puissance.

Popusnokar fondit le fer et n'en prit que la partie la plus dure; des trois *piculs* de fer il ne retira que la quantité nécessaire pour faire une petite épée dont la lame était aussi mince qu'une feuille de riz, mais le tranchant en était tel que si, avec cette épée, on fendait un homme en deux, il ne s'apercevait pas qu'il était fendu; il avait l'impression que le coup l'avait manqué; il pouvait parler comme devant. Mais si on le poussait, il tombait en deux morceaux. Si on remplissait d'eau une jarre de terre, on pouvait couper la jarre en deux sans qu'une goutte d'eau se répande; ce n'est que lorsqu'on touchait la jarre qu'elle se partageait en deux et que l'eau s'écoulait.

Popusnokar trempa cette épée avec le plus grand soin et vint la présenter à Prah Kèt Mealea.

Le roi entra dans une violente colère et fit d'amers reproches à Popusnokar devant tous les dignitaires: « Tu as volé pour ton propre usage le fer que je t'ai confié! C'est pour cela que cette épée est si petite! »

Popusnokar, furieux, répondit:

« Je ne reste pas au Cambodge, je vais retourner en Chine! »

Il s'éloigna traînant derrière lui l'épée dont il avait tourné le tranchant vers le plancher.

Lorsqu'il fut sorti, on s'aperçut que les planches sur lesquelles avait passé l'épée étaient toutes sectionnées. Prah Kèt Mealea envoya aussitôt appeler Popusnokar et lui fit demander l'épée. Popusnokar refusa et la jeta dans le Grand Lac. Ensuite, il s'embarqua sur une jonque et mit à la voile. Il alla se fixer en Chine, son pays natal, et instruisit les hommes.

Telle est l'histoire de Popusnokar ; peu d'hommes la connaissent et, parce qu'ils l'ignorent, ils parlent à tort et à travers, prétendant que ce sont les *deva* qui ont construit Angkor.

# Tales of the Hare

## 27 Classic Folktales of Cambodia

Translated by Chhany Sak-Humphry

ISBN 978-1934431542

Cambodia abounds with ancient legends about powerful jungle animals. But in this surprising book you'll meet an unlikely hero: a small rabbit! As you'll discover in 27 classic folktales, Mr. Hare uses his brain to make up for his size. Time and again he outsmarts huge elephants, hungry crocodiles, fierce tigers...and even men!

This beautiful full color book presents the tales in Khmer and English, with side-by-side translation, so students of both languages can continue his tradition.

**www.NagaPrince.com**

www.ingramcontent.com/pod-product-compliance
Lightning Source LLC
Chambersburg PA
CBHW082126180726
48291CB00010B/2757

* 9 7 8 1 9 3 4 4 3 1 2 1 4 *